1

Love, Gudrun Ensslin

LOVE, GUDRUN ENSSLIN

A Novel

By

SIMON CORBIN

Love, Gudrun Ensslin

Love, Gudrun Ensslin

Published in 2010 by YouWriteOn.com

First Edition

Love, Gudrun Ensslin

Love, Gudrun Ensslin

The revolution says:

I was

I am

I will be again

**Statement of the disbanding of
the Red Army Faction**

March 1998

7

Love, Gudrun Ensslin

Love, Gudrun Ensslin

PROLOG:

KRENDLER'S BLOG (WINTER 2010)

My comrades sacrificed themselves for a cause.

They believed the cause was greater than themselves – the collective value of the enterprise greater than their individual destiny.

The cause was more than merely political. More than mere foot soldiering on behalf of Soviet Communism and Chairman Mao. The true cause was equality and freedom – freedom for all humanity. The enemy was tyranny and iniquity – in the guise of imperialism and gangster capitalism; that which would seek to exploit, repress and control for personal gain; for the squalor that is *profit*.

"From rejection to attack; to liberation."

The embers and ashes of the Cold War may now themselves be cold – but the enemy remains. The enemy – in the person of governments, bankers, financiers, taxmen, bureaucrats, corporations (in a word, CAPITALISTS!; in a word, EXPLOITERS!) – still exists and grows ever stronger, ever more destructive, ever more contemptuous of the remainder of society; ever more cruel and deadly to the needy, the

Love, Gudrun Ensslin

disenfranchised and the oppressed.

My comrades remained uncorrupted by the course of
history and utterly committed to resisting the will of
the ruling powers. They fought for collectivity and
togetherness and against isolation, loneliness and
exploitation in society. And now the enemy believes
that, having 'won' the Cold War, it is open season for
profiteering, asset stripping and the appalling vanity of
personality cult dictatorships. No longer is there any
need for surface PR – a pretence that capitalism
'cares'. . .

Instead, what do we have today? This is what we have:
The military and police deployed against those fleeing
from poverty, war and oppression. A society full of
prisons. Cops and security forces tossing the homeless
out of the consumer shopping areas, as well as youths
and anyone else who upsets the bourgeoisie. Police
batons and other weapons used against those pushed to
the edge; those suffering at the very margins of our
society. Exclusion, repression and displacement as
policy. Only people who don't contradict the efficiency
of the economic system are desired, as well as anything
else which can be capitalised.

There is an idealism at work at the core of German
'kultur'. We Germans don't accept the real world as it
is, so we wish to change and transform it into the ideal
world (as we see it). We are, therefore, eternally on a

Love, Gudrun Ensslin

quest to create both the 'new Germany' and the 'new society' – whether that be the Weimar Republic, the Third Reich, the 'real existing socialism' of the Marxist DDR or today's 'united' Germany after the fall of the Wall; the same Romanticism is reborn in every generation. My comrades were Germans and idealists from the '60s generation – as am I – and the ideal upon the altar on which they sacrificed themselves is this: The International Struggle For A Just And Fundamentally Different Social Reality In Opposition To The Entire Development Of Capitalism.

And so now it is time for a New Revolution. So, CAPITALISTS and EXPLOITERS be warned – I have, from this moment, renounced our 1998 renouncement of violence; I have dusted off my gun and polished up my bullets; imperialists, reactionaries, racists, patriarchs, exploiters, profiteers, CAPITALIST PIGS of the world. . .be warned. . .I am gunning for YOU! The War is Returning. Reality Is Being Brought Back Into The Belly Of The Beast! THE DAYS OF RAGE are upon us once more.

No man can avoid his destiny. Life is a process of becoming.

I was
I am. . .

G.K
Gudrun Ensslin Kommando

Love, Gudrun Ensslin

Love, Gudrun Ensslin

CHAPTER ONE: DER SPIEGEL

Maverick billionaire Rory Carlisle stood in the service elevator, needing to calm down. He was not accustomed to travelling in the service elevator – neither was he accustomed to losing his composure. He felt the panic rising – vile acid shooting through his bloodstream like bile in his throat. How best to calm down? How best to get a grip when you are stuck inside a bleak mechanical coffin, descending inexorably towards the dark subterranean environs of the basement? A bizarre notion suddenly struck him: what if the elevator doors never opened again? What if this was it for Rory Carlisle for all eternity – trapped, conscious and alive, yet also totally alone and confined; imprisoned with only one's thoughts for *all time*? Could there ever be a greater Hell than that? The lower the lift descended, the more Rory's sense of panic rose. At least, he reasoned, he had found a further distraction with which to replace the incandescent anger he was feeling before he even entered the elevator.

He could, he supposed, always calm down by staring at himself in the mirror. It was a trick which had worked for him many times during childhood. Whereas other boys had their 'imaginary friend', Rory always found solace and refuge in his own reflection. Yet this was more than pure Narcissism. For the young Rory, his 'other self' from that magical Wonderland beyond the looking glass was capable of *anything*; no adventure was ever too challenging, no challenge was ever too daunting and there was no enemy who could not be vanquished. And now…there *he* was again, staring right back at him once more: the 'other' him – inhabiting some silent parallel universe; his left-handed, inverse, evil twin. His *doppelganger*; staring him boldly in the eye – holding that gaze proudly; matching him equally; facing him down; never flinching.

His reflected self was so impeccably behaved whenever he was caught in open sight – yet such a man of mystery and intrigue whenever he was out of view. How appropriate. How like the real Rory! Yet where did his *doppelgänger* go when the 'real' Rory moved away from any reflective surface? Did he, perhaps, involve himself in some diabolical double act with Rory's shadow? Did this terrible and unholy twosome plan and plot together in their invisible realm? And, if they did, could they ever – in a millennium of millenniums – have conceived a plan so perfect – and so *devious* – as the one the real Rory Carlisle had spent years creating and only recently set in motion?

Certainly they could not. He doubted *anyone* could devise such a scheme as his – less still possess the inner strength and steel resolve to absent themselves from the picture entirely, leaving someone else to do the dirty work and, in the eyes of the pedestrian-minded, to take the ultimate credit. If Rory was really as vain as this act of staring lovingly at his own reflection suggested, would he be content to remain anonymous and hidden while someone else took the acclaim for *his* masterplan; a plan for changing the whole of society – if not the *world* – for the better? How many people realised the strength of character required to stay behind the scenes – to keep your true self and your true purpose hidden; only breaking cover to act, superficially, as a facsimile of yourself (like a mute reflection in a sideshow mirror)? How many people could hold a mirror up to society and require that someone shatter it (for *all time*) and yet not reveal they were the one to inspire, encourage and *instruct* the stone throwers? How many people could even *conceive* of such a thing as that?

No, there was no reason for anger. No reason for uncertainty. No reason for doubt. Yes, his plan had been threatened, his security system breached – but only in a minor way and only by some minor nuisance – not by any significant authority. He could still look in the mirror and still see it: his plan was still functioning, still operational and still beautiful...and his *reflection* was still beautiful too! All that was required was true strength of character, true strength of purpose and true strength of *will*; the ability to carry on regardless and face down any enemy – however great and threatening, however small and insignificant. And that is precisely what he intended to do; keep on keeping on.

His lackey, his proxy, his *factotum* – the Frankenstein's monster he created – was out there, about to do his bidding; about to make those in society who had enslaved and corrupted it pay the price of their machinations and the iniquity they created. He just needed to hold himself together and watch it all unfold – the game was about to begin.

The elevator 'pinged' to announce its arrival in the basement. Rory laughed to himself – in his anger he had pressed the button for the basement rather than the ground floor and the doors had closed before he realised his error. Although he jabbed frantically at the buttons to correct his mistake, the system had no 'override' facility. That needed to be fixed. He would ask someone to speak to the caretaker the following morning to ensure the man had it remedied at once. It shouldn't be too difficult to arrange – after all, Rory did own the entire building!

He checked himself in the mirror one last time. He saw cold, steel blue eyes. He saw a thick mane of naturally blonde hair with a jaunty fringe, swept casually to one side. He saw skin that was clear and clean and taut – looking far younger than its fifty years. He saw a natural authority and an unassailable, imposing posture. He saw a man of character, experience and status in a bespoke navy *Huntsman* suit, a slate blue *Turnbull & Asser* shirt and a crimson *Hermés* tie covered in the image of dozens of tiny

Love, Gudrun Ensslin

silver 1930s *Mercedes* racing cars. Rory adjusted his tie and repositioned his solid gold tie clip. He considered himself carefully as the elevator doors slid open. He looked pleasingly traditional – clearly a member of the Establishment. Appearances can be deceptive though! For now, it *suited* him to look like this. Ours is a society that operates solely by surface appearance, judges books only by their cover and sees only what it wants to see. And Rory wanted to be seen as the autocratic archetype – the pillar of our global capitalist age – without revealing even the tiniest hint of what lay beneath. *That* knowledge was for him alone – a private pleasure. After all, who would have believed that this arch capitalist was really the greatest Anarchist the world had ever seen? Truth really is stranger than fiction, Rory told himself.

Reinvigorated – and with his sense of purpose fully restored – Rory marched smartly out of the elevator, climbed the stairs from the basement, crossed the lobby and headed out into the grey morning air of London's Docklands.

CHAPTER TWO: PIG IST PIG!

And so here I am on a balcony with a gun in my hands and a finger on the trigger waiting for my target. This is only the second time in my life that I have held a gun. Back then it was a handgun. How I marvelled at its weight and solidity. It was like a piece of chiselled metal; some base totemic sculpture. In many ways such a primitive weapon – and yet still so very deadly. This time it is a rifle. Longer than the pistol. More *balanced*. Seemingly more *sophisticated* – made to seem so merely by the addition of burnished wood for a stock and telescopic sights with crosshairs that perfectly frame your intentions. It was the ideal weapon for a *sniper*; a weapon for staking out your target with infinite patience. Waiting at a distance, disguised and camouflaged, still as the night air; unmoving, scarcely breathing – seeking that fractional window of opportunity; that one fatal moment in which to take your shot. It was the weapon of the *hunter*. I could easily pretend to myself that I was indeed a hunter. That this was the forest – and not a financial district within a major European capital city. That I had painstakingly climbed into a rudimentary 'hide' built

Love, Gudrun Ensslin

into the upper branches of a cluster of trees – instead of lying prone and unmoving on the cold stone floor of a plant-filled balcony attached to an anonymous rented apartment. I could easily have pretended all of this. I could even have pretended that my prey was not human. I could have *pretended* all of these things – but then I would simply be lying. Worst of all, I would be lying to myself – and I wished to be honest; firstly to myself and thence to the world at large (for how else can one avoid the biggest failing of all: *hypocrisy*?)

Many crimes have been committed in the name of building a better society. Was I, Georg Krendler, really about to add to their number? Could I *really* justify these actions to myself? Could the taking of a single human life really improve the lot of *millions*? Did I truly have the *right* to cast myself as judge, jury and executioner? I had hesitated and been beset by doubts before, of course. Back then, when I was in the midst of the action; in the eye of the storm. Back then, when I was surrounded by Gudrun, Andreas, Astrid, Holger, Ulrike – and my other comrades from Baader Meinhof. Back then, when Ingeborg died. Back then, when I fled.

Back then became right now. Decades passed but the world had only turned full circle. What I lacked back then was certainty and conviction. This was something that never troubled my beloved Gudrun. She was always so strong, so sure, so *focused*. Where did she get that confidence? Where did she get that *rage*? So much rage! Yet it was not blind rage. It was not

19

rage turned inward against the self. It was not hysteria. It was channelled. It was directed. It was *controlled* rage. Rage as a *weapon*. Rage against a selected target. If she had to press a button to destroy an entire nation – an entire planet – she had that strength; she had that iron will; she had that RAGE. *She* had it – yes. But did I? When I was right there with her – side by side in her presence as a comrade-in-arms – I had lacked it then. Despite the gun in my hand, what made me think I had it now?

For those who wished to build a better society through the barrel of a gun, the equation was simple: eradicate this or that group of people and you thereby build a better society for all who remain. In the crosshairs: Communists. Jews. Blacks. Gypsies. Homosexuals. Drug addicts. Americans. Financiers. The Government. Fascists. The Military-Industrial Complex. Arabs. Muslims. Kurds. Iraqis. Iranians. Israelis. Russians. Georgians. Oligarchs. Somewhere out there is a conspiracy theory that makes demons of us *all*. However we can be categorised or compartmentalised – *dehumanised* and separated from our individual human worth – there exists a twisted script somewhere that casts us neatly in the role of the villain (and thence as victim). It is the same mistake each side – each *faction* – has made down the centuries. Led only by hatred and fear – to kill in the name of this obtuse equation. They bombed our subways so we bomb their villages. It is the same philosophy – the same rationale; the same outcome;

Love, Gudrun Ensslin

death upon death upon death.

And yet, here I am: waiting to kill – waiting to take a human life. Waiting to commit a crime that can never be undone; a heinous wrong that can never be put right; for which there will *never* be *redemption*. Even killing an animal for food is a *decadent* act; taking the life of another living thing for your own momentary pleasure. How much *more* decadent is the taking of a human life in pursuit of mere political *theory*?

"Your problem is you think too much, Georg," Gudrun once said to me. "And if you think too much, you do not act. You should trust your subconscious mind to rule your conscious mind. You should trust your *instinct* for justice – and then you will *know* how to act. You will *know* what has to be done."

I smiled at the memory. We were both students of Philosophy then – but Gudrun had no time for Philosophy anymore. To her, it was just another distraction – another pointless diversion from daily reality. Thinking was the enemy of action. Action was the means to achieve the goal. The goal was revolution. The justification was already in place – for all to see; our unequal, repressive and exploitative society. Action was the only means to change this situation for the better. What's to think about? The equation was simple!

And still I doubted. Could the killing of one man really make such a difference? What if someone had killed Hitler, Stalin, Pinochet, Pol Pot or Saddam

Love, Gudrun Ensslin

Hussein before they had taken power in their respective nations? How many lives could have been saved? How different might the course of world history have been? And yet how could one justify the *presumption* of the right to take *any* life (even *such* a life) without becoming exactly like those rage-filled ideology-obsessed killers oneself? In other words, how could this be done without falling foul of the sin of *hypocrisy*?

Sin upon sin and death upon death. Would I be helping the situation or merely compounding the situation? So far in my life I had avoided The Mark Of Cain. Did I really now wish to embrace it – to suffer this indelible stain for all eternity? And yet I too now felt the *rage*. And the *shame*. Rage at the continued – and worsening – injustice of our society...and shame at my continued inaction. As the man I awaited walked suddenly into the cross-hairs of my rifle, I had a choice to make – and the equation was simple. . .

CHAPTER THREE: ICH BIN PETE

URBANE GORILLA WEBSITE POST:

The existence of poverty in the world is evidence that greed still exists in the world. Your society is morally bankrupt and increasingly polarised – and you have become wilfully anaesthetised to this fact; turning a blind eye in your corpulent, cosy complacency.

You have been neutered by your own avarice and petty bourgeois aspirations – the pursuit of the 'perfect' colour supplement lifestyle has been the altar on which your own potential has been sacrificed. You are living out someone else's dream – prescribed for you rather than created by you. You are hamsters on a treadmill in a gilt-encrusted cage. Even if your prison is lavishly furnished, it is still a prison.

Yet it is not all your own fault. You are merely a pawn. A foot soldier. Cannon fodder. A mindless lemming. An automaton. A soulless computer program executing instructions. A sheep. A trusting lamb led to the slaughter.

The cost of living is deliberately kept artificially high (and rising) to keep you under control. Greed is actively encouraged as the sacred fuel of this sinister worldview ('divide and rule'). Following taxation (including taxation by stealth) and all your monthly debt repayments (mortgage, credit cards, bank loans, 'consolidation' loans and household utility bills) there is no longer any disposable income in your pocket for the basic necessities of life (such as food, drink, travel and entertainment).

And so you are forced to borrow more – just to complete the weekly shop; just to achieve a subsistence-level existence in this obscenely rich society. And so your debt increases. And so your servitude increases. And so your powerlessness increases. And so your freedom and opportunity diminish. And thus are you marginalised and controlled. Welcome to the bottom of the pile. Welcome to the underclass!

It is time the imbalance of our society was addressed. It is time the wrongs and injustices were rectified. It is time for the marginalised, the downtrodden and the exploited to fight back.

It is time the privileged parasites – the undeserving

Love, Gudrun Ensslin

architects and figureheads of our socially divisive society – heard the clarion call for justice from the hearts of the oppressed. It is time to reset the scales. It is time once again for *revolution*!

Anarchist Pete

Rory Carlisle pressed the return key on the laptop and sat back with a satisfied smile as his latest polemic was dispatched into cyberspace to take its place on his heavily encrypted website. As he relaxed, Rory reflected on two things – firstly, the sense that this piece of rhetoric was his best yet and, secondly, the trivial origins of his internet alter ego: Anarchist Pete.

It was an ID he had devised from childhood memories – an association that had relevance and meaning for Rory Carlisle but no obvious link to him from anyone else's perspective. This was another important factor in making the name untraceable. 'Anarchist Pete' could be anybody. Indeed, it was much more effective for Anarchist Pete to be some mythical, unknown, shadowy figure – a name that could one day become a legend; another Andreas Baader, Carlos the Jackal, Abu Nidal, Osama bin Laden.

For a split second it was the 1970's once more. The young Rory was at the breakfast table at the small semi he shared with his father in South Ealing. On the table was a large pack of Rory's favourite cereal –

25

Golden Nuggets. Rory was addicted to them. His father moaned at him about them – "…nothing but balls of sugar … rot your teeth … make you fat … full of chemicals …" – but he bought them for Rory and allowed him to eat them anyway; it kept Rory quiet… which kept Rory's father happy.

 Golden Nuggets were bright yellow orbs of compacted sugar and cereal. They would crunch and grind as you ate them, testing the ability of your teeth (and fillings) to withstand the effects of chipping away at brightly coloured *ersatz* granite – although they did soften somewhat if you drowned them in sufficient milk. However, it was neither the taste nor the texture that had Rory hooked. The secret truth was that the young Rory mainly loved *Golden Nuggets* for its packaging. *Golden Nuggets* used to have a cartoon character called 'Klondike Pete' on the box. Klondike Pete was a wild, avaricious, gold prospector who had hitched his wagon to the gold trail in the American Wild West. He was accompanied at all times by his toothy, grinning, faithful mule. Klondike Pete and his mule were shown on the front of each pack like a pair of MGM movie stars – a smiling reassurance and happy endorsement of the nutritious and delicious qualities of the 'nuggets' within. They also appeared on the back of the box – often with an embarrassingly simple puzzle to solve: 'Help Klondike Pete choose the right trail to get to the gold'; 'Which of these tangled ropes leads to Pete's mule?'

 Rory would sit and eat his cereal – shovelling

dutifully and automatically without looking at his bowl – while staring fixedly at the images of Klondike Pete and his mule. To the nine-year-old Rory, Klondike Pete represented freedom and possibility – the freedom to travel off on your own and seek your own fortune… and the tantalising possibility of actually finding it! However, it was the freedom to organise his own life away from the claustrophobia of living with his father and the possibility of making something of himself on his own terms for which Rory ultimately longed.

It's not that his father was especially strict nor that his father was directly abusive towards him – but there was a certain tension between them that would never go away and a hierarchy that would never change. Breakfast was a case in point. The Carlisle household – consisting solely of Rory and his Dad – took 'gold top' milk; milk with a thick, heavy, silky layer of cream sitting in the neck of the bottle. Rory would have loved that cream to add to his *Golden Nuggets* – but was expressly forbidden to touch the cream (or even to open the bottle) until his father appeared at the table as the cream was reserved for his father's coffee. It was a kind of ritual.

Rory's father never ate breakfast – just strong coffee and a cigarette. Breakfast was also usually a silent affair – Rory sitting staring at the back of the cereal packet; His father sitting smoking and staring at Rory; the bottle of milk sitting between them; one thought in Rory's mind – that, if his mother had been alive, *she* would have let him have the cream from the top of the milk.

Rory's mother died in childbirth – but he was quite sure his father attached no blame to him personally for this unfortunate consequence; after all, his father told him so repeatedly. As a result of his mother's death, Rory had no brothers or sisters. It was just him and his father in that small semi in South Ealing – the 'starter home' his parents bought together at the outset of their married life; their downpayment on their future as a couple, made bricks and mortar… until Rory arrived (their downpayment on their future together made flesh) to single-handedly tear their dream apart.

It wasn't so bad being an only child. At times Rory would have liked a brother or sister – most of the other boys at school seemed to have them. It would be someone to share your experiences with; someone who could relate directly to your own unique perspective on life as your particular family's offspring; someone to play with, scrap with, spar with, *grow* with. Even an extended family would have been a bonus – Rory's maternal grandparents ceased to have much to do with Rory and his Dad after his mother died and then they died in quick succession shortly thereafter anyway. Still, his father bought him books – books by the bucket load – and encouraged him to read voraciously (not that he needed much encouragement as a lonely, only child). Interestingly, his father was especially keen for Rory to read – locked away in his bedroom – whenever any of his several 'new aunties' came to visit.

"Reading broadens the mind and is the very best kind of education," said his father repeatedly.

He drummed this pearl of wisdom into Rory with great regularity. Rory always found this funny because he never, ever saw his father reading a book! Still, Rory loved reading. Reading meant plucking fruit from the Tree of Knowledge; reading was the acquisition of wisdom; reading was mankind's downfall and yet it was also his salvation. Reading meant access to thoughts and concepts. Reading meant understanding. Reading meant *power.*

His father was a used car salesman. Not the most successful used car salesman – but not the least successful either. He got by. *They* got by. There was food on the table. There was whisky on the sideboard. There was money in the bank. It was a litany Rory's father never tired of repeating. Rory's father was fond of sermonising; and was always preaching to Rory one way or another – handing down arcane knowledge from father to son...repeating the pattern of the generations; following the genetic coda.

Mostly Rory's father taught him about cars. Cars, cars and more cars. When he was small it was a kind of testosterone paradise to be living with his father. It was a world of cars and books and a successive parade of 'aunties' who fussed and fawned and ingratiated with him in an attempt to (temporarily) replace the mother he never had. Rory's father begun his career selling a wide range of cars – in fact, any vehicles he could get his hands on. Indeed, it was the act of selling Rory's mother a car that brought them together in the first place. However, after some years in the business, Rory's father eventually decided to specialise in *Mercedes* – and his devotion to the marque was such that, for Colin Carlisle, *Mercedes* was not so much a brand as it was a religion.

Whenever the adult Rory Carlisle, sitting back in a large leather Chesterfield in his state-of-the-art Docklands apartment closed his eyes, he could immediately transform himself back to a seven-year-old sitting on the leather front seat of his father's trusty old gold *Mercedes*. There he would be, unencumbered by such Nanny State social niceties as a 'seat belt law'.

Little Rory, bouncing around in the seat like a human jumping bean, possessed of an attention span inferior to an amnesiac gnat, participating in endlessly repetitive conversations with his father about life, cars and his father's views on how to treat women. The same conversations would repeat themselves over and over and over so that Rory could always be called upon to interject at the appropriate moment to finish his father's sentences for him. It was another ritual – like the one with the cream in the milk bottle – and there was a curious comfort in it for them both.

"That three-pointed star on the bonnet is a Holy Trinity," his father would say. "It stands for quality, reliability and…"

The gap was left for Rory to fill. Sometimes he would add the expected rejoinder immediately…

sometimes he would let it hang in the air for as long as possible – just to see how pregnant a pause he could make it.

"...style!" Rory would shout triumphantly, and both he and his father would laugh uproariously – sharing some hidden joke only the two of them could understand.

"The Brits love their Kraut cars," his father would continue. "We might have bombed the hell out of them in the War but we buy their motors by the shed load."

Then his father would launch off on a speech about 'the War' – telling Rory how he was evacuated to mid-Wales; what a culture shock it was for a London boy to find himself surrounded by funny-accented villagers and wandering flocks of sheep; how Rory's paternal grandparents died in the Blitz (and what an irony it was that *he'd* then ended up selling *German* cars!); how he'd subsequently been brought up in Dagenham by his Uncle Billy and Auntie Jean (both childless, both long since dead); how he'd then moved back to his native Brentford and begun selling cars for a living (pursuing his first love – he'd learned all about engines by helping to service the truck and the tractor on the Welsh farmstead); how he'd worked his way up from a humble salesman to the owner of his own business; how he was answerable to no-one...

Rory had heard it all a thousand times before and he knew that when his father spoke about the War (and his own parents) he would sometimes get maudlin

– and this was the only time Rory would ever see his father glassy-eyed and wistful. (It was strange, thought Rory, how his father never seemed to display the same set of emotions with regard to Rory's mother). And Rory had to look away at those moments as no boy ever likes to see his own father looking tearful and vulnerable. So, during those War-related speeches of his Dad's, Rory would instead focus on his father changing gear. His father had exceptionally nice hands – naturally tanned (almost caramel in colour) with prominent veins and strong, thick fingers. They were proper man's hands and Rory hoped that, when he grew up, he would have hands exactly like that too.

Eventually, Rory's father would snap out of his wartime reveries and the atmosphere between them would return to 'normal'. Usually, it was something in the traffic ahead of them – or in the opposite lane – that would bring his father back to immediate reality. A *Rover* might fly past in the other direction.

"What's that?" his father would ask, suddenly pointing out the rival vehicle.

"A Jew's canoe!" Rory would reply excitedly – a Pavlovian response inculcated by his father over many miles of motoring.

"What's that, then?" his father would continue, pointing out an *Austin Allegro* or a *Morris Marina*.

"*British Leyland* crap!" Rory would trill – another Pavlovian response.

"Shall we shoot 'em down then, Ror?" his father would ask about any slower car directly in front of them. Rory would nod dutifully and his father would drop a gear and pull out into the opposite lane. As he pressed the accelerator the front of the *Mercedes* would rise and fall in response like the bow of a great battleship cresting a powerful wave in the mid-Atlantic. Rory settled his eye-line behind the three-pointed star on the bonnet. In his fertile child's imagination it immediately transformed into the gun sights of a *Spitfire* (or, perhaps more appropriately, an *Me109*). Through the gun sights, Rory watched the tarmac disappearing beneath the onrushing metal of the unstoppable, invincible *Merc*. The *Mercedes* would cruise past the slower car – inevitably a *Hillman Imp*, *Ford Zephyr* or *Morris Minor* – with an audible purr and a truly regal air. At the critical moment Rory would plaster himself all over the passenger side window and regale the opposing driver with a tongue-fully-out, nose-thumbing, gurning taunt of remarkable dexterity. Then his father would pull back into the correct lane and continue accelerating until the 'loser' was merely a pathetic speck on the horizon in the rear view mirror.

"Left for dead! Shot down in flames!" his father would laugh.

Rory would spin on his seat then, looking back at the disappearing vehicle.

"Should've bought a *Mercedes*!" he would yell at the top of his voice. It was the final expected Pavlovian response.

CHAPTER FOUR: DAS KONZEPT
STADTGUERILLA

Becoming an arch-capitalist – an uber-capitalist – was the smartest move Rory Carlisle ever made in his plan to destroy the system. He saw himself as a 'sleeper' and a fifth columnist. Disguise yourself as one of them, get close to the enemy…and then rip his heart out (without hesitation or mercy). He was the Trojan Horse of corpulent capitalist consumer Britain! He was out to lance a very large boil – and they'd never even see it coming (and certainly they'd never believe who was responsible). It was the perfect plan.

It hadn't always been about subterfuge, however. Long before he became the successful internet entrepreneur they all read about in *Forbes* business magazine, he was an open and obvious anarchist – a proud flyer of the black flag. At university in the 1980's – the very decade of 'greed is good' – he had been a fully paid up member of the Bedford College Anarchist Society. He owned all the Crass albums, he spent hours in the Anarchist Bookshop in Railton Road reading pamphlets about Proudhon and Bakunin, he subscribed to *Class War* magazine, he went on 'Stop The City' demos, he wore black from head to toe.

His alma mater, Bedford College, was a jewel in London University's crown – an imposing Gothic building in Regent's Park's Inner Circle. It was originally a women-only College but went fully co-ed in the 1960's. In 1984 London University sold the entire building lock, stock and barrel to a private American College – cashing in on Bedford's prime Regent's Park location to turn a pretty profit. All the students were dispersed to the faraway rural campus of Royal Holloway in Egham, Surrey – with the sole exception of the Philosophy department (of which Rory was a member). The philosophers were sent to King's College in the Strand – keeping Rory in Central London.

Rory was in the Bedford College Anarchist Society's meeting room on 20th July 1982 when an IRA bomb exploded beneath the bandstand in Regent's Park during a performance by the military band of the 1st Green Jackets. Seven of the musicians were killed and several others seriously wounded. Rory arrived early for the meeting and was alone in the room at the time of the blast. As the rearmost window afforded an expansive view of Regent's Park, Rory initially idled away his time watching the band entertain its audience of foot-tapping pensioners and curious tourists. When the explosion took place, Rory, watching with his head resting lazily against the window frame, saw it completely by chance. He immediately interpreted this coincidence as a 'sign'. This, he thought, was true Providence. He regarded his chance witnessing of the event as showing him the significance, legitimacy and effectiveness of political terrorism – direct action as a form of policy. That was his first and most instinctive thought – a dispassionate and clinical assessment; a *political* analysis of an unfolding event. That this hard-headed response should be his instantaneous reaction to witnessing such an incident was also in itself instructive to him – Providence again showing him that his responses were not the same as those of mere mortals. Furthermore, it was undoubtedly the case that this inner toughness was also in place *for a reason* (and that *reason* was surely in order to ensure his future greatness and decisiveness as the leader of a global revolutionary movement). It was a moment of great clarity; in one instance his entire life coalesced into a *purpose*.

Only as a secondary factor did any sense of shock at what he had just seen begin to register. It was utter carnage, he thought. An atrocity. The instantaneous creation of a human abbatoir in a public setting. The bombing was literally spectacular, his analytical mind further reflected – a sight (a *spectacle*) that, once seen, could never be forgotten. It was something you see that you somehow can't quite believe you're actually seeing – something that transports you to another dimension, another parallel universe, another reality far removed from the humdrum daily existence we are all conditioned to regard as 'normality'. One man was propelled through the air by the blast and neatly impaled on a nearby railing – just like a choreographed stunt from a B-grade horror movie.

When the other members of the Anarchist Society finally burst into the room the hubbub and excitement was enormous and unrestrained.

"Did you hear about the bomb?" one of them asked Rory urgently.

"I saw it!" Rory replied with an ill-disguised tone of pride and admiration.

The group immediately sat down and held a debate about the legitimacy of violence in pursuit of a political cause. Then they had a vote. The split was exactly 50:50 between those who felt that a pacifist, non-violent campaign of persuasion and reason (as personified by Ghandi and Martin Luther King) was the only legitimate (and lasting) means of changing society, and those who adhered to the more dramatic and immediate tactics of bombing, shooting and knee-capping. Only Rory abstained – not because he was undecided on the issue. It was rather that he was already beginning to anticipate the political consequences of his perceived actions – after all, if he was seen publicly supporting either viewpoint then he could also be held to account for it at a later date. (Indeed, it was just this type of growing awareness of public accountability that would soon see him renouncing his membership of the Anarchist Society and adopting the strategy of a fifth columnist – the

Love, Gudrun Ensslin

hidden provocateur he would eventually become).

After the Regent's Park bombing, Rory began
to research terrorist and paramilitary organisations –
studying their tactics, structure and modus operandi
regardless of their cause or motivation. Brigate Rosse.
Red Army Faction. The Weather Underground. The
Symbionese Liberation Army. The Sandinistas. Action
Directe. The Black Panthers. Black September. Israel's
'Hagganah'. The PLO. PFLP. IRA. INLA. UDF. ANC.
The whole alphabet soup of revolution and insurgency.

Now Rory had both direction and purpose –
and case study examples to follow and utilise. One day
– and of this he had no doubt – *he* would also become
the inspiration of a paramilitary Anarchist sect that
would change the entire world.

Following his graduation, Rory was effectively
unemployed. He had no job lined up – and he certainly
wasn't about to join the mindless throng of capitalist
lemmings in Margaret Thatcher's Britain...queuing up
for 'graduate training schemes' at faceless corporate
conglomerates...becoming a small subservient cog in
someone else's money-making machine. A pathetic
serf from cradle to grave?...no, thank you! A 'career'
on a conveyer belt?...*nein danke*! No-one was going to
exploit Rory Carlisle and get away with it. Anarchist
Pete would see to that! Still, there remained a need for
cash and a steady income – at least until the cashless,
centrally planned economy of which Rory dreamt had
been introduced. He needed some sort of job (and,
indeed, a terror group needed funding...). He briefly

considered becoming a drug dealer – after all, he was smoking so much dope already that 'flogging it to fund it' was simply a logical progression. However, this particular 'career option' was rejected for two reasons – firstly, it was really just another form of capitalism (serving some gangland fat cat in his acquisition of personal wealth and empire-building was little different from the dull servitude of working for some blue chip company with its fat cat Chairman and brand-building); secondly, if Rory Carlisle was going to undertake something classified as 'criminal' then it would not be just some pathetic low-level petty crime…it would instead to be something truly… *spectacular*.

Rory was granted an allowance by his father which saw him quite comfortably through his studies at Bedford and King's – especially so, considering Rory opted to reside in an Anarchist commune in Stockwell…saving him the ignominy and ideological distaste of having to pay rent to some odious Rachman landlord. However, relations between Rory and his father were becoming increasingly strained with each passing year. From Rory's perspective, there was a growing divergence in their philosophies and value systems – a polarity exacerbated by age (his father displaying the typical defensive conservatism and adherence to tradition that comes with the ageing process while Rory represented the vigour, righteous anger, radicalism and revolutionary verve of youth). From his father's perspective, Rory was simply a slacker and a scrounger ("typical of today's youngsters") who should simply "knuckle down" and "get a proper job".

On the few occasions they met, they argued. The car sales business had become increasingly successful so that Rory's father now owned several dealerships and showrooms throughout West London and out towards Heathrow Airport – 'Colin Carlisle Cars – The Three C's That Spell Quality'. Whilst the primary focus remained on *Mercedes Benz*, the dealership recently expanded to include *BMW*, *VW* and *Audi*. ("The Brits still love their German metal," his father said. "Especially in silver. I'm shifting tons of 'em, Ror. The Krauts can't build 'em fast enough!") Colin also moved house – swapping the long-ago outgrown semi in South Ealing for a large, five-bedroom detached (with double garage) directly opposite the gated main entrance to Osterley Park (thereby allowing Colin to position himself in the geographical epicentre of his chain of car dealerships like a spider lurking in its web). The contrast of the relative splendour and bourgeois comfort in which his father now lived compared to the daily struggle of the people whom Rory encountered in the sink estates of inner London and the squat he called "home" greatly offended the budding young revolutionary – and he chose to visit his father's house as little as possible (and, in fact, only when money was an especially pressing requirement).

One particular visit, however, shaped Rory's

entire future. He remained unemployed and doing nothing for several months when he discovered his allowance had ceased to appear in his bank account. Rory went into the branch to check on the anomaly and it transpired there was no mistake – the payment order had been cancelled...by his own father! Clearly, the miserly old bastard had cut him off out of sheer spite. Senseless with rage and filled with perceived injustice, Rory travelled to the house to confront the miserable Scrooge. He was fuming and raging so theatrically that no-one dared to sit next to him on an otherwise crowded tube train travelling from Green Park to Osterley.

On arrival at the house he found his father had gone out – no doubt, Rory surmised, doing the rounds of his many dealerships to ensure the salesmen were shifting sufficient 'Kraut' metal. Rory tried his key in the door – and found the locks were changed. Now, completely beside himself with undiluted outrage, the young Carlisle picked up a large stone and prepared to hurl it through one of the windows of the parental home. He intended to break in and trash the place – teach the old buzzard a lesson for his sorry act of betrayal. The stone was raised and ready to be launched when some small voice from the recesses of Rory's mind spoke to him. The voice whispered that there was another way – a *smarter* way to ensure that Rory got longer-lasting satisfaction from this situation than the momentary relief provided by a solitary act of vengeful vandalism. He dropped the stone and turned

41

on his heel.

A couple of hours up the road killing time in a local pub – spending the very last of his cash on 'lager tops' and with only the *Evening Standard* crossword and a roll-up for company – did little to improve Rory's humour. However, he managed to calm himself sufficiently to return to the house with his inbuilt thermometer partially reduced from boiling point. This time, his father's white E-Class *Mercedes* was parked in the driveway. The three-pointed star on the bonnet seemed to be watching him like an evil eye as he trudged up the gravel to the front door. Rory pressed the doorbell. Twee musical chimes jangled mockingly.

The atmosphere between Rory and his father was even more uneasy than usual. They circumnavigated each other both emotionally and physically – proceeding with the utmost caution like armed representatives at a pow-wow. The kitchen counter formed a negotiating table for them. They sat on barstools staring at each other in an extended silence; opposing factions negotiating a ceasefire. It reminded Rory of the ritual of the milk bottle from way back in their South Ealing days.

His father made coffee the old-fashioned way – in a bubbling percolator on the naked flame of the gas hob. Now the coffee sat between them, steam rising, the intoxicating aroma somehow mellowing their mood and encouraging conversation. Rory reflected just how much things had changed between him and his father since the advent of Rory's teenage years. It seemed that

Love, Gudrun Ensslin

since Rory began to develop his own agenda, his own sense of values and his own sense of 'personhood' – since he ceased to be simply his father's adoring minion and servile alter-ego-made-flesh and began to question and challenge his father's authority – that their 'relationship' had begun to break down.

"As soon as things got a little bit tough, you turned your back on me." Rory thought to himself.

He held that thought as they at last smiled benignly at each other as each sipped his coffee with a quiet reverence.

The conversation flowed hesitantly between them – not a points-scoring tennis match of a conversation but a conversational hot potato juggled awkwardly in the search for some common ground. Some small secret part of Rory still hoped for a genuine emotional connection with his father – but that was a remote and forlorn hope. His father had never been one for emotional displays – in his father's eyes emotion was weakness; emotion left you vulnerable; such things were unseemly…unmanly…un- *English*! With his father it always came down to practicalities – food on the table; money in the bank; a task to be completed; a goal to be achieved; annual sales targets to beat. The conversation boiled down to this: his father offered him a deal. The terms were: take it or leave it.

Rory rejected outright the offer of an apprenticeship in the car sales business (barely suppressing the scornful laugh he'd felt like including in his rejection). Hence, this was the deal: Rory's father would sponsor his return to College and/or university – this time in pursuit of a "vocational" course of study. Rory would then be given one further year to find "a proper job" and "gainful employment" and then all funding and allowances would cease…period.

"Enough of all this idleness and wasting your talent," was the phrase that stuck in Rory's mind.

As much as Rory hated to be forced into doing something that someone else wanted him to do…as much as he resented being the puppet for some puppet-master…as much as it *killed* him to be *controlled*… Rory stuck out his hand and shook on the deal.

That night he slept in the back bedroom in Osterley where all his old toys and games and other childhood belongings from South Ealing were now stored in crates and boxes. Unable to rest, Rory sat upright in bed plotting his next move and trying to determine exactly which vocational course might hold even the slightest genuine interest for him. He looked across at the tatty old boxes containing his once treasured *Airfix* planes and *Scalextric* cars gathering dust in the corner before switching out the light, hunkering down, and offering up a silent oath to Bakunin to let him know that Rory Carlisle was definitely not 'selling out'; that he was merely playing a waiting game…and that he had a clear long term plan and a far greater objective in mind than merely towing his father's line.

CHAPTER FIVE: HEIMAT

I don't know if you've ever seen anyone shot. The life goes out of them immediately and they drop like a stone. They instantly collapse and crumple as if commanded; they are like puppets with their strings cut – the blood and life pouring from them as their spirit departs. It is death and gravity combined in an unholy pact. Those who are shot resemble roadkill; bloodied and lifeless; mangled corpses; cold-cast parodies of what they used to be. Skin that has been shed. Such is the fragility of the spark of life.

My father was attached to a German Army film unit during the Second World War. He saw – or, rather, filmed – action on the Eastern front; jubilant, grinning, victorious tank crews and waving foot soldiers; the bonnets of armoured personnel carriers draped in the scarlet swastika flag; men certain of 'final victory' as they swept across the Russian steppes in yet another *'Blitzkrieg'* manoeuvre.

It was my father's job to record the official, Party-approved, version of the conquest of the East. He did so in both movie film and still photography; in black and white and in the rare and novel colour format. Once, he met Leni Riefenstahl. My father produced literally thousands of images – standing behind an assault party and its accompanying tank as they blasted yet another farmhouse (and its occupants) to Kingdom Come in a candid portrayal of genuine front-line action; the posed re-enactment of front-line assaults (photographic fodder for 'patriotic' newspapers, magazines and the Party's Propaganda Ministry) – soldiers smoking casually in relaxed camaraderie, soldiers enthusiastically giving their officers the 'Hitler salute', a soldier poised with a hand grenade in mid-throw…his clear blue eyes filled with ideological zeal.

There were also unofficial images and records of atrocities – both stills and movies – that my father had salted away as his own perverse collection of memorabilia; documentation of an unbelievable time in history; images of naked Jews being shot into pits, Commissars being hung by their obscenely stretched necks from makeshift gibbets. These images were carefully housed in shoeboxes in the attic of our home – mixed up with photographs of myself as a baby, my mother as a young woman (sadly she never became an old one) and photographs of places deemed to be 'tourist attractions' in and around our home town of Wuppertal. The incongruity and anachronism of the juxtaposition between these images of death and murder and our mundane family life always struck me – on some childish and inchoate level – as somehow significant. Yet it was the images of death that

Love, Gudrun Ensslin

obsessed and beguiled me and I would sneak up to the attic alone at every available opportunity during my late childhood and early teenage years and sit and pore over this material for hours.

There was one film in particular that I would play over and over again on my father's rickety old projector – risking burning the film to a frazzle by holding the 'freeze frame' button as long as possible at key moments. The film showed the execution by firing squad of 'partisans' against a wall in a Ukrainian village. There was no way of knowing if these were genuine partisans – the Nazis had a habit of labelling any 'undesirables' they wished to shoot as 'partisans'... these people could just as easily have been Jewish civilians or randomly selected villagers killed as part of the policy of 'reprisals'.

The film (which was a very rare colour example) began with a still – a hand-held blackboard with the title 'Execution of Partisans, Horokhov, Ukraine, 1941' written on it in elegant, tutored script. It then cut immediately to five men in civilian clothing standing against a stone-coloured wall (the side of a house?). The men looked intermittently nervous, bewildered, resigned. None of them had blindfolds. I would freeze-frame at this point to carefully study their faces – to check out the differing individual responses of men about to face certain death...five lives about to be extinguished and recorded for posterity in the act of dying. The camera then panned across to the firing squad standing a short distance away. To my surprise, the shooters were not dressed in SS uniform but appeared to be soldiers of the regular Army – their tin helmets glistening in the summer sunshine. Their rifles at their sides, they stood rigidly to attention…awaiting commands.

Immediately, their Captain – distinguishable by his peaked cap – waved a *Luger* in the air. He barked some commands – lost forever by this silent film recording – and the rifles were raised, cocked and shouldered. The camera swung back to focus on the 'partisans' and panned out so the frame included the condemned men and the dark metal tips of the executioners' rifles. There was a clear puff of smoke from the gun barrels and an instant of recoil – you could also freeze-frame the exact moment of this happening. At virtually the same instant, the five men fell – dropping straight to earth like lead anvils; five marionettes with their strings cut from above. They collapsed in disarray in an inelegant heap – two falling on their sides, two others crumpling in spastic contortions, their arms and legs trapped and twisted awkwardly beneath them; one slumping against the wall as if taking an afternoon siesta in downtown Old Mexico.

The camera began to zoom in, lingering obscenely on the pile of bodies and then the film jumped suddenly – as if cut or spliced – milliseconds of time lost. A microsecond of blackness and then the images returned – a panned-out view of the five bodies once more. Then an officer stepped forward, *Luger*

48

Love, Gudrun Ensslin

pointed directly at the victims. What he did next
always shocked me more than the actual shooting
itself. He quite deliberately leaned over and spat on the
bodies – one or two of which were still twitching.
Congealed phlegm, dragged up slowly and deliberately
for the purpose, rained down on them in their final
moments. You could freeze-frame it travelling through
the air. However, it was the contorted look of hatred on
the officer's face that always horrified me the most. It
was the sheer hellish look of a demon from a
Hieronymous Bosch painting. That face haunted me in
my nightmares for years afterwards. Then the film
went totally black and ran out. In all, it lasted about
two minutes. However, I would always sit for far
longer in contemplative silence after watching it while
the film flapped helplessly as it revolved round and
round in its spool. And *that* is how I spent much of my
youth – my precious 'formative years' – alone in the
attic of our house watching 'snuff movies' before the
term was even invented.

I was born in Wuppertal – birthplace of
Friedrich Engels – in 1949. My mother died in
childbirth and I knew her only through the many
photographs that were taken of her by my father. They
were good quality photographic portraits – as befits a
professional photographer of my father's considerable
experience. Immediately after the War my father re-
opened his camera shop and re-established his
photographic business that had been so rudely
interrupted for seven years by the Reich's attempted

conquest of Europe. The shop was only a short walk from our house in the picturesque Beyenberg suburb and throughout my teenage years I would be left largely to my own devices while my father toiled. To his dismay, I had no interest or inclination to get involved in the photographic business. Apart from watching films and pouring over old photographs in the attic, I read books. I was a small town loner with a common small town loner's disease – I wanted to get away. And I saw education as my route out of the 'Wuppertal ghetto'.

There wasn't much to do in Wuppertal in the post-War years of my upbringing – except to ride the *Schweberbahn* (other than Engels, the *Schwebebahn* suspension railway – a curious hybrid of a monorail and a ski-lift, constructed in 1900 – was Wuppertal's worldwide claim to fame). Alternatively, you could go and stare at the animals in the Zoo. Most of the boys were obsessed with football (which bored me) and resigned to menial jobs in industry... and I got absolutely nowhere with girls – lacking the necessary confidence and bravado that was essential for picking them up. Hence, I had a lonely, drawn-out (and seemingly endless) teenage existence, punctuated only with books, photographs and daydreams – little troubled by daily reality.

My main interest was the War (and its consequences) – a largely taboo subject in Wuppertal (and the rest of West Germany too, for that matter). This interest, combined with my growing disgust for the former Nazi regime (fuelled and exacerbated by my father's secret hoard of photographs) isolated me even further. My father's steadfast refusal to talk about the war years and his experiences (all enquiries were met with a curt "Ach!" and a cursory wave of his hand – the imaginary swatting of an irritating fly) angered me and distanced me further from him with each passing year. It was as though he simply wouldn't let me into his life – as if it were some part of *me* that disgusted *him*…and not vice versa!

Gradually, my own disgust and open hostility towards him came to crystallise and embody our failing relationship. I could imagine him standing at the site of massacres blithely discussing camera angles and lighting – and the superiority of *Agfa* film over *Kodak* – as queues of people waited to be executed. I wondered whether he'd ever wielded a gun himself – borrowed a rifle and plugged a few victims just because he *could*… just to see what it was like to *be* one of the executioners rather than simply photographing them. After all, shooting four-year-old children into pits was just a bit of fun you could pass off as a 'patriotic duty' wasn't it, *Vati*?!

My hatred and resentment – fertilised by his silence and his characteristically taciturn, sanctimonious and lugubrious manner (a posture that somehow ironically and obscenely painted *him* as a victim) – meant that eventually there was no real communication between us whatsoever. We were simply strangers living under the same roof. It was an impasse that could end only one way – with me packing my bags.

I saw university as my way out. The more I learned about the War years, the more I was drawn to the radical Left. The more unrepentant ex-Nazis I saw living off the fat of the land and still running the show, the more I hungered for direct action. This was now the 1960's – the decade of hope and idealism; the decade of youth and rebirth. The student movement was growing all over Europe. We – the young people – could wipe away the sins of the previous generation by revolutionising society. There would be free love... drugs...a fairer distribution of wealth...an end to poverty...racism...capitalist greed...and free concerts by the Rolling Stones! As my intellectual credentials – and my political awareness – grew, I knew it was in university and within the midst of the heart of the revolutionary student movement that I truly belonged (which also meant as far away from Wuppertal and my father as humanly possible).

Shortly before I left to study Philosophy at Frankfurt University, my father made one last gesture towards me. It was a gesture that was hard to interpret – was it simply a benevolent gift? Was it some sort of 'peace offering' designed to reinstate a dialogue between us? Or was it simply some enigmatic attempt to get me to "see sense" and finally accept his own 'pragmatic' "make the best of life as you find it and don't rock the boat too much" worldview? It could have been any – or all – of these things. In any case,

Love, Gudrun Ensslin

what my father did was to pay for me to go and live in England for two weeks.

After the War, Wuppertal fell under the British Zone of Administration and one of their number had established a policy of exchange visits ("encouraging friendship, reconciliation and understanding") between the young people of Wuppertal and those of its English 'twin town' – South Shields. Thus, in 1967 at the age of eighteen, I found myself staying in the industrial north of England for a fortnight – experiencing the 'hospitality' of our conquerors. As a metaphor for my life so far, it was perfect: it was every bit as bleak and grey and miserable as the inner landscape of my youth and it served only to reinforce the notion that my departure for Frankfurt and the company of my like-minded student revolutionaries could not come quickly enough!

In hindsight, one interesting footnote results: little did I know then that I would eventually come to live in England and make it my permanent home.

Love, Gudrun Ensslin

CHAPTER SIX: WIE ALLES ANFING

It began and ended with Frankfurt. In April 1968 Andreas Baader – with Gudrun Ensslin – fire-bombed two department stores in Frankfurt as a direct attack on bourgeois consumer society and in direct revenge for the police murder of Benno Ohnesorg. In June 1972 Andreas Baader was captured by over one hundred policemen armed with machine guns, rocket launchers and tanks. The arrest – in Frankfurt – took place live on German television. This time, however, there would be no daring escape through the windows of the Dahlem Institut. After five brief years, it was over.

These were five years of my life. Five years that could never be repeated, regained or equalled. Five years inside a vacuum of heightened adrenaline, mortal danger and moral, intellectual and physical rebellion. Five years as a seditionary in my own homeland, amongst my own people. Five years as a foot soldier in "the war of the 60 against the 60 million". Five years that were the greatest five years of my life. Five years in which I was more alive than I have ever been before – or been since.

*   *   *

Love, Gudrun Ensslin

When I arrived back in Wuppertal from my two-week sojourn in South Shields I was more eager than ever to escape from my father and my stultifying home life. Student radicalism was on the march. The reactionary fascists of my father's generation were running scared. *My* generation was amounting to something – taking action; righting wrongs; protesting injustice; actively atoning for Germany's many, many sins. My frustration at missing out was incendiary.

My two-week absence in England coincided with the killing of Benno Ohnesorg by a Pig. On my return every young person was talking about it; every student radical was planning revenge. Always a lone wolf, the closest thing I had to a friend in Wuppertal was Carsten – a young waiter with left-wing sympathies that matched my own, who worked in the *bierkeller* I most often frequented. Over a *stein*, Carsten filled me in on the details of the Ohnesorg killing.

On June 2nd 1967 students gathered in Berlin to protest against a state visit by the decadent Western puppet ruler – the Shah of Iran. The *Polizei* – unprovoked and straining at the fascist leash – launched an attack against the student protestors, handing out vicious beatings with batons drawn. In the chaos and confusion one policeman pulled a gun and shot the unarmed Benno Ohnesorg, killing him instantly. I was outraged at Benno's death. I wanted to grab the nearest policeman I could find and smash his brains out against a lamppost. Instead, I had to content myself with yet another beer and wait until I could join up with my fellow students in Frankfurt in a little over a month's time.

In late August 1967 I arrived in Frankfurt with a small suitcase of belongings and took up residence in the student Halls – filled with a sense of having missed out on life for far too long and keen to make contact with the campus radicals at the first opportunity. I managed to hitch-hike all the way from Wuppertal – starting out with a local truck driver and ending up with a like-minded, long-haired hippy couple in an old *VW* Beetle they had painted orange and covered with pink, blue and white flower motifs. The girl of the couple – Sabine – rolled a few joints en route. It was my first experience of cannabis and it made me feel as though my head was lifting off from my body like a gently rising *Zeppelin*. As I smoked in the back seat of the Beetle, I felt splendidly drowsy; happily sedated; at peace with the world; as though my life had finally begun.

Franz and Sabine dropped me off just a few streets from the University campus. I wanted to swap contact details with my new 'friends for life' but Franz casually shrugged off my dope-fuelled enthusiasm with a jovial aside:

"Well, we know where to find you, Georg!" he laughed. "Besides, I'm sure we'll meet up at a demo soon."

Then he turned serious and looked at me conspiratorially.

Love, Gudrun Ensslin

"But before we part," he continued. "Let me give you something interesting you might like to read. Pass me the bag, will you, Sabine."

Sabine reached over into the back seat of the Beetle. There was a holdall lying on the bench next to where I had been sitting clutching my suitcase. Sabine stretched for it and I noticed her lithe and slender shape beneath her yellow tie-dyed dress. Her brunette pigtails swung wildly as she twisted and contorted to haul the bag into the front seat. Once she had done so, she passed the bag to Franz who rummaged inside. I could see that the holdall was filled to the brim with paper – typewritten documents; some bundled, others loose. Eventually, Franz pulled out a clutch of tightly packed pamphlets. He extricated one and handed it to me.

"Thanks," I said glibly – a Pavlov response – without really looking at my gift. Franz smiled broadly. I remember thinking his teeth were very horse-like.

"Peace, brother!" he said, raising his right hand in a clenched fist salute.

"Peace!" I replied awkwardly, clumsily aping his gesture, too embarrassed to use the term 'brother'.

With another toothy grin and an over-revved roar of the Beetle's industrial-sounding engine, Franz and Sabine were gone.

I looked at the pamphlet and couldn't quite believe my eyes. It was a document written by two members of *Kommune 1* – Rainer Langhans and Fritz Teufel – dated April 1967. It advocated the burning down of department stores as a "legitimate response" to the "assault on society" being undertaken by "the Coca-Cola capitalists of America". *Kommune I!* Everyone knew about them! They were an Anarchist squatter community founded in Berlin. They practised *nudity* and believed in "free love" and outraged the surrounding "square" society they were dedicated to overturning. It was total equality and intellectual freedom – with sex on tap! Perhaps Franz and Sabine were members? If I could, *I* simply had to join them! For a start, I decided, I really should let my hair grow long like Franz's. I probably ought to get some beads as well.

It didn't take long for me to ingratiate myself among the radical element on campus. Their inclusive ideology and earnest Left-wing idealism meant they welcomed me with open arms. The fact I chose Marxism as one of the options within my Philosophy degree syllabus also allowed me to quickly burrow my way into the heart of Frankfurt Uni's radicals.

One of my lecturers – Julius Semmler – specialised in Hegel and the Marxist dialectic. He also hosted notorious parties in his apartment attended by all the prime Left-wing intelligentsia and other 'movers and shakers'. And I was a frequent visitor – taken under his wing by Semmler as his keenest disciple. At times it all seemed a bit much for a wide-eyed boy from Wuppertal. To say that my head was turned was something of an understatement – in fact, it turned so much it practically revolved full circle!

By the time March 1968 arrived – a little over

Love, Gudrun Ensslin

six months into my studies – I was totally immersed in student activism and the concept of 'Revolution'. Wuppertal – and my father – were long forgotten; indeed, I resolved never to return there. My father's refusal to see me off – or even to wish me well – when I departed for Frankfurt only served to entrench and embolden my already strong feelings of antipathy towards him. His cold dismissal of Philosophy as "mind games for layabouts" and spiteful rejoinder that I "should have been glad to inherit a trade and now would inherit nothing" only served to increase my contempt for him – and my conviction that he represented exactly what was wrong with Germany every bit as much as the hated Axel Springer. No! If I *needed* a father – indeed, if anyone ever truly needed such a patriarchal, despotic figure – then Julius Semmler would surely be a far better role model for my future development. And Julius thought so too.

However, March 1968 was also memorable to me for a far more profound reason than the final collapse of the emotional ties between myself, my father and my home town. Rather, this was the month and year that I first ever set eyes on the divine and charismatic figure of Gudrun Ensslin at one of Semmler's 'gatherings'. Gudrun attended Herr Professor's party in the company of her boyfriend – Andreas Baader. They made a striking couple even in those early days. She: reed-thin, tall, fiery beyond belief. He: languid, charming…utterly convinced of his own future greatness. They were like characters from

Love, Gudrun Ensslin

French cinema – stepping off the screen and brought to life in an unholy cloud of *Gitanes* and *Disque Bleu*. I couldn't take my eyes off Gudrun. Surreptitiously, I followed every move she made. Every blink of those mesmerising eyes, every transient smile of those wide lips, every feminine flick of that long, lustrous hair. In another era, Gudrun could have been a fashion model; a mannequin of perfection. The imposing height, the natural slenderness, the incredible elegance, the unparalleled charisma; all spoke of a unique figure. Every room she entered was a catwalk for Gudrun – although she would have shot me down in flames for saying as much! Yet she also *knew* it full well – and she *used* that knowledge to her advantage; and that apparent contradiction only served to heighten her appeal in my eyes. She was everything I'd always wanted and hoped to find in a woman. However, she belonged to Andreas Baader – both the man and the movement. And I was too painfully, cripplingly shy to even speak to her that night. So I merely watched; a voyeur; a Peeping Tom; a pathetic little kid with his nose pressed against the windowpane of life's many possibilities.

Gudrun owned such hypnotic eyes. Beyond the wiry, pipecleaner toughness, beyond the utterly engaging smile, beyond the high cheekbones and the balletic grace – her eyes were undoubtedly her most striking feature. The ancients believed it was in the eyes that the vivacity, the fire, the incendiary *soul* of a person actually lived. Given the chance, I could

Love, Gudrun Ensslin

happily look into those eyes for an eternity; marvelling at the real Gudrun Ensslin that lay deep inside. Quite often her eyes appeared permanently wild and staring – and unnervingly penetrating.

She always painted extra thick layers of kohl around her eyes to heighten this very effect. A slender, prominent nose added further character and completed her unconventional beauty and rare allure. Her wide mouth was, by unpredictable turns, either thin-lipped or ravishingly sensual. When she smiled you could see – just for a fraction of a second – the fiercely intelligent and bright-eyed little girl who was once a Protestant Pastor's daughter, model student and direct descendant of Hegel himself. When she raged – thin-lipped and hysterical, spewing political bile and hate-filled rhetoric – you would have thought her possessed. Gudrun, Gudrun, Gudrun. My poor tortured Gudrun. *I* would have loved you as you were meant to be loved – and you would have laughed in my face for such weakness!

Although I was too tongue-tied and overawed to speak to Gudrun, I chatted extensively with Baader that night. Julius made the introduction – pointedly referring to us as "kindred spirits" and calling Baader "one of the few true men of action in the movement". Andreas clapped me on the back and hugged me like an old, long-lost friend. I felt I could learn from his easy amiability and relaxed, leonine demeanour. He seemed to effortlessly charm and captivate everyone in the room with his magnetism. Small crowds would gather just to hear him speak – yet I was later granted a private audience following Semmler's introduction. I felt honoured – yet also scrutinised – and so I dredged up my very best rhetoric and sloganeering to demonstrate that I was a loyal and unswerving supporter of "the cause". I mentioned I had read the *Kommune I* pamphlet – and I even quoted from it. Andreas's whole face lit up. His eyebrows raised and his complexion positively glowed. He leaned in close towards me once more and draped a trailing arm around my shoulders. I heard his leather jacket creak as he pulled me closer to whisper confidentially in my ear. His breath smelled of alcohol and *Gitanes*.

"If you've read the words of the Comrades," he chuckled. "You'll be pleasantly surprised by events taking place in this very city next month."

He gave me another friendly, conspiratorial squeeze. The leather jacket creaked in my ear once more and I searched his eyes to see if this was merely the imagined, boastful confidence of a drunk – yet, despite the heavy alcohol consumption, Baader's eyes remained clearly focused with a steely determination.

"Just don't go too near the *Kaufhaus* for a while," he continued enigmatically.

Then he broke away, chuckling quietly, and called to Julius for "more *Schnapps*, Herr Professor!" I watched him disappear among the crowd of partygoers – effortlessly working the room like a '50's Hollywood movie star. I felt heady – privileged and important with my covert (yet cryptic) knowledge. I felt I'd been

Love, Gudrun Ensslin

blessed to be trusted and bestowed with such information during a rare unguarded moment from the great Andreas Baader. Of all the people in the room, *I* had been chosen and *I* knew information I wasn't even sure Semmler knew anything about! I certainly didn't need the joint a fellow student offered me – I was high enough for the rest of the night at being the confidant of this "true man of action".

As the party finally wound down, Andreas and Gudrun took their leave. Catching sight of me near the door, Baader gave me a smile and a conspirator's wink. I nodded and smiled lamely in return – the star-struck acolyte. Noticing this exchange between us – and despite being momentarily bemused by it – Gudrun also then smiled towards me; a broad, beaming, heart-stopping, girlish smile. I felt my insides melting and turning to mush. Had I died at that moment, I would certainly have died happy.

CHAPTER SEVEN: PRAXIS

DOCUMENT INSERT:
(GQ Magazine)

•AN AUDIENCE WITH RORY CARLISLE
BY DOMINIC KEMBER

Bill Gates. Donald Trump. Roman Abramovich. Lakshmi Mittal. Bernie Ecclestone. Richard Branson. Alan Sugar. *Rory Carlisle*. All of these men are multi-millionaires – some are even multi-billionaires. All are what might loosely be termed 'charisma capitalists' – icons of our consumer age. All are very private men who are largely inaccessible to the Press. Very few grant interviews and speak candidly concerning their innermost thoughts and their role in society. Rory Carlisle, however, is different. Mr. Carlisle answered GQ's request for an interview in the affirmative – and we are happy to present the results of that encounter to you now.

Love, Gudrun Ensslin

Gates: IT / The internet.
Trump: Property.
Abramovich: Oil.
Mittal: Steel.
Ecclestone: Formula One.
Branson: Retail/Mobile Telephony / Aviation.
Sugar: Retail. Carlisle: Cars / The internet.

Oil, Property, Steel and Retail are all tried and
trusted arenas; proven sectors for wealth creation –
established routes to riches for multiple decades, if
not centuries. The internet, however – even in the
21st century – remains the new kid on the block by
comparison. Yet this sector alone retains the
potential to outperform all these other sectors put
together. It retains the cachet and the *zeitgeist* of
'nowness' – the aura of the scientific cutting edge
and the hidden promise of the dawn of a new
technological age revolutionising the way of life of
all humanity. The internet itself might now be taken
for granted – viewed only as little more than a
telephone with pictures – but we are still just
scratching the surface of its possible applications.
Like Bill Gates, Rory Carlisle sees himself as a
pioneer in the field of information technology.

Can there really be anyone in the UK – or within
the 'global village' for that matter – who still does
not know of Rory Carlisle? Anyone who needs his

growing business empire – expanding at a comparable rate to the Universe itself – to be explained? Is there anyone anywhere who has not used or encountered his companies' services? SearchQuest – his search engine – is the only true worldwide rival to Google. His MeMeMeee domain name is bigger than Yahoo or MSN – in the UK at least – as both an ISP and free webmail provider. His auction site – RorySell, modelled on Ebay but specialising exclusively in prestige cars, private jets and luxury yachts is the global leader in its lucrative and prestigious field. The holding company for all of these enterprises – RoryCar Ltd. – is worth more millions than can be counted or imagined. Last week, I went to meet the man behind the myth – armed with my trusty dictaphone and on a mission to interview him on behalf of GQ and its undoubtedly curious readership.

As befits a man of his status, Rory Carlisle has several properties all over the world. The Carlisle property portfolio includes: an elegant Georgian townhouse in Belgravia; a luxury penthouse above his holding company's offices in Canary Wharf; a 'get away from it all' rural estate in Aberdeenshire; an Alpine retreat in the Swiss *Graubunden* canton – complete with swimming pool, tennis courts and private ski lodge; an Upper East Side townhouse and an Upper West Side penthouse (with Central Park views) in Manhattan; a movie star-style mansion in LA's Bel Air. And these are merely the *documented* properties – those owned personally by Mr. Carlisle himself. The list does not include the network of commercial buildings and residences held throughout Eastern Europe, Asia and Africa in the name of corporate subsidiaries of RoryCar Ltd. For the record, my audience with Rory Carlisle took place at the afore-mentioned Canary Wharf penthouse. Read on to discover how it feels to meet one of the richest men on the planet – a man to whom both Midas and Croesus might be tempted to doff the cap and bend the knee.

I stepped off the DLR at South Quay station and walked along the Old Millwall dock until I arrived at a building directly opposite what was once the ill-fated London Arena. Rory Carlisle's penthouse occupies the top three floors of this ten-storey building – to the untrained eye it appears relatively modest compared to some of the 'mini-Manhattan' skyscrapers in the vicinity. The building is a hive of activity during daylight hours – office workers scurrying hither and thither through electronic barriers, armed with hi-tech swipe cards. As you enter, a row of three identikit blonde receptionists seated behind a marble 'Welcome Desk' offer hollow, insipid 'professional smiles'. I approached Stepford Receptionist No. 1, stating my name and the purpose of my visit. She consulted a computer screen, her elegantly manicured fingernails skipping lightly across a keyboard – a secretarial symphony expertly played.

"Ah yes," she said finally. "GQ magazine. You're expected. Mr. Carlisle's valet will be down to collect you shortly."

The word 'valet' stood out in my mind immediately – reaffirming that I would soon no longer be in the company of a mere mortal but would instead shortly find myself in the presence of one of the true super-rich of our mega-rich era. Valet. V-A-L-E-T. I had visions of someone whose job description included the act of placing one's toothpaste on one's toothbrush at bedtime! I took my place on a plush leather banquette and waited. And I waited. And I waited. And I *waited…*

It was a good thing I had the foresight to bring a paperback with me – James Ellroy's fabulous *Cold Six Thousand* – as I was left waiting in the lobby for well over an hour. I twice reminded one of the blonde clones of my "three o'clock with Mr. Carlisle". Each time she replied like a well-trained *Dalek*: "Mr. Carlisle's valet will be down to collect you shortly". On my third time of asking she added: "You *are* expected." The 'are' part of the sentence was supposed to be reassuring – but time nevertheless dragged ever onwards. As the Rolling Stones once famously remarked, time waits for no man – but I certainly waited for Rory Carlisle. Eventually, just as Ellroy had me truly engrossed and speculating about the precise extent of the conspiracy and the exact nature of the Mob's involvement in the assassination of JFK, a tall, thin, gaunt man appeared directly in front of me. He looked like one of those horror movie butlers left alone to guard the castle while the vampire sleeps in the cellar below. Suddenly, all those late nights spent watching *Hammer Horror* films on cable TV came back to haunt me. If this meeting had been taking place in Transylvania, it couldn't have been more fitting.

"I am Jardine. Mr. Carlisle's valet. If you would care to follow me, Sir." he intoned gravely. I stood up to follow him – wondering how people like that always manage to make the word 'Sir' sound so much like an insult!

We took a key-operated private elevator to the top floor. Our ascent was conducted in total silence. I used the time to study Jardine carefully. He really did look like an extra from a *Hammer* movie – only, seeing him now at close quarters, I could tell it wasn't Dracula's servant whom he most closely resembled. He was more like some hybrid of the Igor character who assisted Professor Frankenstein spliced with Lurch from the Addams Family!

The lift arrived with a cheery 'ping' and the doors slid gracefully open. We stepped directly out into a sitting room-come-reception area. The carpet was a plush cream shag pile affair and my first thought was that it must be a real bastard to clean.

I even checked the soles of my shoes – grimy from tramping the London streets. The walls were pale green – so pale that without closer inspection they could almost have been white. The furniture was an eclectic mix of antique and ultra-modern. An antique bergere sofa clung to one wall, upholstered in bold, broad cream and maroon stripes. Jardine gestured pointedly towards it.

"If you will kindly be seated, Sir, I shall inform Mr. Carlisle of your presence."

I sat meekly and obediently – feeling as though I were awaiting either a critical job interview or visiting the dentist for root canal surgery. Jardine disappeared around a corner while I stared at the paintings surrounding me. Now, I'm no art expert, but I recognised at least two of the canvasses as iconic images from major German Expressionist painters. Both were originals.

Jardine eventually reappeared and led me along a seemingly never-ending corridor to Rory Carlisle's study. At last I found myself in the presence of the great man himself. Carlisle stood up as I entered the room. He was stationed behind quite possibly the largest desk I have ever seen. He reached out his right hand but made no real effort to extend it across the oceanic space of the desktop. Instead, I was forced to lean right across, straining my back in the process and almost sprawling inelegantly over the desk. It was one-upmanship of the most blatant kind. The theme continued when we sat down; Carlisle in a magnificent leather throne of an armchair, yours truly in an armless (and considerably lower) plainer number.

Rory Carlisle is immensely fit and sprightly for a man of fifty. He could easily pass for someone ten – or even fifteen – years younger (and frequently does so, "especially when entertaining young ladies" – or so he tells me). His thick mane of blonde hair (frighteningly akin to that of the Stepford receptionists downstairs) is slicked back and his crystal clear blue eyes seem to stare right through you without mercy. In the 1950's he would have been described as possessing 'matinee idol good looks'. I, however, am inescapably reminded of Gordon Gekko – Michael Douglas's go-getting High Financier character in the classic '80's movie, *Wall Street*. Carlisle is wearing a monogrammed baby blue Sea Island cotton shirt from *Turnbull & Asser* and tailored cream slacks. If I could see his shoes beneath the titanic desk, I would expect them to be handmade – probably crocodile loafers (and almost certainly from either *Trickers* or *Lobb*).

"Jardine, will you bring us some tea, please," Carlisle asks pleasantly of the hovering valet. Jardine nods deferentially and leaves.

"Now, I believe you have some questions for me? Please feel free to fire away when ready," he says urbanely, turning his attention back to me. There is neither apology nor explanation for having left me in the lobby for the best part of a lifetime. I suppose, when you are as wealthy as Rory Carlisle, apologies are optional.

With my dictaphone placed between us, looking like a marker for some stranded battleship on the tabletop of the Cabinet War Rooms, I begin:

GQ: Like most people, I'm well aware of your status and success in the IT industry – but why car sales? Where do the cars fit in?
RC: It actually all began with cars. My father was a car dealer in Southwest London for many years – selling all the top German marques. He planned to disinherit me but surprised me when he died and leaving me a substantial legacy. This meant I was in possession of the significant capital I needed to invest in the IT industry at the time I bought into the shell company that eventually became the MeMeMeee ISP.

GQ: Your father planned to disinherit you?
RC: Next question.

GQ: Why invest in IT at all? Why not keep on selling the cars and simply hire someone else to do the donkey work for you?
RC: It crossed my mind, of course – but I also wanted something of my own that I'd created for myself...rather than something I had simply been handed as a *fait accompli*. Furthermore, I happened to be in the right place at the right time. An

acquaintance with whom I'd studied Philosophy at London University had progressed to PhD research in Artificial Intelligence. He knew some people who were desperately looking for financial backers for a new IT company they were trying to launch – and the unadventurous banks and venture capitalists were, as usual, steering clear of things they couldn't understand. I invested – and later bought out both of my two business partners.

GQ: How much was your initial investment?
RC: Look, this is all documented in business archives up and down the land. Better still, put your enquiry into my SearchQuest search engine and see what it throws up! You're a journalist – surely you did your research before coming to see me?

At this point Jardine reappeared, carrying a silver salver containing fine bone china teacups and a piping hot silver pot of tea. Silence reigned as Jardine poured out two cups of golden tea – the stillness punctuated only by a sound reminiscent of a miniature waterfall as the cups filled. Jardine then stole quietly out of the room.

"*Fortnum & Mason* Golden Orange Pekoe," said Carlisle appreciatively, holding up his teacup. "Once you've tried this, you'll never drink any other tea." I smiled and took a sip, even though it was still too hot to drink.

GQ: Do you still take an interest in Philosophy?
RC: (*laughs*) **You cannot be alive and not take an interest in Philosophy, my friend – even if you remain blissfully unaware of the fact. Even your very existence is a philosophical conundrum. Remember Descartes and 'the *cogito*'? Existentialist doubt. All of life inevitably reduces to – and is encompassed by – philosophical questions. Ethics. Physics. Metaphysics. Epistemology. The nature of truth. The existence of God. Politics. Semantics. Linguistics. Mathematics. Quantum Mechanics. Aesthetics. AI. Free will and Determinism. Parallel universes. The paradox of mind-body duality. The inescapable subjectivity of the human condition. There really is only one subject in existence: Philosophy.**

GQ: Wow! And that stuff is floating around in your head all day every day?
RC: I think it's actually floating around in everyone's head – if only they'd stop and listen to their inner voice once in a while. More tea?

GQ: More tea would be lovely, thank you. Now, to talk 'nitty gritty': you're one of a very small cohort of people considered to be 'capitalist icons'. How do you feel about that – and how do you see the responsibilities of this role?
RC: Well, if what you say is true, I'm somewhat perturbed at being categorised in such a manner.

For one thing, I certainly do not see myself as a 'capitalist' – at least, not in the cigar-smoking, top hat wearing, exploiting the workers clichéd way I think you might be implying! Certainly, I am a rich man – but I most definitely do not see myself as a capitalist. In fact, I actually think capitalism is doomed and will die out completely over the next few generations.

GQ: Capitalism is doomed? How so?

RC: Actually, I think I should both amend and qualify that comment a little further. What I meant to say is that I believe a certain *brand* of capitalism is doomed. You see, the flavour of 'capitalism' we have now is effectively a sorry legacy of the Cold War and the demise of Soviet Communism. The checks and balances that were in place between the two competing global ideologies during the Cold War era meant that capitalism was still required to 'sell itself' to the people; to 'care' about the consumer to some extent. Now that the Cold War is over – and capitalism has effectively 'won' – that imperative has vanished overnight. Now, the worst kind of capitalist is running riot and ruling the roost – believing there is no longer any need to provide value or care about anything other than the rapid accumulation of personal profit by any means possible. The former checks and balances are off and it's open season on a global scale for the worst kind of capitalist – the sort who couldn't give a fig for community, society or the ecology of the planet. And that kind of capitalist will pretty quickly destroy both the way we live and the environment on which we depend. And I am certainly not *that* kind of capitalist. I also truly believe that kind of capitalist will eventually be stopped – once the groundswell of global public opinion eventually turns fully against them, that is.

GQ: So, what kind of capitalist are you?
RC: I suppose, if it's a neat soundbite you're after, you could call me a 'caring capitalist' or a 'capitalist of conscience'. I believe very firmly in such principles as the strong having a moral duty to help the weak, the imperative to share one's good fortune with those less fortunate and the concept of 'giving something back'. That's why I'm now setting up the Carlisle Charitable Collective – 'CCC' in honour of my father's memory – to redistribute much of the wealth and profit my businesses generate towards such deserving causes as conservation, medical research, global famine, poverty relief and helping the homeless. And I further believe that I am in a much better position to help from a position of strength – in simple terms, I have so much more to give. And it seems to me it is far better that *I* am left to direct my resources in needy directions than simply to rely on the Government to do it through taxation – I mean, do *you* trust *them* to actively help all the causes I've

just stated to the extent that is required? So, my view is that it's not *being* rich that is a crime and an iniquity in itself – it's *who* is holding the wealth and *what* they are doing with it. Remember, this is not a bad world unless we make it one – and we can easily make it a good world through our everyday attitudes and actions.

GQ: So, you see yourself as another Bill Gates?

RC: Very much so. In fact, I see Mr. Gates very much as a role model. Bill Gates and his wife have publicly pledged to give away 95% of their personal wealth to good causes – and they have begun to put that plan into action. He has already spent billions on Aids/HIV research and in helping Africa. If all so-called 'capitalists' were to adopt the Gates model then our society – and our planet – can look forward to a very healthy future. However, if 'traditional' or throwback capitalists continue to pillage, rape and plunder our resources – both human and environmental – then they risk either destroying the planet or creating an underclass so marginalized and resentful it will one day turn on them like a rampaging Frankenstein's monster and destroy them entirely. After all, such a vision is not without historical precedent, you know – consider, if you will, the French Revolution and the Russian Revolution. It hasn't happened in the UK yet, of course – but frankly, just give it time, the way things are going. You see, as a capitalist society we face a very simple choice – either share the wealth and empower the people around us (and get them on our side and working with us) or continue to repress, exploit and cheat the less fortunate (in which case capitalism will eventually destroy itself). It's pretty much 'reap what you sow'!

GQ: And you really think the British people will rise up in armed rebellion?
RC: Absolutely – if they are pushed much further. We Brits, of course, have an inherent sense of 'fair play' deeply ingrained within our culture. We are also naturally very stoic and resilient. But there's always going to be a straw that can break the camel's back. Once the Brits *realise* they are not being treated fairly but are in fact constantly being exploited and played for suckers, they will rise up angrily in pursuit of something called 'justice'. Of that, I have no doubt. It's as sure as eggs is eggs. It may take two or three generations – but it *will* happen. Unless the really rich folk (like me) and (especially) our Government are *seen* to play fair, share the wealth, help those in need and actually *care* about such issues as iniquity and injustice – then the whirlwind is coming. And that, in a nutshell, is capitalism's central challenge in the modern, post-Soviet era. Frankly, my friend, *[and at this point Rory Carlisle leaned forward in his chair and looked me squarely in the eyes]* the recipe for success is really very simple: equality, justice and

opportunity for all. **Fairness is the easiest antidote to social unrest – and the basis of a stable society. Without it, we are all doomed.** *[With a flourish, Rory Carlisle then switched off my dictaphone. The message was clear: interview terminated]*

GQ: Wow! Some food for thought there! Mr. Carlisle, on behalf of GQ magazine and its readers: thank you very much.

Moments later, Jardine ushered me back into the private elevator and turned the key. All at once I was back in the lobby – feeling as though my audience with The Great Man had never even happened. As I stepped out into the rain that was now falling hard around Canary Wharf only one thought remained in my head: that really was quite exceptional tea.

© **Dominic Kember**

After the journalist left, Rory Carlisle asked Jardine to bring him more tea – and some of those delectable Scottish butterscotch shortbread biscuits. He wondered if he had gone too far with the journalist – hadn't the interview been little more than an ill-judged self-indulgence? Certainly, he'd got quite carried away in places – reducing himself to merely a soapbox rant; quite unseemly. Calm down, he told himself. Dunk another biscuit in the tea. Re-assess. No real damage was done. Yes, he'd been a bit idealistic and outspoken – but there was nothing in there to connect him (or his views) directly with Anarchist Pete. Besides, he'd only spoken the truth. The part about the Charitable Collective was absolutely true – another little project for Jardine to organise on his behalf (alongside the rather interesting *covert* project Jardine was already organising).

Rory pressed the intercom and called Jardine back yet again.

"Certainly, Sir," the valet replied; his voice a perfect rendition of acquiescence and patient, dedicated servitude.

In the moments it took for Jardine to arrive, Rory Carlisle considered his manservant carefully. He represented a degree of loyalty that even money could not buy. In fact, it was not even money that *did* command Jardine's loyalty. No, Sir! Jardine's loyalty was guaranteed even if Carlisle ceased to pay him *any* salary whatsoever. No, Jardine's fidelity was guaranteed through one of the oldest tricks in the book – holding a trump card on him and keeping it locked securely in your private safe. It was a trick learned from countless secret service operations the world over – a staple of the spying game with a pedigree extending backwards from the CIA and KGB to the Roman Empire. It was a trick beloved of blackmailers, extortionists and the Mob. To put it quite simply, Rory Carlisle had the 'dirt' on Jardine – and he used it like a

Love, Gudrun Ensslin

Sword of Damocles over his valet's head to guarantee
unswerving devotion of the most fanatical kind.

'Knowledge is power' says the maxim – and in
this case Rory Carlisle had the knowledge about
Jardine that gave him unlimited power over his servant.
All those sordid little trips Jardine took to Morocco
couched delicately within the euphemism of "one's
little holidays" – trips indirectly subsidised by Carlisle.
The underage boys. The unmentionable practices. The
unusual accessories. The clandestine photographs and
covert film of these activities lodged securely within
Carlisle's private safe – ready for downloading onto
the internet as video streams or galleries of lurid
technicolour stills. Oh, the joys of the digital age! – so
much *easier* to run a smear campaign; so much *simpler*
to be able to destroy credibility and a reputation at the
mere touch of a button. Or perhaps the evidence could
be passed directly to the police? The dutiful act of the
concerned citizen! And rumour had it that life inside
was no picnic for those of Jardine's persuasion. No!
Jardine's loyalty was assured – making him perfect for
every little task that Rory Carlisle demanded of him…
and in particular: BANKER BINGO.

It was all so beautiful. If Carlisle's BANKER
BINGO project ever unravelled then it was Jardine
who would be the fall guy; Jardine who would take the
flak; Jardine who would be held responsible and
publically vilified. Jardine – the rebel manservant who
had misappropriated his Master's funds to set up a
secret fantasy plot to take revenge on the iniquitous

society that kept him in a demeaning and servile role; a mere lackey bereft of equality and opportunity…driven to breaking point to become the worm that turned!

The funds for BANKER BINGO were located within – and operated from – Jardine's personal account. It was Jardine who (operating under instruction from Carlisle, of course) ensured the servers hosting the heavily encrypted BANKER BINGO website (found by a seemingly dead yet actually encrypted link from the URBANE GORILLA website) were constantly on the move from one remote East European location to another – making both websites virtually untraceable. It was also to Jardine that the network of fake brass plate companies registered all around the world that 'owned' URBANE GORILLA would lead – assuming that anyone could actually unravel the jungle of smoke screens, loose ends and incomplete paperwork (additionally fuelled by generous backhanders) that provided cover for the GORILLA website's 'ownership'.

It was even Jardine who personally hired the private investigators to research among the terrorists to find the candidate who would eventually become Anarchist Pete's perfect 'apprentice' – the man (or woman) to put the BANKER BINGO plan into action. Handily, it was therefore Jardine's face that had been seen – even when using a false name – in connection with the entire project. Thus, if it all came crashing down, it was Jardine in the firing line; *Jardine* who would be identified as 'Anarchist Pete' and not Rory

Love, Gudrun Ensslin

Carlisle himself. Even the fact of Carlisle apparently being the one responsible for uploading Anarchist Pete's rants and rhetoric to the URBANE GORILLA/BANKER BINGO websites from his own PC's and laptops would ultimately count against Jardine – after all, who else would have such easy access to Rory Carlisle's personal computer equipment but his faithful servant?

"He must have seen my password over my shoulder whilst serving the tea, Officer," Carlisle could hear himself saying – his voice the epitome of sadness and regret. "I only wish I had been more security conscious – but somehow your awareness drops in your own home among your closest associates…where you least expect betrayal to rear its ugly head."

Then, to ensure Jardine was fully in the frame, it only required one or two evenings when Carlisle had a cast iron alibi for being elsewhere at the time that 'Pete' was uploading his invective from Carlisle's desktop PC…while Jardine remained in the Canary Wharf penthouse alone. And alibis could be bought – especially when you were as wealthy as Rory Carlisle. Hence, even if Jardine tried to double-cross him and confess all (which he wouldn't because of the 'dirt') then even the 'facts' would condemn the hapless valet – and his pathetic attempt to smear his Master would only be viewed as further confirmation of his lunatic secret resentment of the hierarchy of society and his own place within it. Hence, his need to create the persona of 'Anarchist Pete'. Hence, an open and shut case! Poor old Jardine – to be convicted of 'biting the hand that feeds'. How very déclassé!

Rory Carlisle smiled to himself. It was such a perfect plan – so beautifully conceived; so expertly executed. He only wished he could tell someone about it – revel in its glory; reveal *himself* as its true creator…not that craven pederast, Jardine. But, of course, this was the one thing that Rory Carlisle could never do; the one boast he was not allowed to make. Until after the revolution, URBANE GORILLA / BANKER BINGO / Anarchist Pete had to remain a private pleasure; a secret, vicarious thrill.

At that precise moment, Jardine appeared. His face was its usual inscrutable mask. Rory felt an amused indulgence – a condescending warmth – towards his valet as the man stood before his master's desk awaiting his latest set of instructions. Carlisle half-smiled at him.

"You called, Sir?" Jardine enquired solicitiously.

"Yes, indeed," Rory replied. "I'm going out. Have that file we discussed on my desk by six o'clock sharp, will you Jardine?"

"Very good, Sir," said Jardine, with a slight tilt of the head.

As Rory took the elevator down to the basement garage he felt very pleased with himself indeed. Forget the journalist – there had been no real slip of the tongue there. Forget any personal risks – Jardine was still in situ as the fall guy. Later on, there would be something very interesting to read sitting on his desk and demanding his full attention – and then maybe 'the project' would at last advance to its final stage. All was well in Rory Carlisle's world. Arriving in the garage, he looked around among his collection of upmarket cars. So much luxury, so much choice – and all of it belonging entirely to him. A wide selection of vehicles was available to him at each and every one of his properties – with any surplus lovingly moth-balled in a warehouse in the New Forest. For all his hidden anarchist and environmentalist sympathies, the motor car never really left Rory's bloodstream. Perhaps that was one of the few signs that his father's blood and DNA still flowed through his veins.

So, what was it to be? The *Aston*? The *McLaren*? The *Lambo*? Eventually, he decided to take the *Bentley* out for a spin – a quick circuit of the Isle of Dogs; hands luxuriating on the tactile leather of the steering wheel, the merest touch of a foot propelling this sophisticated urban tank…no feeling in the world quite like it.

The file was sitting on Carlisle's desk when he returned. It was neatly bound in a maroon leather folder – making it resemble an upmarket restaurant menu. Rory smiled to himself and immediately headed off to take a shower. He felt exceedingly pleased with himself at having managed to delay the reading of the file – despite an overwhelming temptation to immediately dive in and devour its contents; to greedily gorge on the covert information contained within. No! One must take one's time over delectable pleasures – after all, this was the very characteristic that defined the *connoisseur*. Delaying the reading of the file would only make the event itself more enjoyable – and he wanted to truly *savour* the experience. If the file contained details of 'the one' – unlike so many of the others before it – then Rory wanted to feel at his most relaxed when his plans finally took shape.

Having showered, Rory Carlisle lowered himself once more into his favourite leather armchair. He was wearing *Sulka* silk pyjamas, a Royal blue bathrobe and embossed *Trickers* slippers. He poured himself a large Scotch whisky from the decanter that had been so thoughtfully placed nearby by Jardine, picked up the folder and began to read:

GEORG KRENDLER; ex-Baader Meinhof
Born 1949; Wuppertal, West Germany. Only child.

<u>Father</u>: Wieland Krendler; pre-War photographer; attached to a Wehrmacht Photographic & Propaganda Unit on the Eastern Front – later transferred to the Waffen SS for the Ardennes counter attack and final defence of the Reich. Post-War; owner of a camera shop/photographic studio in Wuppertal. Died Wuppertal, 1979 (cardiac arrest).

<u>Mother</u>: Hannelore Krendler (nee Engelhardt);

seamstress. Died in childbirth, Wuppertal, 1949.

Profile:
Georg Krendler was a studious loner with few
friends during his childhood years in Wuppertal.
He developed radical left-wing sympathies fairly
early in life. These feelings remained – quickly
becoming fervent and leading to frequent
arguments and disagreements with his conservative,
authoritarian father. A fortnight's 'holiday' in
England in 1967 (arranged by Wieland Krendler) –
a student exchange visit to South Shields –
represented the father's final attempt to rebuild lost
ground with his only son. Georg's absence
happened to coincide with the notorious police
killing of student protestor, Benno Ohnesorg, in
Berlin – further politicising the impressionable 18-
year-old Georg on his return to Wuppertal.

Later that year, Georg Krendler left Wuppertal to
study Philosophy at Frankfurt University. He was
immediately accepted into the clique of hardcore
campus radicals. At first, Georg lived in student
accommodation but soon moved in with his
Marxism lecturer, Julius Semmler (see Notes) – a
seasoned radical with KGB/Stasi connections. It
was Semmler who introduced Krendler to Andreas
Baader (see Notes) and facilitated his conversion
from tacit supporter to activist within the Red
Army Faction. At first, Krendler remained a low-

level operative within Baader Meinhof/RAF. Operating under the code-name 'Engels', he delivered messages, transported supplies, organised safe houses, carried out surveillance (etc). Krendler remained dormant during the RAF's 1970 absence in Jordan for training with the PLO.

Krendler was reactivated in January 1971 following a shoot-out with police in Nuremburg (in which two Baader Meinhof operatives were captured). As the Baader Meinhof violence escalated throughout 1971 (peaking in May 1972), Krendler was involved in the thick of things; ostensibly as 'logistical support' (acting as lookout; getaway driver; organiser of safe houses; transporter of weaponry and ordnance; bagman and fence). He is also suspected of direct involvement in at least one murder.

Krendler was not in Frankfurt on the morning of June 1st 1972 – when Baader was finally captured – having already fled to England in the company of his girlfriend, an Englishwoman; Cressida Harris (see Notes). In England, Georg and Cressida married – allowing Georg to remain indefinitely in the UK. They subsequently settled in Cressida's home county of Kent.

Life continued unobtrusively for the Krendlers in Kent. At first, they shared a modest semi in Sittingbourne. Cressida found work as a secretary in the typing pool of an insurance company in Chatham while Georg eventually secured employment as a gardener – becoming extremely dedicated to his new 'profession'. The couple's union did not produce any children. Their relative peace was shattered in 1983 when Cressida suddenly abandoned her job to go and live among her 'sisters' protesting outside the US Air Base at Greenham Common. She simultaneously announced she was a lesbian and would also be leaving the marriage. Thus, Georg was left alone – with no family or friends in Germany to whom he could return (his wider German family having largely perished in the War or otherwise become distanced).

Krendler, who inherited a relatively substantial sum from the proceeds of selling his late father's business, remained in the house in Sittingbourne for several months before securing a new position as Head Groundsman at Cassandra Ladies' College – a fee-paying girls-only boarding school in extensive private grounds near the Kent village of Eastling. The 'live-in' position of Head Groundsman (with rent-free occupation of a small cottage on school land) is a role Krendler occupies to this day. Enquiries show that Krendler is now a highly popular and fiercely loyal employee of the College – readily providing private German tuition to Sixth Form girls studying the subject.

Love, Gudrun Ensslin

Since Krendler's arrival, Cassandra Ladies' College has gained an unrivalled reputation for excellence in German Language studies – with a 100% track record for higher grade A-level passes (of which over 70% have been Grade A).

Attempts to date to engage Georg Krendler in political conversation at local hostelries have thus far been rebuffed.

Rory Carlisle closed the file and pushed it away across the desk. He lifted his tumbler and drained the final drops of whisky, craning his neck right back to do so. Krendler was perfect. It had to be him! After so many high hopes leading only to false starts – a seemingly endless parade of disappointing dossiers on tinpot terrorists and would-be back-bedroom revolutionaries from all over Europe – Krendler appeared to be the real deal. Krendler was definitely 'the one'. Furthermore, he was already living over here in England (where Rory sought to launch his otherwise global plan) – meaning Krendler was accessible.

Certain facts and sentences about Krendler jumped out at Carlisle immediately; they seemingly leapt off the page. They were facts so fascinating and eerily coincidental that they served only to confirm beyond all doubt that Krendler was undoubtedly the man he had been seeking. Indeed, with all the common ground they appeared to share, Rory felt he knew exactly how the German thought and functioned. After all, but for the mere serendipities of age and nationality, they were practically one and the same person!

Consider the Baader Meinhof man's profile: an only child; mother died in childbirth; a poor relationship with an autocratic father leading to eventual estrangement; an unexpected inheritance; uneasy early relationships with women; a loner with strong political convictions; a student of Philosophy.

It was truly uncanny. Beyond age and nationality – was it Georg Krendler or Rory Carlisle who was being described? In the end it was undoubtedly this bizarre synthesis – this mysterious symmetry – that settled it. Georg Krendler was not just 'the one' but THE ONE. It was he who was *The One* who would bring the plans of Rory Carlisle to fruition – THE ONE who would enact the directives of the BANKER BINGO website and at last bring retribution, justice and havoc in equal measure to the corrupt financiers of our shameful era. Rory felt his heart beating faster. It *had* to be Krendler – at *any* cost.

He determined to call Jardine at once to order him to get the necessary wheels set in motion: he would instruct his valet to make immediate contact with *Herr* Krendler and to supply the German with the necessary access codes for the BANKER BINGO website. Rory could then draft some 'Anarchist Pete' blog posts that would speak to Georg Krendler

Love, Gudrun Ensslin

personally. It was time to reinstate the social conscience of 1967. It was time to awaken The Beast from its slumbers...

Love, Gudrun Ensslin

CHAPTER EIGHT: LEBENSWEISHEIT

Baader Meinhof was a misnomer. If anything, it should have been Baader Ensslin. Or, more accurately still, Ensslin Baader. Gudrun was the real brains and driving force behind the group. Ulrike Meinhof was little more than a jumped-up journalist hanging wide-eyed onto the coat tails of the others for the ride. If Ulrike hadn't been so useful and adept in garnering money, favours and 'safe house' accommodation from her trendy chums in the *schili*, then she'd have been dumped on the roadside years earlier. The others often treated Ulrike with open contempt and withering derision – and never more so than when she messed up the Altonauerstrasse bank raid. To me, it was (and always will be) the Ensslin Baader Gang.

In April 1968 the *Kaufhaus Schneider* and *Kauhof* department stores in Frankfurt went up in flames – Gudrun and Andreas skipping up the escalator the wrong way, hand-in-hand, like Bonnie and Clyde, to plant firebombs in *Schneider's* Women's Clothing and Furniture departments moments before closing time. Baader's prophecy to me had been fulfilled – and *Kommune I*'s directive carried out. I was both exhilarated and inspired. The following evening – after a tip-off to the cops – the four fire-bombers were arrested. Gudrun, Andreas, Thorwald Proll and Horst Söhnlein were behind bars. In the space of twenty fours hours my exhilaration turned to deflation. To cheer myself up, I accepted an invitation from Julius Semmler to leave my student accommodation and move into his apartment rent-free. We could then drink, smoke dope and discuss politics until the small hours every night. Furthermore, Semmler's apartment was on the ground floor of a spacious modern block near the University – handily within crawling distance of my studies. It also provided access to picturesque communal gardens in which to relax and temporarily forget the troubles of our invidious world.

Not a lot of studying was done, however. That summer some Nazi swine tried to assassinate 'Red Rudi' and we students came out in protest all over the FDR. I had to help Semmler organise the student sit-in at Frankfurt Uni – arguably my finest hour as a student. The vibe was revolution and anger and fightback – and the high was the high of our own collective power. Still, I kept thinking of Gudrun and Andreas – languishing in custody and missing all the fun. On October 31st the 'Gang of Four' was finally sentenced – three years inside *Tegel* each. It would not be until June the following year that I would see Gudrun and Andreas again.

*   *   *

Love, Gudrun Ensslin

In June 1969 Gudrun and Andreas were released on parole and appeared on Semmler's doorstep. It was I who answered the door to find them both entwined, grinning from ear to ear like naughty schoolchildren. Despite her recent incarceration, Gudrun still looked a vision. I stood there hesitating, blinking at them, not sure if they were actually real or merely apparitions; illusory products of my wishful thinking. It was Andreas who broke the stand-off, stepping forward to hug me warmly (how I wish it had been Gudrun who had taken such a step).

"Greetings, Comrade," he said – his easy charm and wide smile in place as always. "Where's Julius?"

Without waiting for my reply, he pushed past me into the flat – closely followed by Gudrun, who gave me a cursory nod. Semmler was still at the University completing the day's lectures, so I had the pair to myself for a while. We sat in the front room chatting – although it soon turned into a private tutorial. Instead of being the student of Julius Semmler, I was now the student of Andreas Baader and Gudrun Ensslin.

"Have you got any *Schnapps* – or, better still, Scotch?" asked Andreas. "Come on, you must know where Julius keeps it," he laughed.

I began a frantic search of all the drawers and cupboards in the flat. Gudrun sat primly on the sofa next to Andreas – her knees together, her back straight, perched right on the front edge of the seat. My eyes kept darting back to her, searching her up and down, mentally undressing her as much as I could. Eventually, I found a half empty bottle of Cognac in the kitchen and returned with three unwashed tumblers. I set the booty down on the coffee table. Baader poured himself the lion's share. I started to talk about Philosophy – reserving special praise for Gudrun's ancestor, Hegel.

"Academic wisdom is all very well," said Andreas, taking a big slug of Cognac and shaking his head like a dog in the rain, "but what you really need is *practical* wisdom."

"Words are useless without action," added Gudrun – it was the only thing she'd said to me since she'd arrived. I responded to her immediately. I sat forward on the edge of my seat – subconsciously aping her pose – and looked right into her kohl-smeared eyes.

"Whatever it is you're doing," I said. "I want to be involved."

Semmler arrived just as the bottle of Cognac was being drained of its last drops.

"I hope you've been to the grocery store," laughed Andreas, by way of greeting. There was hugging and hearty back-slapping all round. Enviously, I noticed Julius received a hug from Gudrun.

"Listen," Andreas said to Julius, a relaxed arm draped languidly around the Professor's shoulders as though they were best friends on the way home from the local *bierstube*. "Is there somewhere we can talk – in private?"

Love, Gudrun Ensslin

Semmler shot a glance across at me and said with a defiance and determination that surprised me:

"Anything we say can be said in front of Georg – he is absolutely loyal to the cause." All eyes then turned to Gudrun, who nodded her assent. I could have kissed her!

"Well, we're certainly not going back to jail, that's for sure!" said Andreas, sinking back onto the sofa.

"We're getting some people together and raising funds for some more actions," Gudrun added. Now she was centre stage and suddenly animated. Talking about important things – not all those pleasantries, japes and other time-wasting *trivia*. "We'll need places to stay here in Frankfurt – and we'll need money," she continued.

"Right," Semmler nodded, hand on chin, thinking.

"Funds are low!" sang Andreas in a mock-operatic voice. Gudrun sighed and gritted her teeth.

"It looks as though we'll have to resort to writing begging letters to all those liberal shits again," she sneered.

Gudrun and Andreas hung out in Frankfurt for the next three or four months – shifting from one address to another and collecting money from various *schili* along the way. Andreas – a former Borstal Boy himself – had a network of borstal runaways gathered around him...kids who thought he truly walked on water. The boys – known to us as 'The Frankfurt

Apprentices' Collective' – were controlled and politicised by Andreas. They ran around for him like trusty little gophers – fetching this, carrying that, stealing this, selling that. The Boys were funded by students and *schili*. My first role for the Gang – having sworn absolute loyalty to Gudrun herself – was to coordinate the Boys; to ensure that Andreas's directives were accurately received, correctly interpreted and faithfully carried out.

In November, the 'Gang of Four' was summoned back to prison to complete their sentences. Only Horst Söhnlein obeyed.

"Can you drive?" Semmler asked me one day. It was actually one of the few useful things my father ever taught me.

"What do you have in mind?" I asked. "A picnic at Kreuzberg!"

Semmler laughed.

"Not exactly," he replied. "But you're aiming in the right geographical direction at least. Andreas and Gudrun are leaving the country. I want you to take my car and drive them to Hanau. There'll be another car waiting there to take them on the next leg of their journey. I have to be elsewhere tonight or I'd do it myself. It would mean a lot if you could do this, Georg. It won't be forgotten, I promise you."

"Tonight?" I mouthed, shocked.

"Tonight," Julius replied firmly, waving the keys to his *VW* Beetle at me as though he were ringing a small bell. I looked at him standing there expectantly

Love, Gudrun Ensslin

– a small man in a tweed jacket and checked trousers; straggly, thinning light brown hair flying in all directions – every inch the stereotypical 'nutty Professor'. A harmless pantomime figure. It was all I could do to stop myself snatching the keys right out of his hand. It wasn't so much the excitement and the sheer adrenaline kick of helping real-life fugitives on the run that fired me up so much – it was more the opportunity to spend time in close proximity with my beloved Gudrun once again…and in a situation in which she was, to some extent, dependent on insignificant little me! I held out my hand and Semmler dropped the keys into my waiting palm. He looked thoughtful for a moment and then held my gaze with great earnestness.

"Whatever you do," he began, in his deepest, most serious tone. "*Don't* let Andreas drive!"

I picked Gudrun and Andreas up from a safe house in the east of the city – not far from the main road to Hanau itself. It was almost dusk and it was very cold. The heater in the car was broken and you could see your breath in front of you like so much cigarette smoke. I wore a woollen hat, a sheepskin jacket and a Frankfurt University scarf. I also borrowed Semmler's precious calf leather gloves. My legs were freezing in my jeans, though. The car shook and rattled like a World War One fighter plane on the runway.

Gudrun and Andreas emerged from the shadows to meet me as I swung the car into the car park at the front of a large, anonymous-looking block of flats. Andreas carried a *Wehrmacht* kitbag over his shoulder while Gudrun had no luggage at all. I stepped out of the car to greet them. The momentary dousing of the engine brought joyous relief.

"Nice wheels!" smirked Baader. Gudrun, however, looked distinctly pissed off.

"Couldn't you have got something better?" she snarled. "A *Mercedes* – or even an *Alfa*? This noisy heap of shit will draw the attention of the cops like flies! We could hear you coming five kilometres up the road! It sounds like a truck driving uphill with the handbrake on!"

I looked crestfallen and heartily chastened at the fact that 'my Gudrun' was making an angry criticism of me. However, Andreas came to my rescue – goosing Gudrun on the arse so hard she suddenly hopped forward comically, her mouth forming a perfect 'O'. You could see that she momentarily thought of slapping him. However, he shot her his trademark killer grin.

"Relax, honey," he said. "Give the kid a break. We're just three students going for a drive in our kind old Professor's car – no harm in that. Besides, it's only a short hop to Hanau."

We climbed into the Beetle. To my eternal joy – and against all expectation – it was Gudrun who sat next to me in the front seat. A chance to speak to her at last! Andreas spread himself lazily across the rear bench. He produced a pack of *Gitanes* and a pile of *Mickey Mouse* comic books from the kitbag and, despite the rapidly fading half-light, began to read. He was wearing his customary 'uniform' of black leather jacket, white T-shirt, dark jeans with turn-ups and white sneakers. He didn't appear to feel the cold one bit.

I fired up the engine and the old car rattled and wheezed; hopping and spluttering on the spot like a cartoon version of a car that could have leapt straight off the pages of one of Andreas's comics. Gudrun's sneer of distaste reappeared immediately. It was all she could do to stop herself putting her fingers in her ears. I smiled sheepishly at her and wondered if she could tell how my eyes were drawn repeatedly and magnetically towards her.

Of course she knew! Women always know these things. Unfortunately, she didn't give me any sort of encouragement. On the other hand, she didn't exactly appear to object either. She just seemed imperious – naturally regal. Somehow Gudrun always seemed to be above 'all that'. I was only glad she was wearing some shapeless green military fatigues under a baggy old coat – rather than a fashionable short skirt that would have so perfectly showcased her long, slender legs. Had she been wearing such a skirt, we surely would have crashed!

It was hard to converse properly above the mechanical roar of the engine – so we managed only to communicate in occasional bursts of shouting. However, there was one significant outcome to our chatter during that journey – Gudrun gave me my official operative's code-name: *Engels*.

"You come from Wuppertal and you are studying Marxism – so what else could it be?" Gudrun said with a half-smile.

Gudrun was good at nicknames – and pithy sloganeering. It was something of a speciality of hers. Most of the core members of the Baader Meinhof Gang used code-names that had been ascribed to them by Gudrun. Certainly, once they were all imprisoned for the final time, it was Gudrun who began handing out nicknames among her fellow prisoners based on characters from her favourite novel, *Moby Dick*. And most of those nicknames were wickedly satirical in-jokes – just like the lady herself; mercilessly scathing.

Engels: I liked it. It had both stature and gravitas. Not only that but it was the name that Gudrun Ensslin had chosen for me! Thus, as I saw it, it was Gudrun's 'pet name' for me – so I liked it even more.

When we arrived at Hanau, Andreas was fast asleep in the back of the car – snoring sufficiently loudly to almost drown out the engine noise. Gudrun was busily lecturing me on the importance of "dedicating oneself to the cause"; not "showing weakness" and not "becoming seduced by the petty bourgeois values and consumerist trinkets used to pacify the masses."

"You will never truly change society otherwise," she warned.

The changeover of vehicles took place in a small car park behind a rustic-looking tavern. Gudrun was overjoyed to see that, this time, she would be travelling in a *Mercedes*. It was a large, sleek, black executive model – bigger, faster and undoubtedly quieter than Semmler's Beetle. It was practically a diplomatic car. The irony was not lost on the newly-woken Baader.

"Couldn't you stick a couple of flags on the front?" he joked. "A hammer and sickle on one side and a black flag on the other!"

The car sat waiting like a giant poisonous spider with its legs tucked beneath itself. I didn't recognise the driver – a burly young man with an older, weather-beaten face. He wore a leather jacket much like Baader's and a matching grey scarf and cloth cap. As he walked by, I could see his face was scarred and pitted from a teenage bout of severe acne. Andreas and Gudrun seemed to know him well and greeted him effusively. They called him 'Tomas' – but, by now I realised, this was probably just another Gudrun-inspired code-name and not his real name at all. 'Tomas' nodded curtly at me and then put Andreas's kitbag in the *Mercedes'* vast boot. It was time to say goodbye to my passengers. Andreas gave me my now customary hug.

"Look after the Boys for me, will you?" he implored with an emotion I little suspected he possessed. "Tell them I haven't forgotten them." Then he broke away and added: "I'll send word to you via Julius with their next set of instructions."

I nodded – ever the eager serf. Then it was

Love, Gudrun Ensslin

Gudrun's turn. She stepped towards me. At last, I thought, an embrace! However, she only planted a momentary chaste kiss on my forehead and darted back out of reach – a wicked glint in her eyes.

"Take care, Engels," she said. "Study hard – but be *active* for the cause. We won't forget you."

I smiled sheepishly, still tongue-tied and utterly dumbstruck in her presence. How I wish I could have responded further.

Gudrun sashayed away from me and she and Andreas climbed into the back of the *Mercedes* where they curled up together like two small woodland creatures. This time there was no further nod of acknowledgment from Tomas – he simply jumped into the driver's seat and turned the key in the ignition. Compared to the Beetle, this engine purred. I watched the *Mercedes* pull away and resisted the strong temptation to wave – it would have been too much like a child at the end of a visit by his grandparents; not at all becoming for a now active *revolutionary*! I watched until the rear lights disappeared completely from view. After nightfall they would be in Säarbrucken, where another car and another driver would be waiting to whisk them over the border into France during the early hours. There was nothing more for me to do other than return that noisy, rattling jalopy to Semmler.

Julius was overjoyed that his 'pride and joy' had been returned intact.

"I was sure Andreas would persuade you to let *him* drive," he said as I handed over the keys. "I've

Love, Gudrun Ensslin

bitten my fingernails to the quick just thinking about
it."

Certainly, Andreas was not the most sensible
of drivers. He knew only one speed: fast. He knew
only one mode: reckless. On more than one occasion it
was only Andreas's erratic driving that drew the heat of
the cops when otherwise the Gang might well have
gone unnoticed. Yet Andreas loved cars. It was one of
his favourite topics of conversation – besides women,
guns and revolution.

Of course, Andreas's promised instructions for
the Boys never arrived. Out of sight seemed to be out
of mind in the winter of '69. There was little I could do
in practical terms except return to my studies – which I
did with some gusto: planning to write a thesis on
Hegelian dialectics in honour of Gudrun.

Meanwhile, Andreas phoned Astrid Proll and
invited her to join the exiles in Paris – bringing some
useful stuff with her; textbooks, pamphlets and another
Mercedes which was donated by the *schili* wife of a
Frankfurt boutique owner (something for Andreas to
drive at breakneck speeds around the Parisien
boulevards). Astrid also took her camera – snapping
some 'photos on the run' that later became a published
book. A great time was had by all – smoking and
drinking in Left Bank cafés, spending *schili* money and
(verbally at least) setting the world to rights. Then they
hit the road once more, travelling south. Thorwald
Proll turned himself in to the authorities in Strasbourg
– although his sister chose to remain on the run with

105

Love, Gudrun Ensslin

Andreas and Gudrun, her camera shutter snapping away faithfully all the way to Italy and Napoli.

I didn't hear any more about Gudrun and Andreas until the following year. During the interim, I even found myself a girlfriend – Cressida Harris: a radical Left-wing Englishwoman studying German Literature and Language at Frankfurt (whilst writing a feminist critique of *Goethe*). Then, one chilly day in February, Julius walked into my room soon after Cressida left and announced with shocking casualness:

"Andreas and Gudrun are back in Germany. In Berlin. They're staying at the apartment of a friend of mine – a journalist called Ulrike Meinhof. You can join me in visiting them next week, if you like."

Love, Gudrun Ensslin

CHAPTER NINE: KONTAKT

URBANE GORILLA WEBSITE POST:

"Those who don't defend themselves die. Those who don't die are buried alive in prisons, reform schools, the slums of the worker districts. . . and in brand new kitchens and bedrooms filled with fancy furniture bought on credit." Red Army Faction communiqué; June 2nd 1970.

Is it really more than four decades since Ulrike Meinhof and the Red Army Faction so eloquently warned us of the dangers of our consumer society and its pitiless corporate greed? And did we heed the warning? What exactly do we have today – in our brave new 21st century? An end to the Cold War, yes. A victory to capitalism, yes. But do we have a *better* society? Have we eradicated iniquity – or simply encouraged its proliferation?

Just take a look around you for the answers: we inhabit a credit-crunched society in which there is only increasing polarisation; the rich getting richer and the poor getting poorer. And all of this has evolved as the result of a deliberate policy. My friends, is that really *progress*?

For those of you who still have hearts and minds: here is the official CALL TO ARMS for those who truly believe in a just and fair society! Remember: this corrupt and shameful society *can* be changed. You don't have to *passively* settle for THIS! You can *actively* initiate – and *achieve* – REVOLUTION.

Remember the spirit of 1970. Remember Baader Meinhof. The Red Army Faction STILL LIVES!

Anarchist Pete

It had to be the CLS 55 AMG. The *Bentley* was a possibility but the CLS was, when all was said and done, a *Mercedes*. Rory Carlisle was driving himself to his country pile in Aberdeenshire from the Docklands penthouse. Had he opted to be driven by his chauffeur then the Bentley would have been the logical choice. However, for driving himself over long distances, Rory would always choose the CLS. Not only did he feel himself to be following in his father's footsteps by driving a *Mercedes*, but the CLS 55 AMG represented a welcome return to the values and quality of the legendary *Mercedes* marque of his father's era. It was a true piece of automotive sculpture – aesthetically pleasing and with a ground-breaking design. It was obviously lovingly assembled and it felt solid and tank-like. Like a *Panther* or a *Tiger* tank. An impregnable, floating battleship of the tarmac (just like his father's car had been in those glory years of the 1970's). In fact, it was the exact same model Bernie Ecclestone had owned – the same one little Bernie had woken up one morning to find hoisted up on bricks outside his West London mansion. How Rory laughed when he'd read about that! Laughed like a drain.

Ecclestone annoyed Rory. Apart from anything else, it was due to Ecclestone being the very first person in the whole of the British Isles to take delivery of a CLS 55 AMG that ensured Rory had received a car classified only as 'No. 2' off the production line. Even with Rory's car dealing reputation and long-established *Mercedes* connections, somehow the dwarfish Formula One supremo still managed to pull rank and jump to the head of the queue.

A thick mane of blonde hair and hard blue eyes reflected back at Rory in the rearview mirror as he powered the CLS smoothly into the outside lane of the motorway. Rory congratulated himself on what he saw. Indeed, he thought, had it not been a 'career' for vacuous gayboys such as Jardine then he might actually have made it as a male model. Well, that was *something* at least he'd always enjoy over that gremlin Ecclestone – matinee idol good looks.

Rory stamped down on the accelerator and let

the ultra-responsive gearbox propel the CLS from a pleasant high altitude cruise to a scorching Mach One. He felt he could surely drive all the way to Scotland without stopping even once – that was how much of a GT the CLS seemed to be. However, one necessary pit stop was scheduled in York. After all, there was work to be done. The laptop, nestling comfortably in its leather case in the spacious boot, still had a fair few words of wisdom and rhetoric to impart in *Herr* Krendler's direction; just a few further words of encouragement along with a couple of trigger phrases that should soon encourage old Georg to set about pulling a trigger of his own.

Rory Carlisle's CLS was maroon with a cream leather interior. The seats felt solid and overly supportive at first – yet they really came into their own during long distance travel. The car managed 0-60 in fewer than five seconds – an achievement that was, of course, utterly wasted on Britain's roads with its Nanny State speed limits. Here, in fact, was a car ideally designed for Germany's unrestricted *autobahns* – a system that allowed both car and driver to perform to their natural ability and yet was statistically proven to be no less dangerous for permitting such a shocking piece of autonomy to a nation's citizens. You can always rely on the Germans to deliver the goods, thought Rory – especially one German in particular! He could hardly wait to arrive in York. He could hardly wait for Krendler to begin the shooting.

Rory stretched back into the driver's seat and

Love, Gudrun Ensslin

let out a contented sigh. Yes, cruising in the fast lane
was the perfect place for a spot of idle reflection and
calm relaxation. He was completely lost in his
Krendler-related reverie when he became rudely aware
of a white car speeding up behind him and tailgating
the CLS erratically. Rory instantly recognised the
belligerently driven car as a *Mitsubishi* Lancer Evo X.
The *Mitsu* was being driven by a cartoon yobbo – a
closely shaven headed oaf with clenched teeth and
flared nostrils, waving his fist. Some testosterone-
fuelled Neanderthal. A troglodyte full of uncontrolled
and misplaced aggression. The *Mitsu* was now glued to
the CLS's back bumper – its halogen lights flashing
and blazing with menace. The message to Rory was a
simple one: pull over and piss off pal! This simply
won't do, thought Rory, dipping his brakes and forcing
the Evo to momentarily back off in this motorised
game of cat and mouse. The cheek of it – a mere
Mitsubishi expecting to barge a *Mercedes* off the road!
Rory smiled into his rear view mirror and chuckled
benignly as the enraged oik began making cut-throat
gestures. The sight both amused and saddened Rory –
how very useful someone like this could be as a class
warrior once the revolution finally arrived. If only such
primitive, violent urges could be *properly* channelled
against the *proper* targets.

Rory studied the *Mitsu* driver with an almost
scientific detachment. The man really was quite a
specimen – a classic blue collar British yobbo: piggy
eyed; red faced; someone who read *The Sun* on the

bog. A snarling pit bull of a human being. 'Pitbull Man', Rory mused. How very much like 'Piltdown Man' that sounded. Suddenly, Pitbull Man pulled out to attempt to undertake Rory's car. Rory immediately swung the CLS across the lane in a classic Touring Car blocking manoeuvre. Pondlife Man then jinked back sullenly into Rory's slipstream – now apoplectic to the point of spontaneous combustion. Calmly, Rory operated his hands-free mobile. Enough was enough. This had been an amusing sideshow to break his journey but now he wanted to continue on his way to York in peace. *Mitsu* Man would have to learn a valuable lesson – and here it was: by all means take on the rich, sunshine…but do it *smartly* and with *clear purpose* rather than mindlessly and head-on in a blind rage. For, that way, there will only be one outcome; one sorry loser. Furthermore, find yourself a *different* target to Rory Carlisle – who, although you don't know it, is actually *on your side* and *willing* to *instruct* you in the route to *your own liberation* and (more significantly) the ultimate liberation of *your class*. Unfortunately, however, this particular game was over. Rory put through a call to his bodyguards travelling discretely a few cars behind in the smart navy *Audi* RS4 Rory bought for them.

"A few local difficulties with the natives, chaps," Rory quipped.

"We've been watching, Sir," a disembodied voice replied. "Some people have absolutely no manners."

112

Love, Gudrun Ensslin

"Indeed," Rory agreed, once again swerving to prevent *Mitsu* Man getting past him. "Perhaps it's time we taught this fellow some motoring etiquette?"

In a split second, Rory's rear view mirror showed the RS4 pulling alongside his tormentor's *Mitsubishi*. Four burly occupants leaned across and gestured to the lone yob. It was hard to decipher exactly what one of the *Audi's* passengers showed to the *Mitsu* Man – but he instantly turned as white as his vehicle. Immediately, he dropped back and began to drive in a far more docile manner for a few miles before placidly turning off the motorway at the next junction. The RS4 then resumed its place further back in the traffic flow – as discrete as ever. Rory's wing mirror framed an image of the *Mitsubishi* peeling off the carriageway. 'You have to be *smart* when you take on the rich," he mused, shaking his head. 'They can afford better fighters than you with better weapons than you to do all their dirty work for them. They can have the likes of you horsewhipped to within an inch of your life and then still have the law on their side at the end of it. Consider this a lesson learned, my angry friend."

Another sigh. Not for the first time, Rory was grateful to his personal bodyguards. They didn't come cheap, of course – but this was an area in life in which it simply didn't pay to compromise. This latest group of bodyguards was the best yet. They'd been personally recommended to him by a fellow in White's Club. Most of the heavies were ex-SAS – with a couple of retired mercenaries thrown into the mix. The whole outfit was run by an ebullient South African – a no-nonsense, hard as nails, mean-eyed stone cold killer. Rory had used a group of Israelis before that. They were ex-IDF – specialists in *Krav Maga*. They'd been good too – but he'd discovered the South African was far more willing to bend the rules when required. . . if the *price* was right, of course.

Rory pushed a series of buttons and the sound of the *Liebestod* from *Tristan und Isolde* filled the car's cabin. By the time he entered York he had switched to a Chopin piano concerto. He guided the CLS through the quaint stone gates surrounding the old city and headed directly for his hotel. Tomorrow, after a hearty full English breakfast of eggs, bacon, black pudding, tomato and fried slice, he would walk the city walls (an early morning habit whenever he stayed in this compact, historic city) and quietly reflect on events to come. For now, however, there was the small matter of taking out his laptop and uploading something suitably incendiary to the BANKER BINGO website. Furthermore, since Jardine categorically assured him that Krendler had now been contacted, and taken the bait and was now actively accessing the website on a regular basis – his future posts would now need to be a little more direct; and a little more *personal*. A little bit less 'blog' and a whole lot more of a *signal*; more of an unmistakable clarion call – a call to ACTION!

Love, Gudrun Ensslin

CHAPTER TEN: BAMBULE

Berlin, 1970. Our beloved one-time capital. A divided city. Little did I know – and could never have imagined at the time – that one day it would be reunited and serve as our capital once more. In 1970 there was no earthly way you could have known or even suspected this. Only a quarter of a century earlier – and barely four years before my own birth – it had been a city of ruins and rubble; the biggest Fascist swine of all time scrabbling around below ground in his bunker like the sewer rat he was – his Thousand Year dream collapsing all around him, crushed beneath the righteous and avenging boots of the triumphant Red Army. Berlin, 1970: home of Ulrike Meinhof and temporary lodging place of Andreas Baader and the divine Gudrun Ensslin.

*   *   *

Semmler parked the Beetle across the street from an unassuming block of flats in Kufsteinstraße. He was in a remarkably good mood as he had been telling me during our drive about '*Bambule*' – the film Ulrike Meinhof was making about the appalling treatment of

115

young people in custody in our wonderful 'free' Federal paradise. It starred some of the Borstal Boys I helped to look after during Andreas's absence. The movie was apparently a masterwork – an indictment, a testimony and an accusation simultaneously packaged within a valuable historical archive that was also a clarion call for social change. Unfortunately, once Ulrike played out her own starring role in the off-camera production entitled 'Busting Andreas Out Of The Dahlem Institute', the authorities took their spiteful revenge on her by ensuring that ' *Bambule*' was never publicly screened.

As Semmler's Beetle crossed the rural landscape of the DDR en route to West Berlin, he lectured me carefully on the superiority of the Soviet State compared with our own corrupt and uncaring "alliance of fascists and financiers." He became particularly animated on the road from Magdeburg to Potsdam.

"You see these people?" he asked, gesturing wildly as we overtook yet another hay wagon. "They are simple folk enjoying a simple, pastoral existence – exactly what the true Germany has always been about. They may not have the same access to consumer durables – or the same so-called 'standard of living' – that we 'enjoy' in the West but neither do they suffer the same problems. And why? Because the State provides. *They* are not enslaved by the need to afford the latest car or washing machine. *They* are not afraid their children will be left to starve in the streets as they do not have enough money in the bank. *They* do not have to worry that they do not have sufficient funds to pay for either their medical bills or the rent. *They* do not find themselves compelled to slave their whole lives away making one fat capitalist pig fatter and richer! No, no, no, my friend. And why? Because the State *provides*, Georg.

Here at last is a State that truly cares for its people; a State that treats all of them *equally* and with *dignity*; a State that values one individual exactly the same as the next individual. This is a State that does not *allow* any money-grabbing Fascist swine to profit from the servitude and misery of their fellow citizens. Here at last is a truly enlightened State – truly a blueprint for all of humanity's social future. Do not be fooled, my friend, by their supposed technological inferiority or because they so obviously lack the bourgeois comforts that our corrupt and decadent system provides. This is a temporary situation that can be rectified in time – and rectified *fairly* to the benefit of one and all.

They try to pretend in the West that we are the 'free' ones and the people of the East are enslaved – but I say to you that the DDR offers the greatest freedoms available to the German people today: freedom from poverty; freedom from oppression; freedom from exploitation; freedom from injustice and iniquity; freedom from gangster capitalism; freedom from hatred and fascism; freedom from the rat-race; freedom from the demands of consumer greed and the rising cost of living; freedom from private wars of conquest and plunder. These are the *true* freedoms – the greatest freedoms – of the DDR. And still they try to poison us in the West with the idea that we are the 'free' ones? Ha!"

He laughed and snorted at the same time and his eyes looked wild with fervour as he hunched over the steering wheel. Still, I was inflamed with the passion of his rhetoric and truly aghast at the clear evils of the FDR unfolding before me. The next time we overtook a struggling tractor belching its diesel smoke, I felt like saluting it!

My heart was attempting to beat a path through my ribcage when Semmler knocked on the door to Ulrike's flat. It was partly sheer excitement at the clandestine nature of our mission – but mostly it was because I was due to set eyes on my beloved Gudrun once more. Even though I now had a girlfriend, I had been wholly unable to get Gudrun (and her vampish allure) out of my head. For more than six months while she was on the run, she had haunted my dreams. Hours that should have been spent contemplating Ancient Greek philosophical paradoxes were instead devoted to secret reveries involving Gudrun's lithe and slender limbs entangling with my own pallid, over-excited flesh. Scenarios in which I was invited to join her in seedy, run-down hotels in Naples or Strasbourg – only to find a naked and spread-eagled Gudrun alone and awaiting my arrival – dominated my thoughts. In these endlessly satisfying daydreams, she was always more

Love, Gudrun Ensslin

than eager to invite me into the very heart and soul of herself – proclaiming me her saviour and the natural (and only) usurper of Andreas's crown in her devotion and her affections. And now, standing next to Semmler, I was but a few seconds away from seeing this vision in reality once more.

As Semmler's knuckles rapped out a jaunty coded message on the door, it was almost more than my poor heart could stand. Semmler caught sight of my expression, misread it as fear and gave me an encouraging squeeze on the bicep and a sickly little smile. His shrewd professorial eyes blinked rapidly at me behind his round spectacle lenses. I stared blankly back at him as the door began to open slowly – just a fraction at first; a precaution to check whether these really were friendly faces on the threshold. Then, once Julius identified himself, the door swung open.

It was my first sight of Ulrike Meinhof. Standing in the shadows of the entrance hall she appeared to have very dark hair and equally dark eyes. In contrast, her skin was as white and pallid as my own. It gave her a vaguely unhealthy look that those dead eyes did little to alleviate. From this initial sighting she gave me the creeps. Sometimes when you looked at Ulrike you felt as though you were looking at a corpse – an animated corpse, but a corpse nonetheless. There was just something 'dead' about her.

This was a stark departure from my beloved Gudrun – a creature so obviously full of life and verve and vivacity and energy; a vigour and vim and vitality all her own that was truly infectious and life-affirming in itself. Ulrike, by contrast, just made you want to slash your wrists!

At times she was simply a social vampire – draining any gathering or conversation of its hope and positive energy; pouring great gloomy drops of negativity and depression over other people's schemes and ideas; putting a big fat 'downer' on things – always looking for the *problem*; always suggesting the worst case scenario. She was undoubtedly very clever – a gifted wordsmith; a proven journalist; a well-read and genuine intellect. However, try as I might, I just couldn't manage to make myself like Ulrike. I *admired* her, certainly – but I couldn't actually *like* her…and neither, purely by instinct, did I fully *trust* her. On the other hand, I knew that Julius rated Ulrike extremely highly – both personally and professionally – and, for his sake, I always made every effort to get on with her as well as I could. But, for me, it was always Gudrun and, for Julius, it was always Ulrike – I guess there's simply no accounting for taste! Each man to his own.

Ulrike looked mousey and insignificant standing there holding the door to her apartment wide open. Then, Julius moved forward to embrace her and she instantly came alive.

"It's been quite a while," said Julius, clutching her small frame closely to himself and almost losing his wire-framed spectacles in the process.

"Too long," Ulrike replied, breaking free of

Love, Gudrun Ensslin

Julius's clumsy grasp. "Come on in." Then, turning to address me but still speaking to Julius: "Who's your friend?"

"My *finest* student," Julius beamed – every inch the proud father, if only in the spiritual sense. "And *thoroughly* loyal to the cause."

"Glad to hear it," said Ulrike, closing the door behind us and looking me up and down with an amused detachment – as though I were a prize bull brought to market.

"I'm a great admirer of your column in *Konkret*, *Frau* Meinhof," I stammered uncomfortably – not knowing quite how to react under the spotlight of her penetrating stare. The intended compliment came across as awkward, formal and insincere all at once.

"My God," Ulrike laughed, waving away my attempted flattery. "He's not from Prussia is he? That's all we need if we're planning to let our hair down a bit! Come on in, both of you. The others are through here…".

We were ushered into a sparsely furnished but surprisingly spacious sitting room. The utilitarian décor reminded me of Semmler's flat back in Frankfurt. Just like Julius, Ulrike devoted the majority of her space to books, newspapers and magazines. There were rows and rows of books in sagging, overloaded bookshelves – dusty hardbacks in torn jackets were crammed next to battered and yellowing paperbacks. Surely she couldn't read *all* these books? – yet somehow you suspected she did.

Love, Gudrun Ensslin

Andreas was customarily sprawled across the sofa, clutching a whisky bottle to his chest and smoking a non-filter *Gauloise*. The pungent aroma of its strong tobacco permeated the room. Andreas had allowed his hair to grow even longer since I'd seen him last. Now it sat like an unruly mop on top of his head, threatening to spill right over his earlobes while skimming his shirt collar at the back. Even his eyebrows seemed to look more bushy. Of course I didn't dare to tell him but, at that precise moment, he looked positively simian. Even so, it made me think about letting my own hair grow longer – after all, the evidence seemed to suggest that Gudrun liked longer hair these days.

And then, there *she* was – standing with her back to us as we came in, facing towards the reclining Andreas on the sofa. To me, she looked like a sculpture – such was the natural grace and elegance of her stance. She held a cigarette in one hand, a wine glass in the other and one foot ever so slightly arched like a ballerina preparing for a performance. Her long, blonde hair trailed tantalisingly down her back – looking to me to be such a *tactile* temptation. . .

"Hey there, you guys!" yelled Andreas, immediately leaping to his feet on seeing us. Gudrun turned and flashed a smile in our direction that melted my heart in an instant.

"It's Ju-li-us!" Andreas sang happily in the mock operatic voice he sometimes used. "And look, Gudrun – he's brought your secret admirer with him!"

Love, Gudrun Ensslin

I blushed immediately – turning beyond red to scarlet and finally settling on a deep crimson you would not have thought humanly possible. It was Gudrun who came to my rescue – rushing forward to plant a chaste kiss on my forehead.

"Take no notice of him," she counselled.

I could smell the alcohol on her breath and the perfume on her skin. She was just as drunk as Andreas – and equally merry with it. This surprised me greatly as it was one of the very few occasions I ever saw Gudrun drunk. She was usually very, very careful not to overstep the mark and lose her normally iron-willed composure and self-control. My God, I wanted her so much at that moment – with those hot alcohol vapours on her breath signalling to me that, Andreas notwithstanding, her defences were down and somehow she just might be available.

"Hey, Julius," Andreas yelled. "Do you know what Ulrike's kids are calling Gudrun and I?"

Semmler shrugged apologetically, waiting for the punchline.

"Hansel und Gretel!" laughed Andreas, falling back onto the sofa, guffawing loudly.

"Be quiet, *Hansel*!" Ulrike chastised. "You'll wake them up! They're sleeping in the next room, remember."

"Sit down, sit down," Andreas instructed, waving the Scotch bottle in Semmler's direction. "Have a fucking drink!"

Ulrike went into the kitchen and reappeared

with a wine glass for Julius and a cracked coffee mug for me. She shrugged apologetically as she handed me the mug and I smiled sheepishly back.

Andreas poured everyone a large measure of the golden brown liquid. Then he hoisted the bottle and proposed a toast.

"To the worldwide revolution and the end of capitalist oppression! Death to the fascist pigs – wherever they might be!"

Everyone present raised their drinking vessels.

"*Prost!*" I said awkwardly.

They all looked at me.

"He really is from Prussia after all, isn't he?" Ulrike cackled.

"I'm surprised he didn't click his heels!" added Gudrun.

"Are you *sure* he's one of us?" asked Andreas, with mock concern and squinting his eyes so tightly he caused his brow to knit itself into a tight furrow.

"Oh yes," Julius smiled, clapping me smartly on the arm and almost spilling my drink. "I'm *sure*."

It was already late when we arrived, but now the conversation continued deep into the small hours of the night. I tried to concentrate on the discussion – and tried not to stare and obsess too much over Gudrun – but I failed miserably on both counts. I felt utterly fatigued and utterly lascivious at the same time. As my eyes opened and closed involuntarily and an unwanted sleep approached, I made a mental note to myself to lose my virginity as soon as possible on our return to

Love, Gudrun Ensslin

Frankfurt. It was time to 'formalise' my relationship with Cressida and, in so doing, I hoped I might find a 'cure' for my overwhelming Gudrun fixation. It was not long after making myself this promise that I finally succumbed to the twin forces of exhaustion and an excess of whisky and promptly stretched out on the sofa Andreas had previously occupied. I barely had the strength to reach across and turn off the nearby lamp before unconsciousness enveloped me.

It was a fitful night's sleep. I drifted in and out of a semi-wakefulness in which all reality appeared as a mirage and I was scared even to talk or cry out in case I found myself doing so in my sleep and woke the entire household – including Ulrike's precious sleeping children. During my brief 'waking' moments I heard small snatches of the continuing conversation of the others.

They were huddled together in a tight group on some basic wooden chairs Ulrike brought in from the kitchen. In the half-light their silhouettes made them appear to be true conspirators – cartoon effigies of a witches' coven meeting in a forest clearing and planning to poison the villagers' wells. For about a millisecond I felt I was watching Czech puppet theatre or some equally bizarre animation. I was still totally inspired by these people but at that precise instant they also looked horribly grotesque and sinister. I turned to bury my face in the cushions but extracts from their conversation still drifted towards my ears.

"I've been speaking with Dieter," said

Andreas. "He's invited us to join his Anarchist group."

"What? The same ones who bombed the Americans a few months back?" Julius asked.

"Exactly," Andreas replied, his voice now a whisper.

"And?. . ." Julius prompted.

"No, no, no!" Andreas snorted. "I mean, good luck to them – common enemies and all that. . . but we are *proper* Communists. . . we are Maoists. . . we are committed to the Communist cause. We want a *structure* that provides social justice – not wanton anarchy with nothing to replace it."

"Glad to hear it," Julius chuckled. "So what do you propose to do?"

"Horst is putting a group together – *proper* Communist revolutionaries – and we're joining that one instead. We're getting organised at last, Julius. We're looking to get Soviet backing – and we're going to make things happen. . . not just fire-bombing the occasional department store but *real* stuff. Do you think you can help us?"

"Oh, I'm certain I can," Semmler stated boldly.

"What about *him*?" asked Gudrun, no doubt gesturing towards my prostrate form on the sofa.

"Oh, I'm sure he's in too," Julius added blithely. "Certainly he will be if you are, Gudrun!"

Cue much hearty laughter and rowdy hilarity at my expense.

The next morning I was woken by Semmler nudging my elbow and offering me a mug of coffee.

126

Love, Gudrun Ensslin

He was fully dressed and looked heavily drawn. I very much doubted he had been to sleep at all the previous night.

"Get up!" he instructed, handing me the coffee. "Our business here is done."

I sipped the coffee tentatively. It was cheap, nasty stuff – watery at the top with a thick unappetising sludge at the bottom.

"We're going back to Frankfurt," Julius called from the kitchen, from where I could hear him rifling through the cupboards.

I had been looking forward to seeing something of our former capital – Checkpoint Charlie, the Brandenburg Gate and, as utterly bourgeois as it no doubt was, the *Ku'damm*. It was hard to contain my disappointment.

"Where is everybody?" I called back to him, searching for a pot plant in which to tip the disgusting *ersatz* coffee.

"Ulrike's taking the children to school. Andreas and Gudrun are out – God knows where, doing God knows what!. . . Do you want some cake to go with that coffee? It's all Ulrike seems to have in store. The kids have eaten the cereal and Andreas has eaten just about everything else!"

I pulled my jeans and T-shirt on hurriedly and wandered into the kitchen. The cake looked old, dry and thoroughly unappetising. Semmler was sitting at the table resignedly eating a slice. Crumbs dropped into his wispy beard like dandruff, further disinclining me to cut a slice for myself. A wave of nausea washed over me.

"Isn't there somewhere we can *go* for breakfast?" I asked.

"Oh, OK," said Julius, suddenly smiling brightly, throwing down his half-eaten slice of cake and looking for all the world as though this option would never have occurred to him if I hadn't just suggested it.

About two blocks from the apartment we found a kiosk selling *wurst*. We stood solemnly beneath the canopy shielding one of the tables contemplating our extra-long sausages smothered in creamy yellow mustard and breathing in the heady steam vapours from two piping hot mugs of proper, strong black coffee. At that precise moment, it felt like a small piece of Heaven on Earth.

I watched distractedly as Berlin came alive before my eyes. People rushed hither and thither – all looking very important and determined; totally focused on the demands of the day ahead. Mothers dragged complaining children to school. Businessmen in trench coats carrying leather briefcases sailed haughtily past – coat belts and coat tails flapping in the wind.

Delivery trucks loaded with beer or bread revved their diesel engines as they competed in the traffic flow with 2CV's, *Alfas*, *BMW's* and plenty of Beetles just like Semmler's. It was a secret joy to me just to be an anonymous part of that great city awakening; I'd always known that the small town environment of Wuppertal was never right for me and I belonged in a city, and Berlin – divided or not – seemed to have a magic all of its own, with which even Frankfurt could never hope to compete. I bit into my *wurst* and watched the people swarming all around me and wished I could somehow join in; somehow *belong*. As if reading my thoughts, Semmler spoke:

"These are the 'little people', Georg," he said, taking a huge bite from his *bratwurst*. "We're not a part of all that."

I looked at him quizzically and he gulped down his half-chewed mouthful of bread and sausage before continuing.

"As you know," he began earnestly, "the conflict between 'free will and determinism' is one of the fundamental paradoxes in Philosophy. This implies the question: is our destiny pre-determined or does it lie in our own hands? This, then, implies a further question: is your individual nature pre-determined or does it lie within your own power to change yourself?"

I frowned at him – indicating that my incomprehension had only deepened. I took a sip of hot coffee.

"Meaning?. . ." I asked, with no little irritation. Semmler smiled back at me indulgently – it was an expression that coupled a martyred look of infinite patience with the suggestion that what he really wanted to say was 'I thought you were smarter than this, Georg!'.

"Look, do you see that man over there?" he

asked, indicating with the tip of his *bratwurst*.

"The fat guy?" I replied, spotting a rotund businessman in a dark green suit waiting to cross the road.

"Exactly," said Julius. "The question then – simply restated – is this: is that guy a fat capitalist pig by *choice* or is he simply a victim of pre-determined circumstances beyond his control to which he merely reacts. . . like a puppet? The further question is: do we, as Marxists, have any other *choice* but to destroy him and his corrupt society? Can we really refuse our *destiny* to oppose people like him and all they stand for? Or, are we exercising our *free will* by *choosing* to oppose him and actively helping to build a new society predicated on the principle of freedom and justice for all? Like I say, it's a paradox, Georg. What we do; what we are – is it destiny or is it free will?"

He sipped his coffee slowly, allowing time for these ideas to seep into my consciousness. Meanwhile, the fat businessman crossed the road, holding up a podgy hand to thank the driver of the truck that stopped for him.

"But do we have the *right* to destroy this man and his world?" I asked. Semmler laughed.

"*Never* ask yourself that question, Georg! You might as well say: can I refuse my *destiny*? That's the path we're on, my friend – and we're too far along that road to turn back from it or turn off it now. Don't have a crisis of will, young Georg; don't allow fear or doubts to creep in. Think of it like this: we are fighting

130

to create a fair and just society for *all*. The fat guy –
and others like him – are fighting only for themselves;
to make *themselves* richer and fatter and more
powerful; to satiate only their own ego and their own
vanity; to build up only themselves and their own
family circle. And all of that struggle is directly at the
expense of *everyone else* – nothing is done for the
general good; to the benefit of *all* people; only for the
selfish ego of the individual and with no concept of
community. So, you simply need to ask yourself: which
worldview do you prefer? His – or ours? Decide this,
and it's easy for you to decide which side you're on. . .
and then to know what has to be done."

I chewed thoughtfully on another piece of
bratwurst as I carefully digested Julius's latest polemic.
Just as I was doing so, he clapped me on the back so
forcefully that I almost spat out my food.

"Come on," he said. "Finish up your breakfast.
It's time for us to leave."

*   *   *

Back in Frankfurt I was keen to get involved in some
direct action in support of the cause – but very little
seemed to be happening there. All the real action was
back in Berlin with Gudrun and Andreas. Frustrated, I
once again threw myself into my studies. As planned, I
let my hair grow much longer (Andreas-style) and I
grew a wispy beard (Semmler-style). I also lost a lot of
weight as I neglected almost everything but my studies

– the only exception being my campaign to persuade Cressida to get more physical than we had hitherto been. Even Julius seemed to prioritise his lecturing duties over his revolutionary activities at this point.

Cressida – now known to me (at her instigation) as 'Cressy' – also seemed to realise that some sort of sexual congress between us was inevitable; although, despite her 'feminist principles', she left it to me to do all the urging and chasing. I had first been attracted to her because she looked one heck of a lot like Gudrun.

The fact she had left-wing sympathies was merely a bonus – albeit an important one. Cressy had the same long, flaxen hair that trailed down her back and the same mesmeric, piercing blue eyes as Gudrun. She lacked the reed-like thinness and the willowy height of Gudrun – Cressy was not overweight but neither was she a catwalk twiglet like Gudrun. She also lacked the strident vivacity of Gudrun – but she still showed some of the same fighting spirit in her general speech and day-to-day attitude.

Effectively, she was a 'poor man's Gudrun' – which, at the same time, was more than good enough for me. Furthermore, despite being English, she spoke perfect unaccented German – the legacy of a German great-grandparent who had evidently intended to emigrate to America before the First World War but had jumped ship in England and chosen to remain there. Apparently, this heritage caused some degree of difficulty for Cressida's family in England during the

Love, Gudrun Ensslin

Second World War – but the wars between our nations were something we chose to discuss as little as possible. The main thing for me about Cressida, however, was not only that she looked something like Gudrun but that, unlike Gudrun, she was at least *accessible* to me – and I had a certain 'problem' to solve.

It finally happened one afternoon after a lecture on 'Marxist Feminism'. Cressy ear-marked the lecture as utterly critical in terms of her thesis and I agreed to attend on the basis that this was the only series of lectures at the University with the word 'Marxist' in the title that I had not hitherto attended. As it transpired, I was the only man in the lecture hall among a sea of women.

I scanned the lecture hall benches as I entered, quickly spotted Cressida and went to sit beside her. We hadn't met face-to-face for a couple of weeks (maintaining contact solely with the occasional telephone call) as I had been such a hermit over my own studies – consequently my wispy beard and shoulder length hair were entirely new to her.

"Oh, look – it's Jesus Christ!" she quipped as I sat down. I looked at her again for the first time in weeks and my heart skipped a beat or two – sometimes (in the right lighting) she could almost *be* Gudrun!

"Well," I replied, continuing the joke, "what are you going to do – crucify me? Isn't that what all you feminists want to do to us men?!"

"Hmm," Cressy mused, "maybe after the

lecture I'll do just that!"

Just then, the lecturer strode in and took up her position behind the lectern. It was *Frau* Ziegler – a small pocket battleship of a woman. Short, dumpy and middle-aged with wild, black eyes and a mop of equally black unruly hair. She always wore a long black dress paired with a succession of brightly coloured shawls in bold, primary colours. Whatever the weather, a shawl was present – today's was bright yellow. Most of the students on campus – both male and female – referred to her as 'the witch'. I had seen her talking to Julius in the corridor at the Staff Room a few times but had never actually spoken to her myself.

Frau Ziegler – who deliberately kept the *'Frau'* part of her name and delighted in telling people that "yes, feminists can be married too!" – began her lecture abruptly. She barked out her words in a high-pitched staccato which was extremely grating to the nerves. 'Here,' I thought to myself, 'is a woman who will never have need of a megaphone!' To this day, I cannot recall a single word used or concept discussed during that lecture as I spent the entire time slyly eyeing Cressida as she scribbled furiously in her notebook (in English rather than German, I observed). My head was full of lurid imaginings concerning exactly what I would do to her if she really were Gudrun.

Afterwards, we headed to a coffee house off campus. It was a thoroughly *bourgeois* place in which the waitresses, attired in what appeared to be French

Love, Gudrun Ensslin

Maid's outfits, brought all manner of earthly delights to your table on fine bone china or silver platters. It was a venue Cressida clearly knew well for she was effusively greeted and treated like a queen from the moment of our arrival. Cressy sat primly at the table reading the menu card with the same serious contemplation she reserved for her textbooks. For a second, I had a vision of what Gudrun might be like if she were somehow tamed and domesticated. Instead, looking around at the opulence of our surroundings – chandeliers, wooden racks of perfectly ironed pristine newspapers, buxom serving wenches – it occurred to me that this was precisely the type of place Gudrun would prefer to firebomb than patronise!

"This is clearly Germany's most civilised invention," Cressy said, "Coffee and cakes!"

I smiled weakly, shrugged and sank visibly lower in my chair – desperately hoping none of my left-wing 'comrades' spotted me in a place like this.

"Actually, I think the Austrians might have beaten us to it." I replied.

As Cressy ate an extremely large slice of *Sachertorte* and I drank coffee after coffee, we talked about absolutely nothing at very great length. Soon I forgot my surroundings entirely. The longer we were there the more Cressida actually *became* Gudrun (in my eyes at least) – and the more my genuine ardour for her grew. I didn't want to (and although I had been expressly instructed never to do so) – I could not resist telling her about Julius and Andreas…and all about our recent trip to Berlin to see Ulrike. (I did, however, retain the presence of mind to keep Gudrun's name out of it at this stage). However, I had the sudden desire to share my involvement in the revolutionary movement with this beguiling Englishwoman. I desperately wanted to impress her – to show her I was *actively* involved in supporting the cause; not just a distant sympathiser or a well-meaning well wisher – to demonstrate that I was a *real revolutionary*.

"I *know* people," I added enigmatically.

"Tell me more," Cressy said. "But not here – back at my place."

She took my hand across the table and squeezed it tenderly as I looked into her eyes. I knew then that the deal was done and the bargain sealed. And so, I had sex at last – just a few weeks short of my 21st birthday – in Cressida's cramped flat in a rundown student apartment block with paper-thin walls and stinking corridors.

It was both absolutely wonderful and utterly unsatisfactory at the same time. Physically, it *felt* wonderful – and it was a great weight off my mind to finally lose the embarrassing burden of my virginity. However, it was psychologically wholly unsatisfactory as it did absolutely *nothing* whatsoever to 'cure' my obsession with Gudrun (as I hoped it might). In fact, if anything, it only made me want Gudrun *more*!

The first time was very quick. I looked down at Cressy and saw Gudrun's face and Gudrun's hair fanning out across the pillow beneath me – and it had been all too much too soon.

"Don't worry, it's always better the second time!" Cressida giggled, clutching me close to her warm, naked skin. "It lasts longer."

I was embarrassed that she could tell it was my first time. I had hoped to disguise it but she sniffed me out instantly. It made me wonder what else she could tell about me that I thought I'd hidden. We spent the remainder of that night with Cressida 'teaching' me – and it was a lesson I enjoyed rather more than *Frau* Ziegler's lecture! After a largely sleepless night, Cressida suddenly ripped the duvet cover away from me – exposing my thin flesh and skinny frame to the cold morning air.

"Go and make me some breakfast in bed," she purred.

"What did you say?" I asked, incredulous.

"That's what feminism is, Georg!" she laughed, using a foot to lever me towards the edge of the bed. "It's *you* who makes breakfast in bed for *me*. Not the other way around!"

I hoisted myself into a standing position and decided I'd comply – padding naked into the as yet unexplored territory of her kitchen and searching the cupboards and shelves for coffee, crockery and utensils.

'Well,' I thought to myself. 'Life's really not so bad. After all, I have a proper girlfriend now...and, best of all, she looks almost exactly like Gudrun Ensslin!"

Love, Gudrun Ensslin

CHAPTER ELEVEN: JUGEND OHNE GOTT

While I concentrated on my studies – and my love affair with Cressida – Gudrun, Andreas and Julius were busy enough without me. In March 1970 – barely one month after Cressida and I 'cemented' our relationship – the first official 'group action' took place; lobbing Molotov cocktails at the *Länder* administration offices in Berlin's *Markischer Vertiel* during the dead of night. Immediately after this *aktion* Andreas and Gudrun moved out of Ulrike's flat into a *schili* place to lie low for a while. However, Andreas's customary hell-for-leather driving almost proved to be his downfall.

The first time he was stopped, he was lucky. Blasting aimlessly round Berlin, his favourite shades on, a *Gauloises* hanging jauntily off his lower lip, his leather jacket creaking with every finger-tip twist of the steering wheel and every casual flick of the gear lever, Andreas was hauled to the kerb by some traffic cop in Kreuzberg. Andreas sweet-talked him; chatted amiably about the car – said he always liked *Mercedes* but secretly longed for nothing other than a *Porsche*. Swore blind he hadn't been drinking. Clapped the cop on the bicep with that trademark comradely gesture of

138

his. Compared the leather of their jackets. Made the cop feel he was his new best friend for life. Escaped with merely a caution. Drove away – slowly and carefully – laughing inwardly; on a rocket ship high – convinced he could charm the birds from the trees.

Back at the safe house, Andreas laughed off the episode – clowning around for everyone's entertainment; aping the traffic cop as an archetypal music hall *putz*; a one-dimensional cabaret fool.

"Real leather, eh?" Andreas drawled in doltish tones.

Everyone fell around guffawing. In spite of himself, it was Julius who laughed longest and loudest. Only Gudrun refused to laugh, sounding a customary word of caution:

"You idiot!" she hissed. "Eventually that cop will wake up and realise that all was not as it seemed – and we'll have the full force of the Anti-Marxist Brothers down on our heads!"

The laughing reduced to a few strangled, embarrassed hiccups. Silence descended. Gudrun's eyes blazed with cold disapproval, trembling in their sockets from the strength of her anger.

A few days later, Andreas was driving again. This time he was at the wheel of Astrid's *Mercedes* at the head of a two-car convoy. They had been on a fruitless mission to dig up some 'guns for sale' that were apparently buried in a cemetery. It was a complete wild goose chase. The 'guns' never existed – they were the fabrication of a Police informant who had infiltrated the group.

The shadow of betrayal was a lot closer than even Gudrun – with her uncanny witch-like instincts – could have imagined. This time, two *Kripo* cars stopped the convoy. This time, it was no cabaret clown who questioned Andreas. Still, Andreas remained cool, calm and confident – he could talk his way out of *any* situation, he thought. It was easy, after all, he was…he was…*who* was he?! A momentary panic flowed through his mind as he handed the cop his fake ID.

"Peter Chotjewitz," said Andreas, as the cop's gloved hand closed around the documentation. "My father was Polish," he added, the easy smile now firmly back in place.

"I see," the cop deadpanned. "And how many children do you have, Herr Chotjewitz?" the cop continued, leafing through the documents with icy disdain.

Andreas stammered and stalled. Panic was rising within him once more. If only he'd bothered to learn his fake ID that bit more carefully; if only he'd taken things that bit more seriously for once – if only he'd listened to Gudrun's frequent admonitions to "shape up for fuck's sake!" He could see her now, in his mind's eye, finger-wagging and scolding like a schoolmistress or an angry *Mutti*; her thin lips mouthing the phrase: "I told you so!"

"I…I…don't remember!" Andreas eventually ludicrously replied. The cop suppressed a wry smile in favour of a weary professionalism.

Love, Gudrun Ensslin

"Step out of the car please, 'Herr Chotjewitz'," he instructed brusquely. "I'm afraid you'll have to come with me."

As Andreas was bundled into the back of a police car, the others were – amazingly – allowed to go free. However, whilst the cop knew there was certainly something fishy about 'Peter Chotjewitz', he did not know that he was also Andreas Baader.

The others had – apparently – committed no crime; so on they drove. . .*sans* Andreas! Back at the police station, Andreas was still keeping calm; still thinking of some clever way out of the mess.

His strategy was simple: the cops knew that he wasn't 'Peter Chotjewitz' but they had no idea who he actually was. All he had to do, therefore, was to 'admit' to some other false identity – one that would stand up to some routine checking…and he would walk free once more. For now, it was simply a matter of keeping quiet and thinking about which other fake persona to use – and which of his comrades would be smart enough to corroborate a false alibi for an apparent stranger right out of the blue.

"No comment," was the only comment the cops could get out of Andreas for the rest of that night.

Unfortunately for Andreas, the following morning his lawyer telephoned the police station with one simple but badly phrased question: "I should like to know under what charge you are holding my client, Andreas Baader?" After replacing the receiver on its cradle, the cop who had taken the call walked directly to Andreas's cell. He smiled acidly at Andreas.

"Good morning," he said jovially.

"No comment," Andreas replied – returning the smile with equally acidic venom.

"I hope you raise the fee you're paying your lawyer, Herr Baader! After all, he's priceless to us!"

*   *   *

"They've sent him back to *Tegel* to finish his sentence," Semmler told me. "The heat is on all of us now. You'll have to move out – find somewhere else to live as quickly as possible. Speak to me less frequently in university. Keep your distance."

I tried to take in all the things Julius was telling me. I didn't even know Andreas had been arrested. I blinked at him wordlessly.

"Can't you move in with that girlfriend of yours?" he continued. "If I need you, I'll send for you."

He was pacing around the apartment in a blind panic, picking up random items – books, T-shirts, records – and spilling them back onto the floor in a trail of debris. He was a whirling dervish; a human tornado blasting round the flat from the moment he set foot over the threshold on his return from Berlin.

"Sit down, I'll put the kettle on and make us some coffee, " I counselled. "You're not making any sense. You need to tell me all about it – right from the very beginning."

Two days later it was all arranged. I borrowed

Love, Gudrun Ensslin

Semmler's Beetle and Cressida helped me move into her apartment in one of the anonymous streets behind the *Hauptbahnhof*. While I discovered the *bourgeois* pleasures of living as a couple – trawling the supermarket together, collaborating in the kitchen over a rusty skillet, sharing a rickety bed that was really too narrow for two people – Andreas was rotting in *Tegel*. However, I later discovered, he still had visitors – among them a certain 'Dr. Gretel Weitermeier' (aka Gudrun – playing up to the nickname given to her by Ulrike's children) and a certain Herr Professor Julius Semmler. Once I heard this, I was immediately back on Semmler's doorstep – banging on the door with angry ferocity. He did not look pleased to see me.

"What are you doing here?" he hissed. "I told you to keep away – for your own good."

"I want to see him," I demanded petulantly. "Everyone else has – including you. Gregor told me. . ."

"Sssh! Keep your voice down!" Julius admonished, grabbing me by the lapels of my brand new brown leather jacket (a gift from Cressida) and hauling me inside my recent former home. Now it was his turn to make the coffee.

"Yes, I've been visiting him in *Tegel*," Semmler admitted tetchily. "But *you* can't!"

"Why not?" I protested, still furiously indignant.

"Because," Julius smiled cannily. "He won't be in there much longer!"

Love, Gudrun Ensslin

*   *   *

At 8.00am on May 14th 1970, the respected journalist Ulrike Meinhof arrived at Berlin's *Dahlem Institut* to begin 'work' on a book profiling "alienated young people on the fringes of modern society".

At 9.30am the same morning, a prison car arrived outside the *Institut* containing Ulrike's advisor and collaborator on the 'book' – one Herr Andreas Baader; granted temporary escorted leave from *Tegel* to help the socially concerned young journalist and film-maker with her important research.

Watched by prison guards, Ulrike and Andreas settled at a table in the Reading Room and began 'working'. Meanwhile, the doorbell of the *Institut* rang. Two young and innocent-looking girls – fresh-faced, clean-cut, bright-eyed and pretty young German girls – were standing on the doorstep.

They announced their names were Ingrid and Irene – and stated that they wished to enter the *Institut* to "check some facts on juvenile delinquent therapy" for a thesis.

What possible harm could it do to let two such nice, socially responsible young women into the building? Hopefully, the sight of prison guards on the premises would not be too frightening for them? Ingrid and Irene pulled some musty volumes from the myriad of bookshelves. They then sat quietly in the hallway – near the front door – earnestly 'reading'. The *Dahlem*

Love, Gudrun Ensslin

Institut was a hive of intellectual activity that morning; noses were buried deep in books and a scholarly air presided. And then the doorbell rang once more.

From their perch in the hallway, Ingrid and Irene were first to the door. They opened it to admit a tall man in a balaclava – and an equally tall masked woman. The man was brandishing a sleek Italian *Beretta* pistol. The woman was none other than Gudrun Ensslin.

A librarian who was standing close by, Georg Linke, raced forward and was immediately shot in the side. The explosion of sound from the *Beretta* shattered the cathedral-like atmosphere inside the *Institut*. Linke staggered back into his office, fingers pressed tightly over the gunshot wound, blood seeping out nevertheless – turning his hands a macabre crimson. Instinctively, he – and two secretaries – made an immediate escape through a nearby open window.

Meanwhile, the two masked raiders entered a second office – right next door to the Reading Room that housed Ulrike and Andreas – and the *Beretta* was then pointed directly at another librarian, *Frau* Lorenz. Simultaneous to this on-going mêlée, sweet little Ingrid and sweet little Irene drew automatic handguns out of their bags and rushed straight into the Reading Room.

As the shocked and confused prison guards attempted to react, Gudrun and the masked man joined Ingrid and Irene in the Reading Room. All Hell then broke loose – bullets and tear gas filled the room, screams and yells permeated the air. In the confusion,

Love, Gudrun Ensslin

Ulrike and Andreas adopted the *Herr* Linke tactic – and dived through an open window to freedom. All the other gang members followed them – this, in spite of one of the guards managing to gain possession of the *Beretta* in a struggle.

The escapees hot-footed it around the corner to a spot where Astrid Proll sat, revving up a stolen *Alfa* until the engine was red-lining and screaming to be let off the leash. A squeal of tyres, a cloud of black smoke and the fugitives were gone – and 'The Baader Meinhof Gang' was born.

The *Alfa* was later recovered by the *Kripo* – it had been abandoned containing a tear gas pistol and (a classy touch, this, I always thought) a battered paperback copy of *Das Kapital* under the driver's seat. The frustrated and humiliated authorities had no-one to punish so they exacted the only revenge on Ulrike that they could – her movie, *Bambule*, was immediately pulled from the schedules. Just like Andreas, Ulrike was now officially 'on the run'.

News of the escape saturated the television and radio bulletins and covered all of the morning's papers. At 8.00pm on May 14th 1970, Cressida and I opened a bottle of champagne with our *spaghetti bolognese*.

Our toast? "Andreas Baader, Gudrun Ensslin, Ulrike Meinhof and… *Herr* Professor Julius Semmler."

*　　　　*　　　　*

This time I followed Julius's advice to keep a low profile. If the heat had been on us before then, right

Love, Gudrun Ensslin

after Andreas's escape, it was positively incandescent.

For me, the next few weeks passed quietly in further 'domestic bliss' with Cressida – a visit to the Zoo, a trip to the *Kino* to see *Moby Dick*. The highlight of this period was the newspaper's full coverage on June 3rd of the preceding day's first ever official Red Army Faction communiqué: "Did the pigs really believe we would let Comrade Baader languish in prison?...Those who don't defend themselves die... Build up the Red Army!"

Then, on 22nd June, Semmler appeared on the doorstep of Cressida's flat – looking for me. I was astounded. It ran totally contrary to his own advice. Furthermore, if I was needed by the cause at any moment – and I was always more than ready to play my part – then surely some third party was going to be dispatched to send word that I should meet Julius at a pre-arranged location; the plan was never ever that Semmler would simply turn up in person and unannounced on my doorstep. Besides, he looked apoplectic.

We barely seated ourselves on the sofa when Semmler thrust a rolled-up newspaper at me and sat back fuming. I unfurled the paper carefully and was astonished to see a montage of full-face pictures of Gudrun, Andreas, Ulrike and others staring back at me. The banner headline read: BAADER MEINHOF GANG GO TO JORDAN. The accompanying text told the story of the "Gang" escaping from Berlin to receive "terrorism training" in Jordan from the PLO. I was completely speechless. Semmler, however, was not.

"How the hell did the newspapers get hold of this?" he snarled, snatching the paper away from me so suddenly that I was left holding torn shreds. Semmler scrumpled the remnants of the paper and threw them angrily to the floor.

"You know what this means, Georg?" he spat.
I shook my head dumbly.

"Clearly, we have a traitor in our midst."

*   *   *

Unbeknownst to me, the Gang returned to Berlin on August 9th and immediately began putting their 'terrorist training' into practice – planning four simultaneous bank raids for the end of the month to raise much-needed funds.

On September 29th the raids were launched – generating approximately 217,000DM in cash and several more newspaper column inches. However, the raid led by Ulrike was more of a disaster than a success – she fled the scene clutching a bag containing barely 8,000DM, having overlooked a container piled high with in excess of 90,000DM. Andreas, in particular, ridiculed her mercilessly for the oversight – suggesting the next time she went on a bank raid she remembered to take her Guide Dog with her!

Gudrun, however, was less amused. Unable to see any funny side whatsoever to Ulrike's "failure", her verdict was succinct: "The woman is useless – and a liability."

However, the overall success of the raids emboldened the Gang – especially Gudrun and Andreas (now officially West Germany's answer to Bonnie and Clyde) – and a further raid was planned against a military arsenal in Munsterlager. All seemed well – until Semmler's prediction regarding a traitor came true. A tip-off was phoned in to the *Popo* and Ingrid Schubert's flat in Berlin was staked out. The *Polizei* arrested 'sweet little Ingrid' while she was clutching the very same 9mm *Lima* pistol she used in the operation to free Andreas from the *Dahlem Institut*. Five other Gang members were later netted at the same address. Repercussions were sure to follow as paranoia settled in.

On October 10th Andreas presided over an internal inquest to track down the traitor – and pointed the finger of suspicion directly at Hans-Jurgen Bäcker. The two never liked each other – Bäcker regarding Andreas as little more than "a delinquent on a crime-spree ego-trip; more like Jesse James than a proper revolutionary." Meanwhile, Andreas regarded Bäcker as "a leech and an upstart; a do-nothing pants-wetter only seeking the limelight for himself."

"You are the traitor!" screeched Andreas.

"And you are a liar!" shouted Bäcker. Shunned and outgunned, Bäcker was forced to retreat. "I'll have my revenge!" he cried as he fled from the scene.

The subsequent Munsterlager raid was successful. The Gang now had money and guns in significant quantities. Now the *real* campaign – and the real *revolution* – could begin. Yet there I was – marginalized; sidelined; apparently surplus to requirements and immensely frustrated. All I had were my textbooks – and a life of neutered domesticity in a grubby little apartment overlooking the dreary *Hauptbahnhof*. I hardly saw or spoke to Julius any more. Following one brief lecture I attended, he disappeared 'on sabbatical'.

Then, I was astonished one morning when a couple calling themselves 'Ulrich and Marianne' turned up at my front door asking to stay "for a few days" and citing Julius as having directed them to me. I hesitated – my resolve to help the cause somewhat under threat from my newfound *bourgeois* concerns – after all, this was not my flat but Cressida's. A barrage of thoughts ricocheted through my mind. Cressida is sympathetic to the cause, certainly. She knows that I know Andreas – but she does not suspect the depth of my involvement; I had grown far more circumspect since my attempt to show off to her in the café during our early days.

"Julius sent us," said Marianne, hoping to prompt me out of my wavering uncertainty. She was blonde and blue-eyed, ruddy-cheeked and athletic – in another life she might have been an Olympian.

"He said it would be safe here," Ulrich added.

He was dark-haired and olive-skinned. He was shorter than Marianne and very thin – in fact, she looked the stronger of the two. Ulrich was also very

Love, Gudrun Ensslin

young – he reminded me of some of the Borstal Boys I used to look after for Andreas; one of those types who was desperate to grow up as quickly as possible and had attempted to grow a beard and moustache to hasten the process…only to end up with a face full of arse fluff.

Thus persuaded, and somewhat ashamed of my initial hesitation, I invited them both in and made them comfortable. Later in the day, when Cressida returned from her tutorial, I passed them off as childhood friends from Wuppertal who were hitch-hiking round the country and who only wished to stay for a few days "to see something of Frankfurt" before resuming their travels.

Cressida was surprisingly amenable – and greatly enjoyed the role of hostess. There followed a series of strange conversations about life in Wuppertal that saw the three of us ad-libbing all manner of fictitious shared histories purely for Cressida's benefit – anecdotal flights of fancy that grew increasingly more bizarre, outlandish and unlikely as the *Schnapps* flowed and we began to compete in an unspoken game to see which of us could stretch Cressida's credulity to its outer limits. Amazingly, if she ever doubted any of it, she never let it show.

Marianne and Ulrich remained with us for three days and then left to continue their 'tour of Germany'. As she kissed me goodbye, Marianne whispered in my ear: "When you are needed, Andreas will send for you."

Love, Gudrun Ensslin

*   *   *

At 6.00am on December 15th the doorbell to Cressida's flat rang constantly and urgently. Again and again it sounded. Long, determined blasts of tortuous and aggravating sound wresting us from our slumbers; denying us the freedom of that boundless dimension we call sleep.

"Who the fuck is that?" Cressida groaned, digging me sharply in the ribs. Her eyes remained determinedly closed and her nose was pressed tightly upwards into the folds of her pillow – turning one of her most Gudrun-*esque* features into an ugly snout. Even in those circumstances, I found the sight of her looking temporarily pig-like and so unconsciously indelicate hugely amusing and I struggled to stifle a cruel laugh. The bell sounded again; remorseless; unforgiving.

"I said, who the fuck is that?" Cressida repeated. "Go and see Georg, will you?"

This time the flat of her hand snaked out and found my shoulder, pushing me away to do her bidding. I noticed she reverted to English every time she swore. The bell rang again. The Chinese really missed a trick with their 'water torture' – it should have been ever-ringing doorbells instead! Now Cressida's head whipped up from the pillow, her eyes blazing with the anger of sleep deprivation. She stared at me wild-eyed, hair unkempt, teeth gritted – an English

152

version of a *Valkyrie*.

"Will you please go and see who is making all that damned noise, Georg?"

She said it in German this time – as if I somehow hadn't understood her previous English outbursts.

"Alright, alright – for fuck's sake!" I replied, throwing my section of the duvet aside and dragging my naked form to its reluctant feet.

The cold winter morning air hit me like a blast from a refrigerator and I was instantly fully awake. Still the bell rang. I glanced absent-mindedly out of the small high-set bedroom window and saw a train pulling lethargically out of the *Hauptbahnhof*. Even machines seemed to be indolent that morning! It was a proper winter's morning in Frankfurt – with plenty of thick and heavy snow. I looked around the room for something to wear – if I had to go downstairs to the street it would be freezing. The ever-ringing bell provided a soundtrack to my slapstick search for my clothes. I couldn't recall where I'd discarded my things from the night before – or maybe Cressida had tidied up after me? It was only a small flat – how hard could it be to locate my things? On the other hand, I couldn't even think with that damned bell tormenting at me all the time.

I glanced back at Cressida – she had now disappeared beneath the duvet, taking both pillows with her (presumably one to cover each ear) so that the bed now looked like a pile of discarded fabric. A solitary human foot sticking out in the cold morning air was the only indication that a person lay within. I fought an irresistible urge to tickle her dangling foot. The bell rang again – still more insistently. Cressida – saved by the bell – she would never know how lucky she was!

Cressida had left a pair of candy pink tracksuit pants draped over the back of a chair. Finding nothing else, and in great haste, I pulled them on. There was no mirror in our bedroom – but I figured I must look completely ridiculous. Nevertheless, the real priority was ending the tyranny of that hellish bell. I entered the corridor, closing the bedroom door carefully behind me – lest I further disturb my 'beloved' – and padded towards the intercom. The cold of the floor tiles made it feel as though I were walking on ice. I danced from foot to foot against the cold as I picked up the receiver. I also felt a growing and distracting need to piss.

"Hallo," I snapped irritably into the receiver.

"At last!" hissed a familiar voice. "It's Julius – let me in!"

I pressed the buzzer to admit him to the building – then rushed back down the corridor, opened the bedroom door and called out to Cressida: "It's Julius!"

"Go in the kitchen with him!" instructed the talking duvet.

There was no time for that much-needed piss because Julius was already knocking on the flat door – he must have vaulted up several flights of stairs with an athleticism I scarcely imagined he possessed. I hurried back down the corridor, wrenched the door open and there he stood: frazzled, seemingly thinner than before (if that were possible) and with bags under his eyes that were visible even beneath his spectacle frames. He burst out laughing when he saw what I was wearing. I merely grimaced in reply and gestured for him to enter.

"Typical student!" he quipped, as he brushed past me. "Sleeping all the bloody time!"

"In case you haven't noticed *Herr* Professor, term has finished! It's the holidays." I replied grumpily. "Go in the kitchen, will you, Julius – make yourself at home. I'll just take a quick piss and will be with you shortly."

When I returned, Julius had the percolator bubbling up a treat and the aroma of fresh coffee filled the tiny kitchen. Mercifully, I managed to find my jeans and a sweater by then so I no longer looked like a reject from an avant-garde production of *Swan Lake*. As my dignity was restored, so was my good humour – I was now keen and ready to hear what Julius had to say.

"What sort of coffee is this?" Julius asked me, casually. He had the lid off the jar of grounds and was sniffing at it inquisitively.

"Brazilian," I replied distractedly. "I bought it in the Christmas Market."

We had become coffee experts – coffee snobs. All those weeks, months and years spent sitting in various cafés and kitchens talking about – and planning – *revolution*. Now The Revolution was here at last and I wanted to hear about it.

"It's very good," Julius purred admiringly. "Much more subtle than Colombian."

Only when the coffee was placed between us in steaming mugs and we sat down at the folding picnic table Cressida and I used for breakfast would Julius deign to speak to me properly.

"Andreas and Gudrun are here in Frankfurt," he said. "And they have been here for the past three days."

I nearly fell off my chair. My heart immediately skipped a beat at the prospect of setting eyes on Gudrun again. Although my *ersatz*-Gudrun lay sleeping in the next room, my desire for the real thing had still only increased with the passage of time.

"Relax, they're not coming here," Semmler added, misinterpreting my reaction. "In fact, I'm moving them on to Nuremburg tomorrow. But I did want to come here in person and tell you that things are about to seriously hot up – and I wanted to check you're still available to us and on board because we *will* be calling on you, Georg and we *do* want you to do some things for us."

"Of course," I replied instantaneously – offended that my loyalty and dedication had been even indirectly questioned. "You *know* you can rely on me, Julius. I'm surprised you even had to ask."

"Good, good," he smiled, leaning forward to

clap me on the shoulder Andreas-style – an odd gesture from someone normally as reserved as Julius. "I just wanted to be absolutely sure," he continued. "Because things are really going to take off shortly and this time when we do call on you it may be for much more than just driving people around, delivering messages or finding safe houses."

"Julius, please…"

"No, let me finish. We also have a traitor – or even traitors – in our ranks. Someone is informing the *Polizei*. The Frankfurt safe houses are about to be raided any day now. There's a chance the pigs will come here – they may even take *you* in for questioning. If this happens, you haven't seen me at all since I left on sabbatical. We last spoke on the day you moved out of my flat. We argued – and you hate me now; you want nothing more to do with me…make that absolutely clear to the swine. During the 'row' I called you a lazy and below-average student. I accused you of using me and screwing me out of the rent – and I threw you out. You can even call it a 'lover's tiff' if you want – if *that's* what gets them off our backs then I won't deny it."

He was talking at ten thousand kilometres an hour – more to himself than to me. I sat there dumbfounded – although somehow still taking it all in.

"If they don't come for you at all – even better," he continued. "It will mean they're not as clued up about our connection as I fear…which means you'll be free and able to operate. Which will mean we can

157

call on you sooner rather than later."

He lifted his head up and stared at me over the rims of his spectacles – clear blue eyes searching out a response.

"You know I'm in, Julius." I reiterated. "One hundred percent."

"Good," he said, sitting back, relieved. "Because things are about to get seriously hot."

"So you keep saying! How hot is 'hot', Julius?" I asked.

"Hotter than your Brazilian coffee, that's for sure." Julius replied dryly, staring at his empty mug.

*   *   *

Five days later – just as Julius had predicted – the Frankfurt safe houses were raided. *Polizei* booted down the doors of houses and apartments right across the city – even including the countryside bungalow of some *schili* writer where Ulrike had been staying.

I read all about it in the following day's papers. However, on the day of the raids, Cressida and I remained untroubled. In fact, we spent the day strolling hand in hand around the Christmas Market – just another pair of young lovers enjoying the *bourgeois* consumer dream.

My secret shame was I'd always enjoyed Christmas Markets. Right back to my miserable, solitary, neglected childhood in Wuppertal – I'd always somehow naturally liked Christmas Markets and

Love, Gudrun Ensslin

Christmas-time itself. Everything looked postcard-pretty under the snow and the decorations all looked so colourful and cheering. There was a sense of optimism and bonhomie in the air – even if it was fake, it somehow still *felt* real. Christmas was a refuge for me – the one time of year when I felt something even vaguely approaching inner peace and a tentative hope for a better future.

I was seduced by seeing the magic of a Christmas Market through a child's eyes – the little wooden stalls shaped like miniature Hansel und Gretel houses; the carved wooden toys – soldiers, witches, angels, Santa Claus; the food – chocolate, marzipan, *Stollen*; the tree decorations – shiny, glittery baubles like affordable rare jewels. A Winter Wonderland! All the children dressed like garden gnomes – in brightly coloured bonnets; chasing around like pixies.

"Shall we get some of these candles for the flat?" Cressida asked, pulling me towards a stall selling all manner of colourful, intricately carved candles – from elegant and sophisticated Greco-Roman columns to garish, gaudy, fat, jolly Santas.

"Sure," I smiled indulgently. "Get as many as you like – then we'll go for some more *Gluhwein*."

For a second I could see the possibility of another existence: marry Cressida; settle down; get a steady job; have children; go hand-in-hand together to at least sixty more Frankfurt Christmas Markets before we die. And then another voice entered my imagination and spoke to me. It seemed to be a real voice – audible

Love, Gudrun Ensslin

to me just as clearly as that of Cressida or anyone nearby in the Market. It was not my own voice. It was the voice of Gudrun Ensslin, speaking to me…only she was speaking to me inside my head! She said: "Don't be seduced by all this Hollywood *kitsch*! It's all just *shit*! This is all *bourgeois* bullshit – the propaganda they want you to swallow. The distraction of bread and circuses! Remember what Semmler said to you in Berlin. Don't lose your focus. Don't lose your *purpose*. The Revolution needs *YOU*!"

I put a protective arm around Cressida as she tucked her paper bag of candles inside her coat pocket. One candle can light many fires, I thought.

Love, Gudrun Ensslin

CHAPTER TWELVE: ES BEGINNT

Rory Carlisle awoke from a strange dream. A disembodied voice had shown him three objects – a pen, a guitar and a rifle – and asked him a simple question: "Which of these will you choose to change the world?" The question reverberated around and around in his head, disturbing his waking moments. He had slept fitfully – in spite of being ensconced in his favourite suite; the one he kept permanently reserved and ready at a moment's notice to help him break his driving journey to or from Scotland. He was staying in the finest hotel in York – right opposite Clifford's Tower, looking directly out towards the remains of the tower where a rampaging mob massacred the Jews in 1190. Rory thought about that mass murder for a moment – 150 people callously slaughtered...burned to death...simply because of hatred and intolerance. Was that really all he had in mind with his own BANKER BINGO project? Was that *all* his grand scheme amounted to? A Manson-esque incitement to kill based on hatred and intolerance? No! This was no time for self doubt. This was different. These targets deserved it. The capitalists *deserved* it. They were the purveyors

161

Love, Gudrun Ensslin

of iniquity. They brought it on themselves. Someone
had to draw a line in the sand. Someone had to stop
them – and it may as well be Rory Carlisle...with a
little help from *Herr* Georg Krendler, of course.

"Change must come through the barrel of a
gun," Mao Tse Tung once said. "Against the
imperialist hyena there is no other medium than
extermination," were the words of Che Guevara. Rory
now took strength and succour from these
revolutionary words of wisdom. This is no time for
doubt, he told himself. This is no time to be unsettled
by a mere dream.

There came a knock on the bedroom door.
Instinctively, Rory drew the covers up around him,
covering his nakedness.

"Enter," he called croakily.

A young girl, aged sixteen or seventeen,
walked nervously into the bedchamber, carrying a large
silver breakfast tray. Rory watched her complicated
balancing act and tricky manoeuvres with detached
amusement. Her heel flicked out behind her and closed
the door with a practised skill.

She approached Rory hesitantly, the breakfast
things rattling on the tray with an ever-increasing
volume as she approached the bed. Rory nodded to a
mahogany side table and the girl slid the tray into
position as commanded. Then she virtually backed out
of the room.

The reverence people show to those with
money is obscene, thought Rory. Well, that would all

change soon. Once BANKER BINGO began...the
world would never be the same again!

After his 'Full English', Rory showered,
dressed and summoned his bodyguards from the
adjoining suite. He sent the ex-SAS man to pack his
suitcase and threw his car keys at the burly South
African.

"Karl, will you drive me the remainder of the
way to Scotland?" Rory asked. "I'm feeling tired today
so I'll just stay in the back and put my feet up."

"No worries, Mr. Carlisle," Karl growled in his
unmistakable *Boer* tones.

The CLS was every bit as comfortable in the
back. Rory sank into the leather and closed his eyes as
Karl accelerated smoothly. Rory's thoughts now
returned once again to Krendler and 'The Project'.
Every recent report from Jardine indicated the German
was now ready...so it only remained to point him in
the right direction.

The scenery rushed past in a blur as Rory
concentrated instead on the interior landscape of his
own psyche. So many bankers and financiers profiting
from greed and exploitation and holding the world in
chains. So many Government stooges directly in their
pay, operating solely according to their instructions.
We live in the age of the Bond villain – oligarchs and
gangster capitalists owning everything and giving back
nothing. The list of potential targets for Krendler was
seemingly endless.

Rory opened his laptop and prepared a Press

Release. Once Krendler is activated and the game of
BANKER BINGO had begun, an official communiqué
would be sent to the British Government, Scotland
Yard and the national news media. It would read as
follows:

**Notice is hereby served to the UK Government: the
liberating 'game' of BANKER BINGO has begun.
Greedy, profiteering financial manipulators and
plutocratic exploiters will be systematically
assassinated, one by one, as a lesson to those who
are complicit in the greed and profitmania of the
gangster capitalism that is destroying both society
and the environment. This is a cultural lesson to
those in power – and those who support them.**

**These killings will continue each month until steps
are taken to dismantle the unjust system that
presently governs us and genuine practical help is
at last given to those in society most in need of the
true assistance of the State.**

**In other words, to stop the killing we need to see:
housing for the homeless; medicines and funding
provided for NHS care (no more postcode lotteries,
selling medicines abroad for profit or cancer
patients denied vital treatment to save 'funds'); jobs
that pay a genuine living wage; unemployment
benefits that actually meet the cost of living; a
lifting of the tax burden from the workers and the
levy placed on the corporate profiteers who can**

afford it. In short, you must now live up to your fine words and create a fair and just society for all.

You must announce these measures (on national television, the internet and in Parliament) as policy or further action in defence of the oppressed will be authorised. THE PROFITEERS MUST BE MADE TO SHARE THEIR SPOILS! THE SPIRIT OF BAADER MEINHOF LIVES ON! The war WILL be won!

Gudrun Ensslin Kommando

Satisfied with his words, Rory closed the laptop, sat back and shut his eyes. Presently they crossed the Cheviot Hills and the River Tweed to enter Rory's beloved Scotland. Thence, it was onwards to Rory's final destination in Aberdeenshire – where 'Carlisle House' was located.

However, it was still necessary for Rory to make one more stop en route. A tradition he always observed on entering or leaving Scotland was the taking of tea at Spittal of Glenshee. Spittal of Glenshee was a tiny hamlet that acted as a gateway to the mountain road that would eventually lead Rory to his grand Scottish homestead. It had become Rory's private 'good luck' superstition to visit Duncan in his teashop there – a ramshackle building perched on a low mountain ledge overlooking the narrow stone bridge that led out of Spittal towards Braemar.

Love, Gudrun Ensslin

Rory loved Spittal and he loved taking tea at Duncan's Tea Shoppe. To Rory, the simplicity and isolation of Duncan's existence was something to idealise and envy. Rory would have loved to be able to live that way – and to have exactly that disposition by nature – to simply be able to be satisfied with your lot in life; not to endlessly seek, hunger, desire and lust after more and more and *more*. That would truly be a wonderful thing.

An old-fashioned bell rang as the rickety door to the Tea Shoppe opened. To Rory's delight the place was empty; no locals or pesky tourists cluttering up his favourite traveller's rest; he had the place entirely to himself.

Rory looked around carefully and was gratified that nothing had changed since his visit some months ago. He was greeted by the same coir floor mats, the same wire racks of *kitsch* and gaudy postcards of 'traditional' Scottish scenes and images (varieties of Tartan, men in kilts tossing cabers, a close-up of a sprig of heather), the same glass counter displaying tartan-packaged shortbread and Dundee cake, the same glass-fronted fridge packed to the brim with shrink-wrapped locally cured smoked salmon, generous cuts of Aberdeen Angus beef, shiny cans of *McEwans* lager and large glass bottles of *Deuchars* ale.

Hardly had the bell rung but an elderly figure – surprisingly lithe and upright for his advancing years – appeared sprightly from the rear of the Shoppe from behind a floor-length curtain of coloured beads. The

166

man's grey beard hung long and low down his chest, contrasting garishly with his completely hairless pink scalp. He wore a pair of red tartan trews and a mustard yellow cotton shirt.

"Duncan!" Rory exclaimed in delight.

"Hallo, hallo!" Duncan replied, raising his right hand in salutation.

"A pot of your finest, please Duncan," Rory commanded cheerfully. "And a good helping of some of your splendid shortbread as well, if you will."

"Coming right up, Sir," Duncan replied in his thick Scottish brogue as Rory's instructions sent him spinning in a new trajectory towards the glass counter. "Please, gentlemen, make yourselves comfortable."

The Shoppe boasted the grand total of two tables – both comprising garden furniture crammed in near the entrance. Rory and Karl squeezed around the first table while the ex-SAS man sat alone at the corner table looking somewhat forlorn. And there they sat in contemplative silence, listening to Duncan's tuneless whistling. Presently, Duncan reappeared, carrying a large tin tray on which was balanced a chipped china tea pot, chipped mugs and chipped plates containing some generous rounds of home-baked sugar-coated shortbread fingers. The crockery rattling, Duncan placed the tray on the table before Rory.

"I'll be Mother, shall I?" Rory chuckled, taking charge immediately and passing mugs and plates to the two bodyguards who quietly murmured their thanks. Duncan remained – hovering over the scene, smiling

167

appreciatively.

Once the tea was poured and everything was 'just so', Rory bit deeply into one of his shortbread fingers.

"Tell me," he said, looking up at Duncan and mumbling through a mouthful of crumbs. "Is my namesake still with you?"

"Surely, surely," Duncan replied, nodding eagerly. He stepped back a few paces and called loudly in the direction of the bead curtain. "Rory, oh Rory!" Almost immediately a stocky, old black Scottie dog waddled into view, wagging its stumpy tail furiously.

"Marvellous!" Rory beamed, leaning forward and clicking his fingers to encourage the animal to approach him. Rory walked faithfully towards Rory. As soon as the dog was close enough, Carlisle held up one of the shortbread fingers – dangling it above the dog and enticing it up onto its hind legs, the shortbread remaining tantalisingly out of reach.

The dog began to dance in practised, circus-style pirouettes, performing eagerly for its sugary, buttery reward. All eyes were fixed on the spectacle of the dancing dog. Eventually, Rory lowered the biscuit sufficiently and the dog's jaws snapped suddenly at it, wolfing the shortbread down its gullet in one fell swoop. Everyone laughed indulgently before the same process was repeated, Rory's eyes showing a childish delight in the dog's antics.

After the second piece of shortbread had been devoured dog-Rory was banished back behind the bead curtain. Meanwhile, Rory Carlisle carefully wiped his fingers on his paper napkin.

"I'll bring you some more shortbread, Sir," said Duncan hurrying away. "Free of charge, of course."

Rory leaned over and whispered confidentially in Karl's ear. The burly South African rose and left the Tea Shoppe. On his return he handed Rory a white carrier bag that Rory stored carefully under the table. After all three men had enjoyed their fill of tea and shortbread, the party rose to its feet as one. Rory summoned Duncan once more and handed him the carrier bag. Duncan reached in and pulled out a bottle of *Edradour* whisky.

"For you, my friend," Rory smiled.

"Oh, I couldn't possibly *counsel* such a thing, Sir!"

"But I insist. Consider it a down payment on my next instalment of shortbread," Rory laughed, clapping Duncan amiably on the shoulder.

"Thank you, Sir. Thank you, Sir. Most kind," Duncan replied, admiring the bottle in his hands as though it were a rare artefact just unearthed.

The afternoon's formalities completed, Duncan held the door open for his departing visitors, Rory nodding companionably to Duncan as he left.

"See you soon, my friend," Rory said.

"The pleasure will be all mine, Sir," Duncan replied. If he had worn a cap, he would have doffed it.

Rory settled back into the rear seat of the CLS.

Love, Gudrun Ensslin

"Right then, foot down, Karl," he commanded. "Let's get the trip done with now!"

The CLS pulled away abruptly, continuing a rapid traverse of the Cairngorms. Rory looked back as they passed over the narrow bridge to see Duncan waving cheerily at him, dog-Rory tucked awkwardly under one arm. How absolutely *wonderful* to live like that, Rory thought.

The stoicism, the acceptance, the simplicity. Ignorance really *is* bliss! What a marvel Duncan was! Cairngorms born and bred – never once set foot outside of Scotland. Never owned anything as 'new-fangled' as a computer. Never even heard of the internet! Incredible!

The car progressed onwards, passing seemingly endless craggy rocks and docile, impervious sheep. One by one, Rory ticked off the main route markers – Braemar, Ballater, Aboyne – until, at Bridge of Canny, the two cars swung left and headed sharply north. Shortly afterwards, at Milltown of Campfield, an overgrown dirt track led upwards towards the summit of the Hill of Fare.

This was the stage of the journey at which Rory regretted he was not travelling in the Range Rover Sport (just one of many vehicles awaiting him in the garage at Carlisle House). A short way up this steep incline another roadway presented itself on the left-hand side. Following this winding tree-lined road until it swept majestically around a corner on the hillside led eventually to a clearing that emerged onto a wide gravel driveway and at last revealed a panoramic view of Carlisle House in all its splendour.

This was always Rory's favourite view of his Scottish hideaway – perched atop a small, sculpted hillock with the verdant tree-covered terrain of northern Aberdeenshire and the Cairngorms framing a dramatic backdrop. The architectural style of Carlisle House was Gothic and imposing; slate grey pointed minarets sat astride tall turrets – eight in total – like witches' hats, surrounding the austere building. Admittedly, the overall effect was probably more Castle Bran than pure Scottish baronial – a fact that led the locals to refer to it routinely as 'Castle Dracula'! Still, Rory liked it that way. It was precisely this slightly sinister aspect to the building's appearance that attracted him in the first place. Ever jealous of his privacy, Rory concluded that any notion among the locals that suggested to them that, by trespassing, they might put themselves in danger of encountering vampires, werewolves or perhaps even the roaming Hellhound of the Baskervilles was a further security feature he was happy to encourage.

Rory was grateful to see his dark green Range Rover Sport sitting proudly in the driveway – clearly lovingly prepared and awaiting his arrival. Later, he planned to take the B roads up to Garlogie, back through Tarland to Aboyne and then home for supper – valuable thinking time for him to prepare yet another incendiary message to Krendler. The mounting excitement regarding the launch of his project was

171

almost unbearable – so great he could feel his fingertips tingling with anticipation.

The house was now fully staffed in expectation of his arrival – an extra compliment of locals had been drafted in for the duration of his residency: supplementary kitchen staff, cleaners and housemaids. However, there was only one employee Rory hoped would already be *in situ* – an employee he looked forward to seeing above all others; Jardine. Rory enjoyed the satisfying crunch of the gravel beneath the leather soles of his handmade shoes. As he approached the heavy oak front door, it seemingly opened all by itself and out stepped the slender and sober-suited figure of his greeter – Jardine. Jardine nodded solemnly as his Master approached.

"Your room is ready, Sir. Everything is as you would desire it."

Rory, understanding the code that Jardine's greeting implied, was ecstatic and nodded enthusiastically towards his faithful factotum. He then entered the building, pausing on the black and white marble flagstones in the entrance hall to inspect the staff – all of whom had assembled (including the gardener) and lined up as though it were the 1920s.

"How very nice to see you all," Rory beamed. The assembled staff bowed or curtsied as appropriate. Jardine snapped his fingers and a pair of local lads rushed outside to fetch the baggage.

"Allow me to show you to your room, Sir," Jardine said.

Love, Gudrun Ensslin

"Thank you, Jardine," said Rory. "That really would be quite splendid."

After a hot shower and an invigorating drive in the Range Rover, Rory settled to a Scottish banquet in the wood-panelled dining hall. He enjoyed Cullen Skink to start, followed by venison in rich gravy and a selection of local cheeses with oat cakes for dessert. Replete, Rory retired to the library. Presently, Jardine appeared – bringing a crystal glass containing a large cognac and a humidor containing a wide selection of *Cohiba* cigars. Rory picked the largest cigar in the box and reached for his silver cigar cutter. Soon the library filled with a heavy fog of blue smoke. Jardine then appeared a second time, reverently carrying Rory's laptop computer, which he placed beside his Master on a mahogany side table. Jardine then exited silently from the room – stage right; like Banquo's Ghost.

Rory set his cigar down in the ashtray and lifted the lid of the laptop. The machine – previously left in 'sleep' mode – now sprang into life with an eager electronic bleat. The screen – a small ocean of turquoise – was punctuated by one solitary icon, entitled BANKER_BINGO. Rory double-clicked the icon, leant back and sighed deeply. He needed a moment to compose himself. He was about to write the final words that would unleash *Herr* Georg Krendler (and the Gudrun Ensslin Kommando) on a complacent and unsuspecting 21st century Britain. Once he linked to cyberspace and clicked 'send' there really would be no going back. Rory took a deep breath, swigged some cognac and puffed at his cigar. Then he pressed 'Enter' on the keyboard.

BANKER BINGO ENCRYPTED WEBSITE POST:

This is *your* moment. This is YOUR time. This is when YOU are called upon to do your duty – unflinchingly, unswervingly, unquestioningly – for the good of *all* peoples against the forces of evil; the forces of CAPITALISM; the forces of control, iniquity, greed and oppression.

Soon a game card will become available to YOU on this unique website – downloadable and ready to 'play' – containing the targets you will need: the financiers, hedge fund managers and asset strippers operating behind the scenes to rape nations and suppress millions in their relentless and unprincipled pursuit of unending profit.

YOU will be the one to seek out, hunt down and destroy these TARGETS. Only then will the lessons of Karl Marx have been learned and a true and enlightened era of Real Existing Socialism finally be established.

Know also, that these actions will also be a final vengeance for Petra Schelm, Tommy Weisbecker and the martyrs of the Todësnacht. Happy Hunting, Comrade!

Anarchist Pete

Love, Gudrun Ensslin

CHAPTER THIRTEEN: DER TEUFELSWERK

Semmler's promised 'hotting up' did not materialise as quickly as I anticipated – at least not in terms of *praxis*. Instead, the first half of 1971 was characterised by several bank raids on our part and a spate of apartment raids by the BKA in response.

The RAF raided two banks in Astrid Proll's home town of Kassel (netting us approximately 115,000DM towards 'operational funds'). The BKA replied with raids on our safe houses in Hamburg, Bremen, Gelsenkirchen and, of course, Frankfurt. Exactly as Semmler had predicted, I was hauled in for questioning as a 'known associate' of Andreas Baader, Gudrun Ensslin and Julius Semmler.

As instructed, I derided Semmler in the foulest and most overt terms, describing my involvement with "all that" as peripheral and "certainly over" – mere "idealistic student folly" which I had "certainly outgrown". I emphasised my relationship with Cressida – my desire to get married, to settle down, to join in with 'normal' (*bourgeois*) society. The cops lapped it up. I didn't think they'd go for it but my act came over as so sincere that I almost managed to fool myself!

Love, Gudrun Ensslin

Cressida's testimony helped too. They also hauled her in for questioning – although, as an Englishwoman with no obvious connection to Baader Meinhof, they treated her with kid gloves by comparison. They started out being snide, though – asking her why she was studying in Germany ("Don't they have universities in England?") and why she was so apparently obsessed with German '*kultur*' ("Why choose Goethe when you already have Shakespeare?").

Their tone softened a little when she described our relationship as a "true love affair" and "the real thing" in such saccharine terms that even some of the cynical, hard-hearted bastards of the BKA were reaching for their hankies in response to the *schmalz*! The only difference between Cressida's testimony and mine was that I don't think *she* was acting. They let her go shortly after questioning her over my relationship with Semmler.

"Georg doesn't see Julius any more," she said flatly. "They had a row. Neither of us has seen or heard from Julius in months."

After that, it was 'business as usual' for the pair of us – shopping, studying and enjoying occasional trips to the cinema. A period of 'domestic bliss' ensued – with no communication from Semmler or any of the Gang until, on July 15th 1971, all that changed once more.

July 15th 1971 was the day Petra Schelm died. The BKA planned a 'day of action' throughout the entire *Bundesrepublik* in an attempt to tighten the net

Love, Gudrun Ensslin

on the "criminal renegades of Baader Meinhof". Accordingly, some three thousand cops were manning roadblocks throughout the whole country. In the lazy afternoon haze of a Hamburg summer, a speeding *BMW* crashed through one of fifteen roadblocks established throughout the northern port. At the wheel: Baader Meinhof operative Werner Hoppe. In the passenger seat: nineteen year-old hairdresser Petra Schelm.

Some cops in a larger, more powerful *Mercedes* gave immediate chase and forced the little *Baader-Meinhof-Wagen* off the road. Werner and Petra threw open their doors and fled, on foot, in opposite directions. Werner, pursued by a helicopter and eventually surrounded by some eighty armed cops, surrendered immediately. Petra Schelm, similarly surrounded, stood and screamed a hysterical defiance – and was shot dead in cold blood for her efforts. A nineteen year-old girl screaming a nineteen year-old's naïve defiance shot dead in cold blood by trigger-happy pigs for failing to toe the authorities' line and sing prettily (like a good girl) from the State's hymn sheet.

The result? Tacit – and overt – support for us! Our cause was now at an all-time popularity high throughout West Germany. More than this, the authorities – in the form of the BKA – declared open war on us. The blood-letting had begun. Now it was our turn to respond – and indeed, we all felt we *needed* to respond. . .if only as catharsis. All Hell was truly about to break loose.

Reprisal came on 25th September when two cops were shot and wounded approaching a car containing RAF members Holger Meins and Margrit Schiller on the Freiburg to Basel *autobahn*. Later, on 22nd October, a cop was shot and killed by Baader Meinhof operatives in Hamburg – the scene of Petra Schelm's demise. Once again, Margrit Schiller was involved – although the very next day she was captured. On both sides, the stakes were rising.

In late December the bank raids resumed. On 22nd December three of our people launched a raid on a bank in Kaiserslautern – netting us 134,000DM. . .and shooting a cop dead. One of the three bank robbers was a young blonde secretary called Ingeborg Barz. Ingeborg joined the RAF back in 1970 at the invitation of, and in support of, her politically active boyfriend, Wolfgang Grundmann (himself one of the Kaiserslautern bank raiders). Little did I know then, but my life was soon to become linked with that of Ingeborg Barz...and linked for all eternity.

The killing of the cop weighed heavily on Ingeborg's mind. She hadn't anticipated such violence, such finality; such an irreparable consequence. Suddenly she felt sick to her stomach. In the space of one gunshot, the excitement and adrenaline that living outside the law and 'the revolution' had supplied to her turned to a sordid, naked horror and a nihilistic sense of emptiness. The mask slipped – whereas before the cop died Ingeborg had the sense of being a true

178

Love, Gudrun Ensslin

liberator fighting for the oppressed, there now appeared only to be a desolate black void in her heart and the overwhelming stench of death in her nostrils. It was all too much. The merry-go-round was spinning too fast – she was feeling both dizzy and sick. She wanted to stop but the centrifugal force holding her in place was simply too great. She wasn't sleeping, she wasn't eating, her relationship with Wolfgang had deteriorated to a barely functioning sham. Ingeborg Barz simply wanted out.

On February 21st 1972 Ingeborg telephoned her mother and told her she wanted to come home. For her, the revolution was over. That same day, the bank raids resumed – with eight Baader Meinhof members helping themselves to 285,000DM from the Ludwigshafen Mortgage & Exchange Bank.

"I want to come home, *Mutti*," said Ingeborg.
Ingeborg Barz was yet another young girl in the Gudrun mould: tall, slender, graceful, attractive; long blonde hair and clear blue eyes. However, whereas Gudrun's character was hewn from the hardest diamond, Ingeborg remained, deep down, sugar and spice. Whereas, for Gudrun, time and experience served only to sharpen her beliefs – harden her resolve, deepen her fanaticism – for Ingeborg, time and experience served only to dilute her faith, diminish her commitment; finally persuade her it had all been a terrible mistake.

"*Mutti*, I want to come home."

Love, Gudrun Ensslin

*   *   *

On the morning of 25th February 1972 the telephone rang in Cressida's flat. Still munching on my breakfast of bread and cheese, I ran down the hall to answer it.

"Georg!" a voice said cheerily. It was a voice that sounded familiar but which I still couldn't place. "Surely you haven't forgotten?" It was a laughing, friendly chastisement – as though to say: silly you! "See you at the museum at noon." Then the caller hung up. It was all very quick and surreal – over in seconds and leaving me half wondering whether I'd actually had a conversation or not.

I placed the receiver back in its cradle – and instantly it all made sense; the fog was clearing from my half-awake mind. I had just been contacted by Baader Meinhof. 'See you at the museum' was code – and it didn't mean a museum either. It was Semmler's code for me to meet him – or someone else from the RAF – on the steps of the *Paulskirche*; someone had phoned the message through on his behalf. Twelve noon? I looked at my watch. Best get a move on, I thought.

My instructions from Semmler were to sit on the front steps of the imposing pink-brick church and wait to be contacted. I was told I should read a book, a newspaper or a magazine and show no outward reaction to the approach of anyone I recognised. Speak only when spoken to. I arrived at the *Paulskirche* with barely fifteen minutes to spare. I sat dutifully on the steps twiddling my thumbs and glancing nervously at my watch – wishing I'd remembered to follow the advice to bring a newspaper or a magazine.

Presently, a man approached – dressed traditionally in an Austrian hunting cap (complete with feather) and a dark green *Loden* coat. A scarf was wrapped around most of his face – even though it was not especially cold that day. Despite the disguise, as he came nearer my heart skipped several beats and I struggled to resist the urge to leap to my feet and rush towards him – for, the rapid, bird-like gait and round, silver-rimmed spectacles told me unequivocally that this was Julius Semmler himself!

Julius walked up the steps and passed me by – taking absolutely no notice of me whatsoever; as though I were a ghost he could not see – or as though he were the ghost, unaware of my observation of his ethereal presence. He stopped at the top of the stairs and made a great show of reading the plaque beside the door of the *Paulskirche* – ostensibly as engrossed in its message as any tourist. I had already glanced at this plaque shortly after arriving. It read:

"The Paulskirche is the birthplace of German democracy. In 1848 the first German constitution-sanctioning National Assembly debated here 99 times before it was dissolved by the Prussian Empire in 1849. In the Second World War bombing of 1944, the Paulskirche burned down to its foundation walls. As one of the first Frankfurt

**buildings to be reconstructed, it stood again in 1948
as a symbol of – and a monument to – much abused
democracy.** "

As Semmler backed away from the plaque he pulled a
camera from his inside coat pocket and pointed it
directly upwards at the towering edifice of the
building. Squinting through the viewfinder he looked
every inch the fascinated, affluent Viennese tourist. As
he backed past me, clicking the shutter, he mumbled
from beneath his scarf – almost hissing at me.

"Inside the *Alte Nikolaikirche*. One hour."

Then, shutter still clicking, he backed away
completely – out of range of any further
communication. Once the camera disappeared inside
his *Loden* coat, Julius spun on his heel and was gone –
swallowed up by the crowd.

I had the presence of mind not to leave
immediately, remaining on the steps for a further ten
minutes (with no little difficulty as, lacking any
reading material, I was already heartily bored by the
act of sitting vigil – and was now more than desperate
to reach our next assignation to hear exactly what
Semmler had to say).

Still, I continued to stare ostentatiously at my
watch and exhibit outward signs of impatience and
frustration – a pantomime act of a man left on a limb
by his date that would have been worthy of Marcel
Marceau. At last, I got to my feet, glared angrily at my
watch, looked all around me one last time, hands

Love, Gudrun Ensslin

planted firmly on hips – before stalking off in apparent dismay. It was ham acting, of course – but I figured you couldn't be too demonstrative where the BKA were concerned; you wanted to be sure they – or their spies and informers – clearly got the message!

The *Alte Nikolaikirche* was only a short stroll from the *Paulskirche* – so I had some time to kill. With a full half an hour available to me I fancied a beer and a *schnitzel*. There was nothing so effective in building an appetite as the start of a mission.

The *Alte Nikolaikirche*, located on the south side of the *Römerberg*, was traditionally the church of merchants and councillors. The interior was a dark, quiet haven from the throng of people in the square outside. It took a full second for my eyes to adjust to the half-light inside the church filtering through the stained glass depicting biblical scenes. Once acclimatised, I spotted Semmler, his hunting cap now removed, sitting a few rows from the front, facing the altar. Instinctively, I went and sat in the pew directly in front of him, bowing my head in a facsimile of prayer and contemplation – exactly as Julius had already done.

"Later this evening you will have a visitor," Julius whispered.

"I like your outfit!" I chuckled in reply.

"Shut up!" he hissed. "This is serious and I don't have much time."

Suitably chastened, I suppressed my mirth.

"A young girl will come to your flat this

evening. Keep her there. Chat to her, entertain her – do whatever you have to do – but do not let her out of your sight. She believes she is being taken to see Andreas tonight for a debriefing to be set free of her responsibilities to our merry little gang. Shortly after midnight a car will arrive to take you and the girl to the countryside just outside Frankfurt. The driver will tell you what has to be done next."

The details of my 'mission' were racing through my mind so quickly I could barely take them in. A young girl. Midnight. Andreas. Debriefing. Driver. Countryside. A cold shiver went up my spine. I could see through Julius's euphemisms and I was truly horrified – here we were, sitting in a House of God, discussing and planning a *murder*! Before I could say anything, Julius stood up and crossed himself ostentatiously.

"Don't fuck this up, Georg," he warned. "If you do, we could both end up in a ditch somewhere."

I remained seated in the pew – immobilised by the sheer horror of my situation. When I turned around, Julius Semmler was gone.

The bright daylight and routine bustling of the crowds outside did not register with me as I left the church. Suddenly, I didn't feel a part of that world anymore. It was as though I somehow sleepwalked my way into another reality – a different dimension that looked exactly the same as the world I already knew but which now contained a new and sinister quality which was only just revealed. It was as though I had gone through the Looking Glass – or taken a bad acid trip. My dilemma was immense – and I did not know which way to turn. I could squeal to the authorities, have Julius arrested, the 'driver' arrested and 'the girl' taken into protective custody. But then, where would that leave *me*? With my previously denied involvement with Baader Meinhof now fully exposed, a judicial sentence was a certainty. Even if I managed to strike a deal with the BKA – to tell all I knew in return for clemency – I would be a marked man for what remained of the RAF. An informer! A traitor! I might as well pin a target on my back!

No, I had no 'choice' at all – my only option was to go through with it: to 'do my duty'. But how? Maybe by telling myself repeatedly – until I honestly believed it – that perhaps Julius was simply being a bit over dramatic. Maybe all we *were* going to do was simply 'put the frighteners' on the girl – warn her what *could* happen if she was tempted to talk to the authorities herself. Maybe she really was only attending a 'debriefing'? Maybe Andreas really would be there? Maybe she really would be 'set free'?

When I returned to the flat I found Cressida sitting in her bathrobe, one foot on the kitchen table, painting her toenails with a towel wrapped tightly around her head like a *fakir's* turban. She had just stepped out of the shower and was humming joyfully to herself in happy-go-lucky tones. Her merriment instantly offended me. It was not the fact of it that annoyed me – it was the sub-text that ran beneath it:

she was flaunting her right to her 'ignorance is bliss' happiness right in my face at the very moment when I faced a moral dilemma she couldn't possibly imagine and I couldn't possibly disclose.

"There's a girl coming here tonight," I snapped at her. "A friend of some friends. We have to look after her for a few hours – then I'll take her to another flat later on."

Cressida's bare feet dropped to the floor. Her relaxed smile replaced with an angry scowl.

"Not more of your silly games with Julius," she moaned. "I thought you were finished with all of that."

I waved my arms frantically at her in a hushing gesture. I didn't want her speaking Julius's name out loud – even in our flat, which I still couldn't be certain wasn't bugged.

"Look, it's only for a few hours, for fuck's sake!" I shouted, banging my fist so hard on the table that a jug of flowers toppled over, spilling water across the English newspaper Cressida had only recently abandoned.

"Fine," she yelled in reply. "I'll go and stay over at Sigrid's place tonight – leave you people to it, shall I?" She attempted to brush past me and rush out of the kitchen. I grabbed her, pinning both her arms to her sides and holding her close.

"Cressy, look, I'm sorry," I wheedled, immediately changing my tone from angry to needy. "Don't go. I *need* you here. This is important, that's all.

Love, Gudrun Ensslin

It's just something I have to do."

Cressida struggled free of my grasp.

"I'm going to Sigrid's. I may or may not be back tonight."

She stalked into the bedroom to get changed. I didn't have the strength of will to argue any further. Instead, I put some Colombian coffee in the percolator and lit a flame on the stove. Before the coffee was poured, I heard the front door slam.

*   *   *

I sat in the flat attempting to read my Philosophy textbooks and a bunch of *Mickey Mouse* comics – but I couldn't concentrate on either. Instead, I thought about Cressida – and where we might be heading. I thought about Gudrun – and how we might never get there. I thought about the mystery girl – and wondered how I might face her without hanging my head in shame. I made myself a sandwich using a large block of stale cheese. The sandwich remained uneaten. I felt like a prisoner.

At precisely six o'clock the doorbell rang. My first thought was that Cressida had returned. I ran to the intercom. Then, I realised – Cressida would have a key. I answered the persistent ringing in a cautious tone.

"Yes?"

"Hallo?" It was a female voice – sounding every bit as nervous and hesitant as I did. "Hallo, is that Georg?"

"Yes, who is this?"

"It's Ingeborg. Ingeborg Barz. A friend sent me..."

Without replying, I pressed the entry buzzer.

I waited at the open door with baited breath for Ingeborg to climb the stairs. There was an old-fashioned cage lift but it had been out of order ever since Cressida moved into the block.

"Not very German to leave it like that," Cressida complained to me. "I thought you people were supposed to be ultra-efficient?"

"Don't believe *all* the stereotypes," I replied. "Lazy landlords are the same the world over – especially when it comes to spending money!"

A tall, blonde girl with a slightly boyish frame, carrying a bulging navy blue kitbag slung casually over one shoulder, now stood before me. Her clear blue eyes were alert pools of intelligence – not as mesmeric as Gudrun's, nor so artfully accentuated with kohl, but captivating nonetheless. Ingeborg attempted a nervous smile and thrust a hand out towards me in formal greeting.

"Please, call me Inge," she said prettily. "Everyone does."

"Georg," I replied, shaking her hand a little too enthusiastically and then suddenly releasing it. "Please, come in."

We talked for several hours at the kitchen table – asking awkward questions about each other's

Love, Gudrun Ensslin

backgrounds (home towns, brothers and sisters, pets, favourite movies); all the usual clumsy attempts by strangers suddenly thrown together to establish common ground. However, our conversation remained vague and neutral. We seemed to be complicit in an unspoken pact to avoid talking about politics, Baader Meinhof, death and killing…or any of *that* stuff.

"Would you like something to eat?" I asked suddenly, springing to my feet and glancing at my watch (nine o'clock – three hours to go!). "I'm sorry, it was very rude of me not to offer you any food. I should have thought. I can do better than endless cups of coffee! Here, let me see what I can find…"

Inge watched with amusement as I raced around the small kitchen opening and closing cupboards and drawers like a lunatic. Eventually I turned back towards her.

"Pasta with cheese is the best I can offer you, I'm afraid. Although I'm sure there's a tin of tomatoes somewhere I can chuck in with it."

"Sounds great," Inge smiled, without any trace of irony.

When the food was prepared I put two cereal bowls full of the unappetising mixture on the table between us and added a couple of glasses of tap water as an afterthought. Inge dived straight in – wolfing the spaghetti down as though she hadn't eaten a meal in days. She finished hers almost before I'd even started mine.

"I can make some more, if you like," I offered.

Love, Gudrun Ensslin

"No thanks," she said, pushing her bowl away across the table. "That was fine."

She seemed perfectly content to just sit and watch me eat.

"Do you have a girlfriend, Georg?" she asked suddenly.

The question caught me completely by surprise. It made me realise I hadn't yet mentioned Cressida at any point – in fact, I was perfectly content to allow Inge to think this was my flat rather than someone else's.

"Yes, as a matter of fact, I do," I answered. "She's English," I added as an afterthought.

"English?" Inge repeated, in an astonished tone – as though it were the most exotic nationality possible.

"Yes," I said, flatly. "Although, maybe she's not my girlfriend any more. We had a row shortly before you arrived." Inge smiled.

"She'll be back," she said authoritatively.

I cleared the bowls away, wondering how she could be so sure – and secretly hoping she was right. (Another glance at my watch – ten o'clock. Still two hours to go – what to do now?).

"Do you play cards, Inge?" I asked lamely. "I think we've got a pack somewhere…"

"Not really," Inge replied, shrugging her shoulders. However, I was off again on another of my mad searches – eventually locating the cards in the bottom drawer of Cressida's bedside cabinet. I

Love, Gudrun Ensslin

reappeared in the kitchen triumphantly holding the cards in my left hand and an unopened bottle of *Schnapps* in my right.

"Found them!" I announced boldly. "Here, let me teach you an English game my girlfriend taught me – it's called 'Gin Rummy'."

"Oh, all right then," Inge said, swayed by my bonhomie.

I poured each of us a decent measure of *Schnapps* and shuffled the cards. Suddenly, Inge burst into tears, holding her head in both hands. I sat there paralysed by my inability to know what to do next, clutching a fanned-out hand of cards like an imbecile while mutely watching the girl's heaving shoulders.

"Do you really think they'll let me go, Georg?" she wailed.

Stung into action by the prospect that, in this highly emotional state, she might try to flee my custody, I dragged my chair around the table and set it close to hers. I poured her another extra-large dose of *schnapps* and put my arms around her as benignly as I could. She felt warm and fragile to the touch.

"I'm sure it'll be OK," I lied. It even sounded like a lie to me. She looked up at me – tearful and hiccupping.

"Have you known Andreas long?" she asked.

"Right back to '68," I boasted, unable to keep the note of pride out of my voice – and forgetting any paranoid suspicions about the apartment being bugged. "Look, he just wants to speak to you – to tell you what the authorities might say and do to you if they drag you in for questioning; coach you a bit in how to act and what to tell them. The same thing happened to me – they questioned me, you know. And Cressida. And here *we* are! Trust me, it's nothing serious – just a quick chat and then you can go."

I felt sick to my stomach at myself. I didn't know where those awful lying words and half-truths had come from but they just tumbled out of me in a disingenuous freefall. I have never hated myself as much as I did at that precise moment. Inge, however, seemed reassured.

"I'm sorry," she said, drying her eyes on her sleeve. "Forgive me, I'm just being silly."

She picked up the tumbler of *schnapps* I poured and drank it down in one go, and shook her head like a dog just stepped out of a rain shower. Then she poured herself another large *schnapps* and immediately downed that too. By 11.30pm, when the doorbell rang half an hour early, Ingeborg Barz had consumed the best part of an entire bottle of *Schnapps*.

*   *   *

"Step outside, I need to talk to you," said the man at the flat door. He was thick set and unshaven with dark, close-cropped hair and too much cheap aftershave that barely covered his alcohol-laden breath. He was also wearing Andreas's uniform of leather biker jacket and jeans. I'd never seen him before – although he

192

Love, Gudrun Ensslin

reminded me vaguely of one of the mechanics Andreas
recently recruited to modify and maintain the Gang's
getaway cars. He introduced himself to me as 'Anton'
– although I would bet my dying breath that it was not
his real name. Someone, however, had clearly told
Anton *my* real name.

"Listen, Georg," he sneered, suddenly pinning
me to the wall outside the flat – an act of such
unexpected violence that I almost pissed my pants.
"You bring her out and sit in the back with her. Keep
her quiet but keep her *occupied*. When we get to where
we're going, bring her right up to the door and then
you can go back and wait in the car. Got that?" Even
his whispering was somehow violent.

I nodded my compliance – like an eager
cartoon character captured by a much larger bully.
Anton's knuckles were pressing on my windpipe and I
was struggling for air. I just wanted to get away.
Eventually, he let me go.

"Well, bring her downstairs then, *shithead*!" he
smiled, patting me on both cheeks with brick-like
hands. "It's the black *Mercedes* parked directly
outside."

With that, he was gone – retreating silently
down the stairwell like a vanishing spectre. I walked
unsteadily back towards the kitchen and paused outside
to compose myself – trying to prevent my knees from
knocking or my voice from shaking when I faced Inge
once more.

"It's time to go, Inge," I announced. "Andreas

is waiting."

Fortunately for me, Inge's booze-addled state meant she was in no condition to notice anything amiss with my demeanour. She rose unsteadily from her seat, swung the kitbag around her shoulders and grabbed onto me for support. In the grip of her alcohol haze, she suddenly found everything tremendously funny. Girlish giggles rang loudly through the kitchen.

"Shh, shh Inge," I soothed. "Here, I'll help you to the car."

We made slow, giggly progress down the staircase. By the time we reached the street, Anton was pacing furiously up and down, a cigarette bobbing on his lower lip, eyes bulging maniacally.

"Where the fuck have you been?" he hissed.
We both stared at him blankly – then Inge burst out laughing.

"Who's Mr. Angry?" she chuckled.

As Anton stormed forward I winced and shrank backwards. I felt sure he was about to hit her. Instead, he opened the rear door of the car and jerked a thumb towards the dark interior.

"In there. Both of you. *Now*!"

Instinctively, Inge and I both hesitated.

"Come on," Anton sneered. "We don't want to keep *Andreas* waiting, do we?" A sickly smile spread across his rough features. Obediently, Inge fell forwards into the car, the kitbag rolling away under the rear seat. Anton slammed the door shut after her, almost catching her feet.

Love, Gudrun Ensslin

"You, *arsehole* – round the other side!" he barked at me.

Inge and I barely adjusted ourselves into an upright position before the car roared off – sending our heads back on our necks and threatening to return our spaghetti to the outside world. For the most part we remained silent – passively watching the lights of downtown Frankfurt becoming the lights of the suburbs. We headed southwest to Bingen and then further west into the remote farmland of the Hunsrück.

"How fucking much has she had to drink?" growled Anton from the driver's seat, noticing in the rear view mirror that Inge was now dozing on my shoulder.

"Enough," I replied, humourlessly.

Anton snorted derisively in response and lit another cigarette from the pop-up lighter on the dashboard. When the cigarette was only half-finished, Anton swung the car abruptly onto a dirt track leading towards an isolated farmhouse surrounded by several decrepit outbuildings – no doubt another convenient bolthole arranged by a sympathiser. The jolting of the car as it bounced uneasily over the farmyard potholes and loose rocks woke Inge and she lifted her head from my shoulder. She looked around – blinking uncertainly and squinting through the car's tinted rear windows into the darkness to try to gather some sense of where she was.

"I feel sick," she moaned. I stroked her hair softly.

Love, Gudrun Ensslin

Instead of driving up to the front door of the
farmhouse, Anton pulled the car wide of the main
property and drove around to the rear – eventually
stopping outside a large barn. He killed the car's lights
and cut its engine. Total silence reigned as
impenetrable darkness enveloped us all.

"Give me a few minutes to speak with Andreas
alone – then you two follow," Anton instructed,
twisting around in his seat to face us. As he said this, I
noticed for the first time that he had a gold tooth. It
glinted at me in the thin moonlight, to which my eyes
were now steadily adjusting. I remained with Inge in
the back seat for a while – huddled like two naughty
children while Daddy popped into the tobacconist's.
For a while we said nothing, merely watching as Anton
strode away from the car towards the barn – the
glowing tip of his cigarette giving the only real clue to
his progress away from us. I didn't really know what to
say so it was Inge who broke the silence first.

"Why would he choose here?" she said
suspiciously.

"Who?" I asked crassly.

"Andreas, of course," she replied, incredulous
at my stupidity.

"Well, the city's becoming dangerous," I
replied quickly. "All those raids on our safe houses, so
many people arrested…the countryside makes perfect
sense these days."

Inge looked relieved once more. After all, she
could see the logic behind my words – cold logic is

196

Love, Gudrun Ensslin

always reassuring...even when it substantiates an outrageous lie.

"Still," I continued, impressing even myself with my quick-thinking. "It must have been difficult getting hold of this place. After all, we don't have anywhere near as many supporters in the rural areas. The *schili* are nearly all urbanites."

Inge looked agitated again.

"Let's go," she said, reaching for the door handle. "Let's get it over with. What's the advantage to anyone in this delay? I just want to go home."

I wanted to tell her to run – simply to take flight across the fields; vanish into the darkness and keep going. Run and run and run and keep running and don't stop. Get as far away from this wretched place as possible. But, of course, I said nothing. Instead, lamely – and like a coward – I stepped out of the car with her, took her gently by the arm and led her to her doom.

Once we reached the barn door I knocked twice, as previously instructed. The heavy door slid open on its rails and Anton stood before us once more. In a split second, before either of us had time to even think, pistol in hand, he clubbed Inge several times about the head and face as she stood beside me – pistol-whipping her into sudden unconsciousness. It all happened so quickly I was rooted to the spot with shock.

"Go and wait in the car, *idiot*!" Anton snarled at me, as he dragged Inge's prone body into the barn and closed the door once more. It banged shut with an

197

awful finality.

Shocked and horrified, I stumbled back to the *Mercedes* and let myself into the passenger seat. I desperately wanted to be physically sick but feared the consequences of spoiling the interior of Anton's car. To try to take my mind off what was happening, I opened the glove box and felt carelessly inside. Road maps, a pack of cigarettes and a lighter – ironically shaped like a miniature pistol. Even though I didn't smoke, I took a cigarette from the packet with trembling fingers and lit it with that grotesque lighter – anything, *anything* just to distract myself.

Then, I got out of the car and paced around – dragging the smoke deeply into my lungs, coughing and spluttering, willing it to somehow nullify both my conscience and my consciousness; to batter my brain into submission. And that's when I heard it – the 'bang'. Only, it wasn't a 'bang' as such – it was a loud, sharp 'crack'. Closely followed by another 'crack' – and then another. I jumped and shook at each sound. All I could think of was that horrendous movie in my father's attic. A gap appeared in the barn doorway and Anton strode out. He looked angrily at me.

"I said 'wait in the car' *shitbrain*!" he spat.

I showed him the cigarette – now almost just a butt – by way of explanation and tried to shrug as nonchalantly as I could manage.

"Get in the fucking car!" he ordered.

I threw the butt down and crushed it underfoot. Anton was already in the car, starting up the engine. I ran over and jumped into the passenger seat beside him. He carefully executed a three-point turn, spinning the car around so that it was now facing directly away from the barn. I noticed, as his hands grappled with the steering wheel, that he was now wearing gloves. He reversed the car towards the barn door. Once it was fully backed up, he turned to me.

"I don't know if you've ever seen anyone shot," he began menacingly.

I stammered incoherently in response. I was thinking once more of those films and photos back in my father's attic in Wuppertal – and how those secret hours spent pouring over those awful images had at last come back to haunt me in a way I could never have imagined. In my mind's eye, I could see myself fiddling with the old projector. Flickering nightmarish edits of a nightmare past merged with a nightmarish present.

"I didn't think so," Anton continued contemptuously. "Still, you mustn't piss your pants – or throw up! There's enough clearing up to be done already. You'll have to control yourself, *shitbrain*! I need you to help me get her into the boot. She'll be quite heavy now – heavier than she looks and heavier than you'll be expecting…dead people always are."

I felt like screaming but I simply nodded mute assent.

"OK, let's go, *shithead*!" Anton said, swinging the car door wide open.

I didn't want to walk into that barn. I feared

what I might see. I genuinely feared that Inge might somehow rise up – resurrected as a vampire or some other demonic spectre, hell-bent on seeking revenge and swooping down on us both to tear us limb from limb. I didn't want to see the poor girl's body – but, most of all, I didn't want to be confronted by the consequences of my own complicity; the wages of my own damnable sins of commission and omission.

An eerie flickering light emanated from the barn's interior that only added to the dreadful impression already formed in my mind. It looked like a Horror movie set.

Anton opened the car boot to its widest point, turned and marched confidently into the barn – untroubled and business-like. Cautiously, I followed. The source of the flickering light was soon identified as an old-fashioned oil lamp suspended on a chain from a roof beam. Now the scene, with its *ersatz*-strobe lighting and tall, distorted shadows, suggested Expressionist cinema – *Nosferatu* himself climbing the staircase to claim me in my sleep.

Poor Inge lay sprawled on the floor in a spastic, heavily contorted position – her bloodied head lying on a bed of straw. There was a great deal of blood leaking out – thick and coagulating; staining the straw and congregating around her shattered skull like a mocking halo. Despite this evidence of grotesque violence, her face appeared to be in repose – as if enjoying the most peaceful sleep. Only at that moment did I fully understand the true meaning of the word 'obscene'.

"Come on, let's get her in the car," Anton barked.

It was a major act of will for me simply to approach the body. All my instincts told me to flee – to run away as far and as fast as possible from this terrible vision. To reach out and touch her like this was unthinkable. Bizarrely, I still feared she might transform into a vampire, grab me and sink newly grown fangs into my neck – so completely had my grip on reality been damaged by this experience. Yet, the presence of Anton – a very real rather than merely theoretical threat – persuaded me to override any such reservations. After all, here was a man who, without a moment's thought was capable of rendering me into the same condition as poor Inge if I did not comply with his instructions.

I edged forward and crouched down near the body. Trying to avoid looking at her face, I reached out and grabbed her right wrist. To my horror, it still felt soft and warm – although simultaneously limp and lifeless. A wave of nausea and revulsion swam over me and I thought I might pass out, the hideous scene swimming around me in a whirlpool of indistinct shapes and colours. Suddenly a boot kicked me hard in the ribs – sending me toppling backwards onto the straw and a knife-sharp pain began arching through my chest. Anton, patience not being his primary virtue, stood directly over me.

"Take her feet, College boy!" he commanded.

Love, Gudrun Ensslin

"And pull yourself together – or I might have to shoot you as well."

It was exactly what I feared most – now I too was considered to be in his firing line. And then it dawned on me: what was there to suggest he wouldn't shoot me *anyway* – whether I complied with his instructions or not? Yet, what choice did I have? Still in pain, I scrambled to my feet and scuttled round to the lower half of Inge's corpse. Now, without a second thought, I grabbed hold of both of her legs and tucked them under my armpits, ready to move her wherever he wanted. Anton grunted his satisfaction.

We carried the dead girl to the boot of the car and tipped her unceremoniously inside whereupon she curled obscenely into a foetal position. Anton banged the boot shut and clapped his gloved hands together briskly, as though to say: a job well done. He went back into the barn, extinguished the oil lamp and fastened the door with a padlock.

"Someone will be coming by later to clean up," he winked. "Come on, get in the car – let's go." He seemed to be in a horribly cheerful mood.

Once we were back in the *Merc*, Anton hesitated before turning the key in the ignition. Instead, he turned to me and looked me straight in the eyes.

"You realise I did this for you, Georg," he said.

If I had been standing up, I would have fallen over!

"*You what*?" was all I could blurt out.

"I just did you a big favour," Anton continued

calmly. "They wanted *you* to do it. I was only going to be the driver. They wanted you to *prove* yourself – the leadership thought it was time you were *properly* tested."

I listened, astounded. 'The leadership' – who did he mean *exactly*? Andreas? Ulrike? *Gudrun*?

"I knew you couldn't do it, College boy!" Anton continued. "I knew you'd piss your pants – so I did it for you."

"Th-thank you," I stammered. Even as I said it, I realised it was such an odd thing to be saying – to *this* man, in *this* context.

"Fuck off!" Anton sneered. "I didn't do it for *you*. I'd shoot you myself right now with pleasure if I had my way," he added.

"Then what?..." I began. I didn't understand. None of this made any sense.

"I did it for *Julius*!" Anton exclaimed. "For some mad reason he thinks the world of you. You're like a son to him, *shithead* – the son he's never had. Julius has been protecting you for *years*, Georg. Without him, you'd be in the boot with your girlfriend here!"

"You know Semmler?" I blurted.

"I know a lot of things," said Anton, starting the engine.

*   *   *

We drove back to the outskirts of Bingen in total

silence. I was thinking of our cargo lodged pitifully in the boot and trying to make sense not only of what just happened to Inge before my very eyes but also regarding the revelation that, had it not been for Julius, I might already have been 'silenced'. Anton was simply smoking yet another cigarette. Suddenly, he pulled the car to the side of the road, killed the lights and switched off the engine. As he turned to me, I feared the worst.

"This is as far as you go," he said, blowing smoke in my face.

I shrank back against the car door as he reached inside his jacket and pulled out the pistol he used on Inge. He emptied the last two bullets, replaced the empty chamber and handed the gun to me – placing it firmly with his gloved hands into my bare hands. My first impression was that it was so much heavier than I could ever have imagined – a solid piece of metal sculpture. I gawped at it stupidly – it was the first gun I had ever held. I looked at Anton quizzically.

"Take it," he said pleasantly, suddenly greatly amused. "Now your prints are all over it and mine are nowhere to be seen. After all, it *was* supposed to be *you* that did the deed, wasn't it?" He gave a low chuckle. "All right, out you get. Go on, fuck off *shitbrain*! This is as far as I take you. I'm not going back to Frankfurt – not with this one in the boot, that's for sure. So, I'm afraid you've got a bit of a walk ahead of you. Still, look on the bright side, at least it's not raining!"

Love, Gudrun Ensslin

I tried to tuck the gun into my jeans pocket but it was too big. Instead, I put it through my belt and slotted the barrel into my pocket – then I pulled my sweater as low as possible over my thighs. I stepped wordlessly from the car. I watched as Anton spun the car around and disappeared into the night – red rear lights becoming two Satanic eyes staring at me through a canvas of blackness. I stood stock still in the cold night air. I was shivering – more from my sense of shock and horror than from the cold.

My greatest horror, however, was reserved for myself – and what I learned about myself on that fateful February night. For, there was no escaping from the fact that I had been complicit in an irreversible and evil act of betrayal. A young girl who trusted me, consoled me about my row with Cressida, drank my *schnapps*, laughed at my stupid jokes and slept innocently on my shoulder – was now *dead*...and I had played an unforgivable part in her demise. I was invisibly – but indelibly – stained with blood I could never wash off. I had a long walk home ahead...and plenty of time to think about my next move.

Love, Gudrun Ensslin

CHAPTER FOURTEEN: ES IST SO SCHÖN…
ENGLANDER ZU SEIN

I arrived back at our flat dishevelled and bleary-eyed –
looking, smelling and feeling worse than any tramp.
My horror and fatigue diluted my grip on reality even
more during my long march and the interior of the
apartment now seemed to be rushing in and out of
focus of its own free will. I experienced a strong urge
to throw up and only just made it to the bathroom.

As I crouched down spewing my guts up I
sensed the presence of someone standing over me.
Terrified, I whipped around, dribbling pungent orange
bile down the front of my sweater. Relieved, I fell back
in a crumpled heap beside the toilet pan – still
dribbling like some rabid animal. It was Cressida.

"Georg!" she screamed. "Where the fuck have
you been? What the hell has happened to you?"

I just laughed – laughed until my guts ached.
Pure hysteria! Now Cressida was horrified rather than
simply shocked. She looked at me suspiciously.

"Are you on drugs?" she asked. "Are you
tripping?"

It wasn't a rebuke, however. She was just
trying to make sense of what she was seeing. I

clambered to my feet and moved to embrace her. Immediately, she shrank back, holding her palms out to fend me off.

"No! Don't touch me!" she shrieked. "Look at the state of you!"

I didn't really hear a word she was saying. Now I was again a man on a mission. This time the mission was to make her – my beloved Cressida – understand what I was telling her; I had to get her to appreciate the seriousness of it all.

"We have to get out of here, Cressy," I told her. "We have to leave. We have to escape. It's not safe."

My rising sense of panic was now panicking her.

"What are you talking about, Georg?" she wailed. "You're not making sense. I don't understand what you're telling me!"

"Someone died last night," I yelled. "I helped to kill her! And, if we don't leave, we'll be next!"

"You're joking!" she cried. In her disbelief it was the only exclamation she could manage.

"Do I look like I'm joking?" I asked.

"I don't believe you," Cressida replied.

"Then, where the hell did I get *this*?" I shouted, pulling the gun from my waistband and brandishing it above my head.

"Oh Jesus Christ!" Cressida screamed, holding a hand over her mouth to stifle her shock. "Georg, what have you done?"

When we both calmed down a little we sat at

opposite sides of the kitchen table to talk – Cressida occupying the seat that was so recently vacated by poor Inge. I sat uneasily opposite her, still wearing my vomit-stained clothes. With our minds so focused on our situation, neither of us any longer seemed to notice the acrid stench. The gun lay on the table between us like an accusation – incongruous to her but already an inescapable part of my damaged psyche. Cressida reached for it – a natural act of curiosity.

"No, don't touch it!" I screamed. Her hand shrank back almost immediately. "My prints are all over it already – there's no need to add yours!"

She sat there looking at me – a perfect picture of misery. There was nothing else for it; I had to tell her *everything*. She listened in silence as it all poured out of me – from the very beginning: my father, my childhood in Wuppertal, the visit to South Shields, getting to Frankfurt, Semmler, meeting Andreas, the Borstal Boys, the 'bagman' work I'd done, the delivery of messages between safe houses, Inge, Anton, the barn, the gun, my long walk home.

I couldn't look her in the eye during my confession – I knew if I did I wouldn't be able to continue – so my entire speech was addressed to my own feet. I sat there blurting it all out – a schoolboy confessing to his Priest. Only when I finished did I look her squarely in the eyes. She returned my stare unblinking. She looked inscrutable, enigmatic. When at last she spoke, she said only this:

"I always knew Semmler was trouble."

Love, Gudrun Ensslin

Later, after I'd showered, our response to the crisis was to take ourselves to bed. There, we made love – slowly, tenderly and silently to the dour soundtrack of rainfall on the windowpane. Before, we only ever had recreational sex. This was *different* – this was 'making love'; an unspoken language that passed between us; the physical expression of an inner longing for true union with our 'other self'.

Afterwards, spontaneous tears streaming from our eyes, we lay naked, holding each other close, feeling as though we had somehow been expelled from the same womb – born again anew; two innocents seeing the world together for the first time. Without speaking, we both knew – for us, this was either the end...or the beginning of forever.

*　　　　　*　　　　　*

I wanted to leave for England immediately – pack our things and go the very next day; an overnight moonlight flit. However, Cressida, ever practical, persuaded me to remain a while longer to make 'arrangements'. She also rationalised we needed to make it seem, for now at least, that we were simply carrying on with our lives as normal – and displaying no signs of panic. The last thing we wanted was to show either the RAF or the BKA any hint of erratic or unpredictable behaviour. It was a lot for me to ask Cressida to give up her studies at this late stage and flee with me – *because* of me.

Love, Gudrun Ensslin

"You don't have to leave," I told her. "I'll find somewhere else – here in Germany – where I can lie low."

Cressida shook her head.

"Do you seriously think I can stay here if you just disappear?" she asked. "Knowing what I know? Think again, Georg! No, I'm coming with you – or, rather, you're coming with me!"

I was humbled by her reply – her acceptance of the situation. It made me realise something both profound and uncomfortable. It made me realise she truly loved me – and it made me realise this was the first time in my entire existence I could truly say that of another. My father? No, unless I was conforming to his 'rules' and his 'vision' he didn't really care if I lived or died. Semmler? No, that was something different altogether. But Cressida? It seemed to be the 'real thing' – which made me ask myself if I *truly* felt the same for her. As with much of the Philosophy I was studying, it was a question with no answer.

We remained in Frankfurt for another fortnight – zombies acting out a pretence of normality yet frightened to death by every ring of the phone, every blast of the doorbell. At night a wardrobe was dragged across the hallway and propped against the door, an escape route was planned across the rooftops in case it was suddenly needed. Then, on March 2nd 1972, our paranoia and panic reached its apex. That day, in Augsberg, Tommy Weisbecker was shot dead by the cops and Carmen Roll was arrested.

210

Love, Gudrun Ensslin

Meanwhile, in Hamburg two more of our people were arrested as a cop was shot dead. It was all over the papers – and the atmosphere stank of witch-hunts and repercussions. One week later – on March 9 [th] 1972 – Cressida and I boarded a plane at Frankfurt airport bound for London Heathrow. As we climbed through the clouds, holding hands, I thought only of the gun – cleaned with bleach and buried in a field on a return visit I made to the blood-stained Hunsrück. I breathed a sigh of relief and smiled at Cressida. A new chapter of my life was about to begin – in England.

At first we stayed with Cressida's parents – Clive and Caroline – remaining under their roof for a full six weeks. They lived in a large, timber-framed house in historic Canterbury – the guest bedroom (my room) provided an uninterrupted view of the world-famous Cathedral. At first, Clive could barely disguise his antipathy towards me as a German – telling me pointedly after my arrival that Kent was "Spitfire country". Clive served in the British Army throughout the War – surviving Dunkirk to become part of the unit that liberated Belsen. He wasted no opportunity for telling me about German atrocities and inhumanity – "something rotten is bred into *your* people," he said. I thought of Anton and couldn't disagree.

"When I was at Dunkirk an advancing SS unit captured two of our boys – and I mean boys…lads of seventeen or eighteen," he told me one morning at breakfast, waving a slice of toast and marmalade as he spoke. "To save ammunition, the SS tied those two lads to a tree and bludgeoned them to death with their rifle butts." His eyes took on a glassy, unfocused look as he re-lived this tale. "One of the boys was calling constantly for his mother during his ordeal – until he mercifully lost consciousness. *Your people* simply laughed – they actually found that *funny*. I was hiding in some undergrowth nearby and saw it all. I had been about to surrender – but there seemed little point after that display by *your fellows*. I was lucky to escape with my life. Then, there was Belsen. *Your people* had no regard for the Geneva Convention. Savages…absolute *savages*!"

I sat and listened – appalled and ashamed – and yet also outraged to be held culpable; after all, such fascists were the same people I was fighting myself.

"As a Communist, they would have beaten me to death too," I said.

However, Clive had no time for my Communist views. He was an 'Empire' man who dismissed my (and his daughter's) Left-wing sympathies as mere "youthful folly".

"About time you two grew up, isn't it?" he asked. "Especially if you're going to be married."

Our engagement was as much a practical as a romantic affair. We discussed it at length and it seemed the obvious thing to do. After all, how else might I be legally allowed to remain – and work – in England unless we were man and wife? Even so, it was strictly 'separate rooms' for Cressida and I as long as we remained under her parents' roof.

Love, Gudrun Ensslin

The arrangement didn't bother me as much as I had anticipated. In fact, I relished the opportunity for some temporary isolation and thinking time. There was still so much turmoil inside my head that I needed to come to terms with – and the strain of trying to constantly maintain the image, in front of Cressida's parents, of a light-hearted, happy-go-lucky beau on the cusp of married life (while still grappling internally with my guilt over poor Inge) was something which resulted in bouts of childish sobbing into my pillow.

One afternoon, when I was lying on the bed, immersed in self-pity (my mind filled with images of a laughing Inge, holding my hand as we descended the staircase), the door to the guest room opened tentatively. It was Caroline, her hair piled high on her head in a tight bun, her eyes filled with concern as she peered nervously around the door. Embarrassed, I turned and buried my face in the mattress. Nevertheless Caroline approached me and sat on the bed next to me, gently stroking my hair in a consoling fashion – as though I were Rupert, the family's elderly Beagle.

Caroline remained there – comforting me until the full misery broke free from me at last in silent screams and unfettered convulsions; until I could cry no more and an uneasy silence reigned supreme. Still her hand remained on my head, petting and soothing as though tending to a frightened, wounded animal. And then, she simply stood up and left. After she she left, I swore from that instant onwards I would never, ever cry again – not for anyone or *anything*...and, least of

213

all, for *myself*. As Clive said, it was indeed time for me to "grow up".

*   *   *

By the time the Baader Meinhof Gang unleashed its 'month of Hell' on Germany – in May 1972 – Cressida and I were ensconced in our new home: a small, redbrick one-bed 'starter' house on a brand new development off a main road in Sittingbourne. It might only have been rented – paid for by Cressida's parents – but at least it was 'ours'; a 'home of our own' allowing us the privacy and independence to build a future together. My rediscovered decadent, *bourgeois* jubilation knew no bounds! On parting from Cressida's parents to move to our new property, I was deeply choked with emotion – but still determined to hold myself to my promise never to cry again. I hugged Caroline like the mother I never knew. To my knowledge, she never spoke of what passed between us – allowing me to recover my full dignity.

Clive and Cressida looked on astonished as I clung to Caroline like a small boy about to be sent on his first day to *kindergarten*. Eventually, I broke away and shook hands with Clive. Every time I set eyes on him since our breakfast table conversation I imagined that, some thirty years previously, if he had caught my father – standing resplendent in his sleek black uniform chatting amiably to the coldest of cold-blooded murderers beside some freshly dug pit in eastern

Love, Gudrun Ensslin

Europe – he would not have hesitated to pull the trigger. And now, as he stood before me in his tweed jacket, grey slacks and brown brogues – looking every inch the traditional English gentleman – I knew that, even though such an act would have cost me my very existence, I would not for one moment have blamed him.

*   *   *

Throughout May the stories came in from across the Channel via the detached filter of the British news media about Baader Meinhof's final activities. It was lacking the detail and full sensation of the German news media – leaving me tantalised and tormented; hungry for more information and wishing I could somehow contact Semmler. Both Cressida and I bought every imported German newspaper and magazine we could find – but they were always many days out of date and incredibly scarce. Still, the main events as reported on the news bulletins on our TV set gave me a clear idea of the sheer horror of the 'month of Hell' I so narrowly avoided.

On 11th May 1972 three Red Army Faction pipe bombs exploded in the headquarters of the 5th US Army Corps in Frankfurt. Thirteen American soldiers were killed in this one action, the 'Petra Schelm Kommando' releasing a communiqué proclaiming "Victory to the Vietcong!" The following day, in Augsburg, two Baader Meinhof bombs exploded in the city's police headquarters – injuring five cops.

Meanwhile, on the same day in Munich, a massive car bomb in the BKA's own car park destroyed some sixty cars and all the windows in the pigs' building – our 'Tommy Weisbecker Kommando' claiming responsibility. Only four days after the initial Frankfurt blast, on 15th May in Karlsruhe, a car bomb aimed at Judge Buddenburg exploded – crippling his wife by mistake.

Our 'Manfred Grashof Kommando' issued a statement announcing this was "payback" for the isolation torture being inflicted on the RAF prisoners Buddenburg jailed. Still the killing and the chaos of the 'month of Hell' continued. On 19th May, in Hamburg, two of our bombs hit the hated Axel Springer building (while a further three bombs at the same location somehow failed to detonate). Seventeen office workers were injured. The '*Zwei Juni* Kommando' said:

"To capitalists, profit is everything and the people who create it are dirt." On 24th May two car bombs exploded in quick succession at the US Army European Headquarters in Heidelberg. Three American officers were killed and five GI's wounded. The '*Funfzehn Juli* Kommando' thus hoped everyone would now remember the date on which Petra Schelm died. With this last double blast, the actions of the 'month of Hell' were over. It would not be long before the authorities hit back.

On June 1st 1972 I sat transfixed as British television

Love, Gudrun Ensslin

showed me brief moments of something I previously thought unimaginable – edited highlights of an event earlier shown live on German television throughout the *Bundesrepublik* by a Frankfurt TV crew that had simply been passing through the *Hofeckweg* district on their way to a racetrack but instead stumbled on something truly significant: the capture of Andreas Baader.

A tip-off at the tail end of the 'month of Hell' led the BKA to arrange a stakeout at a lock-up garage for the best part of a week. In the early hours of the morning of 1st June, an erratically driven Porsche Targa screeched to a halt outside the lock-up. Andreas and two other occupants – Holger Meins and Jan-Carl Raspe – emerged. Holger and Andreas went inside while Jan-Carl kicked his heels next to the Targa. Almost immediately, the cops pounced. Jan-Carl legged it as fast as he could yet was easily overpowered and arrested in a nearby garden. A stand-off then ensued between the pigs gathered outside and Holger and Andreas, holed up inside the garage.

The siege began with Holger and Andreas defiantly waving their guns at the pigs and taunting them – shouting slogans, pulling childish faces and questioning both their manhood and their parentage. The pigs' response was to fire a wagonload of tear gas into the building. Then, a police sniper stationed in a nearby flat, put a bullet in Andreas's thigh. At this point, Holger emerged from the building, hands high in the air, ready to surrender. He was ordered to strip to his underwear and then to walk slowly towards the police line – an order with which he readily complied, providing a pitiful spectacle; his thin, bony frame in oddly large Y-fronts – like a giant nappy – tottering uncertainly towards line upon line of heavily armed police. Meanwhile, Andreas – although both gassed and injured – remained steadfastly inside, defiant to the end.

A full ten minutes later an armoured car surged forward, shielding a whole bunch of cops in bullet-proof vests who rushed into the garage like a swarm of demonic locusts. Moments later four cops emerged, carrying a bleeding Andreas strapped to a stretcher. His shades were still in place and a wry smile played across his lips as he nonchalantly gave a two-fingered 'Victory' sign to the watching cameras. It was the same old Andreas those of us close to him had always known!

Only six days later, on 7th June, my beloved Gudrun was in captivity as well. Attempting to buy some clothes for a new disguise from a Hamburg boutique, an eagle-eyed shop-girl spotted Gudrun's pistol half-hidden in her handbag. The wide-eyed girl immediately blabbed to the manageress and the older woman wasted no time in picking up the phone to the cops while Gudrun busied herself in the fitting room, turning this way and that, checking out her new image. When Gudrun emerged she discovered quite a reception committee: a bunch of armed pigs waiting for her! By all accounts, it still required two of them to

Love, Gudrun Ensslin

overpower, subdue and arrest the wild, kicking, scratching, screaming, fighting tigress that was Gudrun Ensslin. All involved admitted that, true to form, she put up one hell of a catfight – and to those of us close to her, *that* was also the same old Gudrun we had always known!

By 15th June 1972 it really was all over – as this was the date of the capture and arrest of Ulrike Meinhof. Some *schili* schoolteacher who was supposed to provide Ulrike and fellow Gang member Gerhard Müller with a safe house in Hannover turned traitor and shopped them. Now, the entire 'leadership' was behind bars.

For me, however, it began and ended in Frankfurt – from the April 1968 bombing of the department stores - to the June 1972 capture of Andreas - the Baader Meinhof Gang being born - lived and died in the city of Frankfurt-Am-Main. Another generation would appear and attempt to continue the fight but, for me, and for the original '68 generation, the 'revolution' was over.

*   *   *

Back in England, all my attention and effort was focused on my forthcoming wedding to Cressida – and the task of building a new life in a new country. On 15th November 1972 – five months after the capture of Ulrike Meinhof – Cressida and I married at Maidstone Registry Office. It was a short service before a small, informal gathering. All the guests hailed from Cressida's side of the family. Her parents were very surprised that not a single soul from my family was present – not even a lone friend from Germany; no-one at all.

"Georg has no family," Cressida explained, on my behalf. "And none of his friends can afford the air fare."

This information made Cressida's mother even more protective of me – and she fussed over me like a Mother Hen right up to the wedding; even more so on the day itself.

The reception was held in Clive's favourite pub, 'The Wheatsheaf', in a small village just outside Canterbury. I had to endure plenty of good-natured Spitfire jokes from Clive's golf club friends – several of whom viewed me, as a German, as some sort of walking, talking museum exhibit; incredibly exotic just by the mere fact of my existence! During his speech, Clive declared that he had pre-paid for a honeymoon for the pair of us in a small town in Scotland called Pitlochry.

"Absolutely beautiful at this time of year," said Clive. "Plenty of romantic walks for you both to look forward to."

At first, the plan was that we would borrow Clive's Rover and drive up there. However, even after seven months in 'Blighty', I still couldn't get used to driving on the 'wrong' side of the road – and, as Cressida didn't drive, it was decided we would take the train instead.

After the honeymoon, our focus switched to the practical matter of finding work and generating a joint income – if nothing else, simple pride made me determined to repay Clive and Caroline as quickly as possible for the generous support they had given us. I felt it was imperative for me to cease to be a burden on them – and their retirement savings – at the earliest opportunity. Our honeymoon in Pitlochry had indeed been spent in taking long romantic walks in the fresh air beside the banks of Loch Tummel.

However, the topics of conversation during those walks were far from romantic – dealing instead with the aftermath of the demise of Baader Meinhof, an analysis of the levels of risk involved in a return to Germany and the question of what sort of work either of us could get if we remained in England. One thing at least was decided – neither of us planned an immediate return to our studies. Despite having been so very close to the finishing line in our respective degree courses, neither of us retained any appetite whatsoever for the ivory tower world of academia; it now seemed too isolationist, too hermetically sealed, too non-participatory in terms of the real world – about as far away as you could get from '*praxis*'.

Cressida soon found herself work in a secretarial typing pool at an insurance company in nearby Chatham. It was a menial, serf-like functionary's position – way below her intellect, qualifications and capabilities. However, at least it was employment – and an income. Finding work for me, however, was less straightforward. There wasn't much call for an unqualified German philosopher with strong left-wing sympathies in 1970's rural Kent. Driving jobs were out of the question due to my discomfort with driving on the left. Bricklaying and building site labouring was not something that suited my impractical, dreamy, idealistic mindset – nor was it an area in which I could claim any experience. Shop work remained a vague possibility – but, given my absolute detestation of commerce, it would have been an ideological compromise too far. I toyed for a while with the notion of teaching German – but, at that time, the appetite for German language tuition in the heart of 'Spitfire Country' was minimal, to say the least!

It was one of our neighbours on the housing estate who came to my rescue. Barry worked at a Garden Centre located a short drive off the main road between Sittingbourne and Faversham – and he seemed certain he could talk his boss into giving me a "try out" there.

"Kent's the 'Garden of England', mate," he said cheerily. "Become a gardener! We always need an extra pair of hands at the Centre – the boss is always moaning about it. Look, I'll have a word with the gaffer tomorrow and let you know."

And so, each morning for the next eleven years, Cressida and I would rise, eat breakfast and disappear in opposite directions – she, on the train, heading due west to Chatham and I, sprawled across

Love, Gudrun Ensslin

the passenger seat of Barry's van, heading due east towards Faversham. For a while it seemed a blissful, carefree existence. Little did I realise, however, that our diverging daily journeys were the perfect metaphor for the emotional distance that was – insidious and unseen, like a cancer – growing between Cressida and myself.

For me, gardening was the perfect work at the perfect time. For a start, it focused on life and natural beauty – planting a seed, nurturing that seed, watching it grow; tending and caring for something that was alive yet also incredibly delicate and fragile. After my experience with Inge and Anton, this was undoubtedly the best kind of therapy.

Here was a world I could create – a world upon which I could impose order and control…and a world in which the end result was always beauty, tranquillity and harmony. It was a world away from raw, ugly commerce and rampant capitalist greed; an open air, clean living, pastoral idyll; a sanctuary for both body and mind. Even the academic side of my personality was satisfied – by learning the names of the plants in both English and Latin, understanding the different effects of the many diverse soils and growing conditions and studying the life cycles and functions of the myriad of insects that surrounded and supported the plant life. I loved to feel the soil flowing through my fingertips, the tactile sensation of the heavy clay or the powdery earth as I shaped it to my will. I became both obsessive and perfectionist about my new 'career' –

Love, Gudrun Ensslin

gradually working my way towards becoming Head Gardener and even something of a minor celebrity among the people of northern Kent.

"If you want gardening advice, ask the Kraut!" they would say.

*   *   *

1977 was a difficult year. During the previous year, and on Mother's Day, Ulrike Meinhof hung herself in her prison cell. The television and newspapers were full of it – even in England. It stirred up all sorts of thoughts and memories I hoped I had buried below the topsoil of my psyche.

The Baader Meinhof Gang were on trial since May 1975. Ulrike's death only punctuated the proceedings as the entire process did not conclude until April 1977 – in fact, it was the longest trial in German legal history.

During this period, I sought refuge in the distraction of my dahlias, hollyhocks and tomato plants more than ever. Meanwhile, the unspoken distance between Cressida and I grew ever greater. By then, we were no longer acting as a married couple – nor could we even be classed as 'like brother and sister' or 'just good friends'.

Instead, we were cellmates, struggling to make the best of our circumstance of enforced cohabitation and battery of joint commitments. Then, on 18 [th] October 1977 came '*Todesnacht*': Death Night.

Love, Gudrun Ensslin

On the night of 18th October 1977, Andreas, Gudrun and Jan-Carl Raspe 'killed themselves' – or were murdered by the State – in *Stammheim* prison. My fervent belief is that the State killed them. They were becoming a liability in custody: new generations of terrorists were taking action and committing hijacks to put pressure on the authorities for their release…not least the PLO hijacking of a *Lufthansa* plane bound for Frankfurt that instead ended up on the red hot tarmac of Mogadishu. To the authorities, the equation was simple: no more Baader Meinhof prisoners alive in captivity = no more terrorist acts committed in the name of having them released.

The news of the deaths in *Stammheim* stirred up feelings in me I didn't know remained. It was the same teenage anger and sense of outrage I'd felt all those years ago at the killing of Benno Ohnesorg; the same desire for action, change (and, yes, *revenge*) that led me to Baader Meinhof in the first place. For a few days – surprising myself at this latent fury – I seriously contemplated a return to Germany and some direct action of my own. However, the feeling passed – and my anger was quelled, replaced with a deep, deep sadness at the realisation of one terrible, irrefutable fact: my beautiful and beloved, angry and mesmeric Gudrun was *dead*.

Bizarrely, and against all reason, I still carried a blazing torch for Gudrun. In 1968 the flame may have burned with a volcanic incandescence I found impossible to hide – but in 1977 the torch still glowed and flickered, its hidden embers very much alive. Even as a married man domiciled in another country, even with Gudrun imprisoned behind the maximum security bars of *Stammheim* – I *still* nurtured the fantasy that *somehow* we might be together one day. And now she was dead. Gone. Never to return. Now I had to face facts and accept, once and for all – that 'Gudrun and I' would never be.

All around me England carried on its daily business – impervious and disinterested; gripped by the competing cultural phenomena of Punk Rock and the Queen's Silver Jubilee. Meanwhile, I became a mute, inert automaton – clinically depressed and sheer hell for Cressida to live with…but, thankfully, somehow still able to function at work; focusing even more intently than before on my new *religion* of gardening. In my mind, every new blossom I planted was a token for Gudrun's grave.

That Cressida and I did not actually split up during this time of crisis was something of a miracle – although, ultimately, it proved to be merely a delay of the inevitable. The simple truth is we were still financially mutually dependent but, socially, we never saw each other anymore. Cressida was out most nights with her friend, Judy – known to me simply as "Judy from work". They had regular "girlie nights" with Cressida sometimes staying over at Judy's place in Rochester. For my part, I mostly sat in the house on my own reading endless books on gardening borrowed from the Garden Centre or sprawling in front of the TV

Love, Gudrun Ensslin

– fascinated and appalled by the plethora of TV game shows the British seemed to love; the ritual humiliation of dreadful imbeciles in tear-filled states of rapture and delirium at the prospect of winning a washing machine! These shows seemed to say everything about the society Baader Meinhof fought so hard to change.

On other evenings I drank and played darts with Barry and a few of the regulars in our local. These evenings always followed a strict pattern that was almost a ritual. Barry would go up to the bar, insist the first round was on him and further insist that I drink a beer of his choosing.

"Have to wean you off those German lagers and onto some good old English bitters," he would say each and every time.

Through these 'booze and darts' sessions, I soon discovered I was very partial to *Guinness*.

"Never the same outside Ireland though," Barry would intone sagely as I supped my pint.

Thus did 1977 become 1983.

Love, Gudrun Ensslin

CHAPTER FIFTEEN: ALLES IST IN ORDNUNG

During the 1980's the pattern had become firmly
established in our household whereby Cressida and I
were leading totally separate lives – sharing only the
household bills and our left-wing convictions.
However, I at least graduated from the sofa (to which I
was initially banished during my major depression
brought about by Gudrun's death) to a single bed in our
spare room. Thus, I would only see Cressida briefly
during the week – usually at breakfast. At weekends –
and at most other times besides – she was usually "at
Judy's." Certainly Clive and Caroline, having expected
to become grandparents soon after our marriage, had
given up entirely on any such development by the '80s.
Their invitations to Sunday lunch also ceased – a great
pity to me as I had grown very fond of roast beef with
Yorkshire pudding and all the other traditional British
Sunday fare provided by Caroline.

In truth, I should have realised our life together
was unsustainable from the moment we set foot on that
plane in Frankfurt. However, I genuinely had not
anticipated that Cressida would be the one to leave me.
Thus, it came as a complete shock when Cressida

Love, Gudrun Ensslin

appeared back at our house one Sunday morning, dropped off by a rather owlish woman who sat resolutely behind the wheel of her old *Ford* Granada waiting for Cressida's return, while inside the house Cressida made an undoubtedly much-rehearsed announcement:

"I'm leaving you, Georg," she said, standing over me as I lay dumbly on the sofa in a beer-stained T-shirt and track pants, surrounded by empty crisp packets and *Guinness* bottles. Her pronouncement barely registered with me.

"Stand aside, will you?" I said. "You're blocking the TV." It was a *Tom & Jerry* cartoon – something that, even though I was an adult, I nonetheless loved to watch. Cressida switched the television off. I swung my legs angrily to the floor.

"I said; I'm leaving you, Georg," she repeated, waiting for some reaction.

"And?..." I replied, unimpressed.

"And..." Cressida sighed. She took a deep breath before continuing. "And...I am going to live with Judy. She's my lover, Georg."

I sat there open-mouthed. I tried to speak but nothing came out; I ended up doing an impression of a goldfish ejected from its bowl. Then I began to laugh – incredulously, uproariously; leaning back and kicking my feet up in the air.

"Please, Georg," Cressida began.

I walked over to the window, still hiccupping with laughter, and stared out at Judy who was waiting patiently in the driver's seat of the *Ford*.

"You're leaving me for *that*…that owl…that librarian…that fucking *spinster*?" I shouted.

"I knew you wouldn't understand," Cressida replied, staring at her feet. "That's why I wasn't going to tell you. I was just going to leave you a note – and simply vanish. It was Judy who persuaded me to be honest and upfront. It was Judy who reminded me that I owed you that much at least."

"Well, bully beef for Judy as you English say!"

"Georg," Cressida said, taking a step towards me.

"No," I yelled, shrinking back. "I can't believe you're actually a fucking *dyke*!"

"It's not just about *that*, Georg," Cressida said calmly, suddenly seating herself on the sofa. "It's about *us*. It's much bigger than just *that*. We are right for each other – that's the only way I can explain it. We've both resigned our jobs…and we're going to live at Greenham Common."

"Greenham Common!" I spat. "This just gets better and better!"

"Nuclear proliferation has to be stopped. This nuclear madness could kill all of us. It could destroy everyone and everything on this entire planet – you know that just as well as I do."

And so I let her go – in pursuit of her 'greater cause'; something I *could* at least understand.

"This isn't just student politics and the antics of Baader Meinhof," she pleaded on the doorstep.

Love, Gudrun Ensslin

"This really is about life and death."

"Tell that to Ingeborg Barz!" I replied, closing the front door.

After Cressida left me I lurched straight back into another black depression. Once more I became inert, sloth-like, almost catatonic.

I lay on the sofa most days, drinking my way through the entire supply of alcohol in the house – getting dressed and venturing forth only to visit the off licence to replenish my booze stocks. Household bills remained unpaid, the telephone unanswered, the doorbell ignored. I learned sometime later that Barry had been covering for me at work – telling our boss of my "highly infectious illness" and "necessary confinement to bed with no visitors." (Cressida contacted him and explained our break-up, asking him to "keep an eye on Georg for me"). After a few days Barry ambushed me one afternoon on my return from one of my many trips to the off licence. He pleaded with me to "put all that self-pitying shit behind you Georg and return to work."

"Plenty more fish in the sea, mate," he said, ever the sophist.

This happened several more times over the next few days. Each time my answer was the same: "I'll return as soon as I can."

One afternoon the incessant ringing of the doorbell was accompanied with loud knocking and a voice speaking to me…in fluent German!

"*Herr* Krendler, are you inside? *Herr* Krendler,

231

if you can hear me, please open the door. It is most urgent that I speak with you."

Fear and paranoia gripped me. I thought of running out the back door but concluded that *they* would have one of their accomplices waiting for me in anticipation of that precise response. Instead, I went to the kitchen and rummaged desperately through the cutlery drawer. Pulling a sharp carving knife from the pile, I crept back to the front door and listened, ear pressed against the wood, knife secreted behind my back.

"*Herr* Krendler, please, it really is very important I speak with you," the voice continued.

Panic was rising. I felt almost unable to breathe, as though I might faint or choke at any moment. This was exactly what I had always feared – *they* had finally tracked me down; *they* had come for me. To them, I was just like Inge – a 'loose end'; someone who had to be 'silenced'. Furthermore, my flight to England at that particular time would have said only one thing to them: *traitor*!...and whether or not that was actually the case, the mere act of leaving Germany would have been enough to convict me in their kangaroo court. And traitors must pay...however long it takes to catch up with them.

Yet it didn't make sense – not with Gudrun, Andreas and Ulrike all dead; the key players from our generation were either dead or held in captivity; pieces removed from the chess board. Why should it matter to any of the peripheral figures who remained – or to the new generation – to track down a petty bit-part player like me who fled all the way to England? It just didn't make any sense. It didn't seem real. Unless…Julius! My God, of course! Semmler was still alive – and free. I scanned the minutiae of every report I had ever got my hands on and there was no news of Julius's arrest or capture or demise; like the slippery eel that he was, he evaded every dragnet and bear trap…and wriggled free to hide once more in the shadows. And now he had evidently returned – and dispatched some lackey (…some Anton!) to England to finish me off. He probably thought I was the one who squealed about the garage – tipped off the pigs as to Andreas's latest Frankfurt hideaway and then hot-tailed it to England… no doubt with the help of the BKA's pay-off money! To him, I represented the worst kind of betrayer – his very own '*et tu Brute*' – and now he had sent someone after me to even the score!

"*Herr* Krendler, I know you're in there! Please, open the door. You'll find it's to your *advantage*."

There was nothing else for it – I was going to have to fight my way out of there! The door was on a chain. I opened it a fraction, not even allowing the chain to gather its full slack. Shrinking back, keeping myself wholly out of sight and the knife at the ready, I called out unsteadily in German:

"Who's there? Identify yourself at once!"

"*Herr* Krendler, my name is Johann Fleischmann. I'm an attorney at law – specialising in probate. I represent the estate of your late father,

Love, Gudrun Ensslin

Wieland Krendler of Wuppertal, some time deceased. *Herr* Krendler, your father has left you a substantial sum of money in his estate."

"Bullshit!" I yelled. "My father hated me! He considered me a disappointment. He wouldn't leave me so much as a pot to piss in! Who are you really?"

My hostility and suspicion seemed to unnerve Fleischmann. For an extended moment there was an awkward silence. Then Fleischmann spoke again, in careful, soothing tones.

"Herr Krendler, I am going to pass my business card to you through the door. Please let me in – I have to return to Germany tomorrow."

A small piece of embossed white cardboard appeared in the gap between door and door-frame. I snatched it greedily, closed the door and examined it carefully. It seemed authentic enough – I even recognised the logo and address of a top Frankfurt law firm. I decided to take a chance – after all, with Cressida gone and my life completely in ruins…what did I *really* have to lose? Still clutching the knife tightly behind my back, I slipped the chain and opened the door. The small bespectacled man in a crisply pressed white shirt and checked trousers who stood before me didn't look as though he could threaten an ant – never mind a psychotic drunk who had armed himself with a knife.

"You'd better come in," I said, sheepishly.

"Thank you," Flesichmann replied, nervously smoothing his raincoat.

Love, Gudrun Ensslin

I now had the embarrassment – and considerable difficulty – of trying to usher him into the sitting room while somehow disposing of the knife that was clutched behind my back without the lawyer seeing it. Still holding the unseen knife, I showed Fleischmann to the sofa. As the man advanced to his seat, I let the knife tumble silently onto the carpet behind an armchair.

"Please excuse the mess, *Herr* Fleischmann, I've not been well recently," I said, noticing his eyes surreptitiously scanning around the roomful of empty beer cans, soup cartons, half-full milk bottles and upended cereal packets. Fleischmann smiled back at me wanly.

"Normally we would write to you about such a matter, *Herr* Krendler," he began, primly crossing one leg over the other. "However, I was in London on other business and we have only recently been able to track you down and your father, who died in 1979, has left you really quite a substantial sum. You see, his business expanded greatly in the latter part of the 1970s. Until his death he owned a chain of photographic stores throughout the *BDR*."

I sat opposite him, my head buried in my hands and began to laugh hysterically – an action wholly misinterpreted by Fleischmann as a son's grief. However, it was not grief but simple astonishment at the immense irony suddenly confronting me. Now, for the first time in my life – and, completely out of nowhere, I had money – and plenty of it. Not only this, but the source of those funds was my miserable Nazi pig of a father – belatedly doing me the only good turn he'd ever really condescended to do for me. Beyond this, Cressida had walked out on me only a matter of *days* before this dramatic revelation – and had thus missed out on the opportunity to share in my sudden fortune. And, to end it all, I was now a capitalist pig myself – a petty bourgeois owner of a business with workers under me to exploit and from whose sweat and toil my profits now derived! How could you *not* laugh at all of that?!

As I showed Fleischmann to the front door and apologised profusely for my eccentric behaviour, I decided at that very moment there would be no more lounging around on a sofa in a string vest – life for Georg Krendler was about to become very different.

*   *   *

I had been back at work for some ten months, my brief period of absence forgotten, my spell of drinking and depression now under control when an advertisement appeared in the local press: 'Wanted: Head Groundsman. Accommodation supplied. Apply Cassandra Ladies' College, Eastling, Kent'.

As soon as I saw it, I knew I had to make an application. It was perfect – absolutely ideal for me: an opportunity to start again on my own – away from the home Cressida and I had shared – with no ties and no reminders. I thought it through very carefully. There was no way I would *ever* go back to Germany. What would be the point? There was no-one and nothing there for me – just a latent degree of risk from the 'old days'. Besides, I had grown to like living in England – especially Kent with its rural backwaters, quaint pubs and traditional villages. I loved gardening too – and, as Barry said, where better to be a gardener than the 'Garden of England' in this 'green and pleasant land'? No, the answer was straightforward – I must remain in England and remain in Kent.

Yet I knew I had to get away from Sittingbourne and its ghosts. The house I still occupied was a daily reminder of Cressida. It was bad enough watching news bulletins of unrest at Greenham Common – searching the crowds of women chained to fences or being dragged away by the police – to try to spot a glimpse my own wife! I was overjoyed, therefore, when I received a letter from Lady Madeleine Hartley-Brewer, Principal of Cassandra Ladies' College inviting me to an interview.

I have never been so relaxed in a situation in which one is expected to be tense. I went into that interview *knowing* the position was mine. Having instructed Fleischmann to sell my father's business on my behalf and transfer my share of the proceeds to my British bank account, I had no financial pressures resting on my ability to land the job. Furthermore, from the moment I spotted the advertisement, I felt a strong sense that this job was my destiny. As it transpired, I was offered the job on the day of the interview itself –

237

Love, Gudrun Ensslin

a highly impressed Lady Hartley-Brewer inviting me to stay for tea and look around the school grounds.

And so began twenty-two years of loyal service to Cassandra Ladies' College – during which time I became "part of the fabric and furniture of the place" as Lady Hartley-Brewer's successor, Dame Catherine, used to say. These were happy years in which I grew accustomed to my isolation and fully accepting of my lot in life. I lived in a small stone cottage on the outskirts of the school grounds – beyond the playing fields used for hockey in the winter and ladies' cricket in the summer. I think my offer, at interview, to provide extra-curricular tuition in German to the school's sixth form students was the clincher. This offer was keenly taken up during my first year of service and groups of senior girls would duly report to the cottage on Sunday afternoons and spend a few hours with me there – during which time all conversation would be conducted in German; not a single word of English was tolerated. These were always especially joyous occasions for me – the absolute highlight of my week and the closest I came to true companionship. I would buy tea and cakes and make sandwiches for the girls every Sunday and a regular party would ensue. I imagined myself to be Ludwig Wittgenstein with his tutees at Cambridge.

Scores of students passed through my hands over the years, many of whom would remain in contact for years thereafter. I was inundated with Christmas cards every year containing long letters (written in

German, of course) detailing their many adventures and escapades since leaving the College. One or two of them even detailed travelling to Germany and reading Goethe at university – sparking more than a few painful memories. A cork board on the wall of my kitchen, as well as the door of the fridge, was plastered with photographs of students I had once taught who were now enjoying their post-College lives – snuggling up to husbands or boyfriends, proudly displaying new babies; in their eyes their *real* achievements since completing their formal education.

For over twenty years I was once again a man on a mission – and this time my mission was *redemption*. For me, each of those girls who came to me for tuition – and every girl I encountered in the College grounds – wore the face of Ingeborg Barz. And each of those children deserved the same care and attention as I lavished on my roses and hydrangeas; each was as fragile and as precious, requiring the same constant levels of care and nurturing. And each must blossom and thrive and succeed – and only thus, I thought, through a lifetime of such selfless care and dedication, might my debt to poor Inge one day be paid.

I had only two interests besides gardening and teaching. I kept tropical fish – enjoying the further opportunity it gave me to create another small world I could manage and control, although this time populated by tiny colourful living creatures as opposed to inanimate plant life. 'Aquatic gardening' I called it. I

Love, Gudrun Ensslin

also bought myself a computer and, through long hours of study and experimentation, became quite proficient at surfing the internet; travelling all over the world without even once having to set foot outside my cottage. I became a regular on gardening websites and related forum boards – asking arcane questions and distributing authoritative advice. By the time I turned fifty – albeit a very fit and active fifty – I was well known to the girls I taught as a 'silver surfer'. Over time the photographs I received of my ex-students in their wedding dresses or proudly displaying their cherubic infants would arrive as jpegs and nestle on my hard drive rather than the fridge door.

And so it continued – an idyllic existence, after a fashion. Until, one day, I received a series of letters (by snail mail) from someone signing themselves as the 'Gudrun Ensslin Kommando'. These missives directed me to a website address and provided a time-limited access code on each occasion. They were written in such a way as to stir up memories I thought were long forgotten. The rhetoric was extremely clever – fiery and motivating like the speeches of Gudrun or Ulrike of old. Sometimes it really did seem as though Gudrun herself were talking – *directly to me* – from beyond the grave.

I tried hard to resist – dismissing it as a cruel prank; wondering which of 'my girls' had somehow discovered my past and why they now wished to torment me thus. Yet, over time, curiosity got the better of me and one evening I decided to access the website.

Love, Gudrun Ensslin

From then on it became my furtive little secret – and I greedily drank in the words of 'Anarchist Pete'; an orator who reminded me that, for years, I had been deliberately blind and withdrawn from the injustice that was taking place every single day in the wider world around me. Anarchist Pete questioned my passive inactivity for the past thirty-four years in the face of increasing capitalist crimes and exploitation; he reminded me that the evils of capitalism were still very much alive and still needed to be actively fought…and now more than ever before. Moreover, Anarchist Pete reminded me that I was not yet dead and I could still make a difference if I chose once more to be *active* – to be once again the Georg Krendler I was in 1968.

And so, perhaps against my better judgement, I decided to download the BANKER_BINGO game card and play Anarchist Pete's 'game'. Gradually the concept of redemption was forgotten – instead, it was once again time for *REVOLUTION!*

CHAPTER SIXTEEN: WAHRHEIT

BANKER BINGO ENCRYPTED WEBSITE POSTS

Profitmania!

Have you ever asked yourself why poverty still exists in an era in which untold wealth and riches proliferate across the planet? Have you ever wondered why the gap between rich and poor is widening rather than decreasing in this age of plenty?

The answer is Profitmania! This is the ideology of global capitalism. This is the new religion. Just like a religion, its orthodoxy must be accepted without question. If you dare to question (...if you dare to ask *why*) you are branded a heretic – and you are treated as such.

Profitmania knows the price of everything and the value of nothing. It cares nothing for the value of

life, dignity and the natural resources of our finite world. It knows only profit and the pursuit of profit at all costs. It knows only the love of money: the root of all evil. Profitmania must be fought...and it must be defeated!

A History Lesson!

When the Cold War ended and Communism in Europe was declared to be dead, a few naïve souls believed this would herald an age of prosperity and freedom for all masses. There would be a better standard of living, better healthcare, better pay, greater opportunities. But what did the people get instead? Profitmania!

The capitalists no longer needed positive PR – a pretence that Profitmania was somehow morally superior. All bets were off! The war had been won! Now it was time for the capitalists to asset strip to their heart's content. So the capitalists bought up all the prime real estate on the cheap. They moved their manufacturing bases to those areas where wages could be most easily suppressed. They coerced women and young girls into the white slave trade. They did what capitalists always do: they plundered and they used – and all in the pursuit of profit. They brought homelessness, unemployment, increased poverty, rising crime. Like the locusts and the parasites they are, they preyed on the innocent and grew fat. Like the locusts and the parasites that they are, they must be destroyed!

New Lie-bour!

Once upon a time the Labour Party of the UK was a socialist party. Once upon a time the Labour Party cared about social justice and social equality. Once upon a time it believed in hospital care for those in need – without examining 'budgets' and 'balance sheets' to determine 'profits' and 'cost'. Once upon a time it believed in social justice rather than social engineering. Once upon a time it served the people rather than the bankers.

The Goebbels-style lie at the heart of New Lie-bour is that it is a socialist party and that it cares. It is the party of the plutocrat; the party of the banker and the global financier who put it into power and whom it serves.

When New Lie-bour was seeking power it sent its emissaries to the CEOs of the investment banks to tell them of its plans: this is 'New Labour' it said. This is no longer the Labour of the Unions, of Arthur Scargill, of walkouts and pay demands. This is NEW Labour: the preening lapdog of the global capitalists. Help us to seize power, it said to the bankers – and we will give you free reign to profit in any way you wish. We will give you hands-off regulation, we will make the City the fulcrum of our *entire* economy...and (the punchline!)...we will require all the little people earning £40k or below to subsidise *everything* through the tax system. This was the Faustian pact that New Lie-bour made with the plutocrats of the City.

And so began thirteen long years of plutocracy; and so began the continuously widening gap between rich and poor; and so began the degeneration of the infrastructure (and the creeping erosion of YOUR civil and workplace rights); and so began the supremacy of the financier class (at the expense of wider society); the supremacy of ego-driven tyrants and blood-sucking locusts!

What Democracy?

Does anyone really believe they still live in a democracy?! You live in a plutocracy! The capitalists deny you all your freedoms. The capitalists seek only to control – and to profit. If you do not pay your taxes – you are put in jail. If you do not pay your mortgage – your home is taken and you are put on the streets. Everything has a price – *everything*! You are given money for the work that you do – but (unless you are a financier) the money is not enough; you are denied a living wage and a viable salary. This is a deliberate act – with a dual objective: to increase the profits of your (capitalist) employer and to keep you under control (too busy working to pay your bills and trying to keep your nostrils above the waterline to give the State any problems).

A percentage of *your* money (for which *you* have worked) is taken – by law (and by force if necessary). With the remainder you must pay for all that you need – food, clothing, travel, healthcare. The price of these items is kept artificially high – by the financiers and the politicians – in their pursuit of profit and control. Their ideology says that everything must be paid for – parking, garbage removal, water, life-saving drugs... *everything*. If they could charge for air they would have done so by now! Even your freedom of movement is dictated by your ability to afford a train or bus fare – so your freedom of movement in your own city, your own country of birth...is dictated by price and privilege! Do you really still think this is a democracy? THINK AGAIN my friend!

You have no control over the money that is given to you. You have no control over the money that is taken from you. You have no control over the prices that are set around you. If you have no money the State will not support you; the State will not protect you. The State will see you only as a problem. The State will prosecute you; the State will lock you in jail; the State will happily see you die! This last option will save the State more 'funds' – and thus will help to maximise its profits! Face facts: you no longer live in a democracy – you live in a plutocracy. You must *fight* for your true freedom! True freedom is freedom from the plutocrats: the bankers, the financiers, the politicians; the global capitalists who have you LOCKED IN CHAINS!

Stop the City!

The financiers and global capitalists have ring-fenced profit. There is no 'trickle down' effect from the City into our wider society. That is PR. That is a LIE! The stock market is predicated entirely on the pursuit of profit (and those profits are not intended to be shared). By its own charter, any publicly quoted company must put the interests of its shareholders (and their dividends) first. In order to generate dividends the company must make a profit – even if that profit is only one penny more than the year before. The company must make a profit to retain 'investor confidence'; to keep its share price buoyant. So, by its constitution, the company *must* make a profit year after year after year – into the future ad infinitum. Although this objective is both insane and impossible – the company, by its nature, will pursue it.

And how does the endlessly profit-seeking company achieve (or *try* to achieve) the impossible? By cutting corners. By cheating. By sharp practice. By gangster capitalism. By doing everything the Communists ever warned us about! They do it by suppressing wages and forcing redundancies, by putting pressure on their suppliers to lower *their* costs while simultaneously raising prices to the consumer at the point-of-sale; they do it through genetic modification, by factory farming, by price manipulation. This is global capitalism. Society – and the environment – are its VICTIMS.

The financiers in the City gamble on prices – share prices, property prices, commodity prices. The commodities game is the most insidious of all. In this game the capitalists bet on the price of a sack of rice – and celebrate with champagne when their TV shows the image of starving children who cannot find even a handful of rice because it has 'somehow' become scarce...and its PRICE has consequently rocketed upwards...delivering a big fat PROFIT to the men in suits!

It is these same capitalists who manipulate the prices. You don't think they are really betting blind in a game of chance do you?! That would be far too honest! No, they fix the odds; they mark the deck.

Love, Gudrun Ensslin

They instruct that ship to stay offshore a week or two longer until the price of oil moves into the spread of values they desire. They finance that coup in the Third World nation that will thereafter offer lucrative contracts to their preferred 'business partners'. This is the 'gangster capitalism' of the plutocrat. They are nothing but locusts who spread poverty, corruption and misery – and profit from each and every blight they create. They are locusts and parasites who must be stopped!

The con of 'National Debt'!

To whom do we owe the money that is being repaid after the global crash of the 'credit crunch'? Read the papers, watch the news – they will never tell you. They can put a figure on it – so they must know to whom it is owed. They are financiers and accountants – so they must be able to produce a balance sheet; they must be able to quantify precisely to whom this money is owed…and at what rates of interest these repayments are being charged. Yet they choose not to do this. They CHOOSE not to tell you. Ever ask yourself WHY?

Could it be because the people to whom you are making these repayments are the SAME people who caused the 'crash' in the first place? Could it be because they do not want the public to know they

249

are profiting twice over from your misery and your dumb, unquestioning servitude?

The 'debt' is due to the 'credit crunch' – the economic collapse was caused by the GREED of bankers who deliberately sold home loans to people they knew could not afford the repayments – knowing they could seize the properties of these people when the repayments stopped; it was a cynical 'property grab' CON all along; it was no accident – it was *planned*; that the duped home owners and their families ended up on the streets and that cities like Cleveland, Ohio were devastated was of no concern to the bankers and financiers – just so long as they turned a PROFIT.

They played pass-the-parcel with the toxic debts they had created – inventing new 'financial products' containing these debts...which they then sold to other financial institutions around the world. It was simply a global pyramid selling scheme! The only question was: who would be left holding the baby when the music stopped? Who would be caught with their pants down having shelled out billions for a worthless asset? They didn't care – because, when it happened...when the conned banks collapsed...the governments forced the people to bail them out. And the bailout happened not once but twice! Tax was taken and given to the banks and new money was printed...and given to

Love, Gudrun Ensslin

the banks. And more money was '*borrowed*'...and given to the banks.

So, who loaned all this money that must be repaid? Who are the *creditors* behind the so-called 'National Debt'? And are they charging interest and making a profit from their loans? The last question is the easiest to answer: yes...they ARE charging interest and making a profit – and they are doing so directly from keeping YOU in financial servitude and denying YOU a decent standard of living in an age of *plenty*. Who are they then, these creditors? As stated, those in power do not want you to know. There is no transparency or 'Freedom Of Information Act' being applied to this question. But the truth is easy to see: it is the SAME people – the bankers and financiers who caused the credit crunch – who are re-lending the money they have been given in the bailouts...and lending it at a PROFIT with swingeing rates of interest that will keep generations in poverty purely to feed their continual GREED!

This is *why* the newspapers and the TV will never tell you to *whom* you 'owe' the money that is being 'repaid' – or even disclose the interest rates that are being charged. It is another CON operated by the financier class. YOU suffer so THEY can live in luxury.

Love, Gudrun Ensslin

It is time, however, for the bankers to reap the only dividend they *truly* deserve: to reap what they have sown! It is time for the bankers to learn that cheating and exploiting the poor and the oppressed carries a PRICE.

BANKER BINGO!

Soon I will make a game card available on this website for you to download and play. The game is BANKER_BINGO! The objective is social justice, revolution and a fair society – a society freed from the chains and the machinations of the financier class. You must assassinate ONE TARGET PER MONTH…until the government is forced to take practical steps to reduce the widening gap between rich and poor; until the financiers and the profiteers are forced to share their obscene wealth. All of the targets will have been carefully chosen for their complicity in the poverty and the misery that has been created for millions solely in the pursuit of PROFIT. Shed no tears…unless they are tears of joy at building a new and just society. Let the capitalists reap what they have sown – pay them their due dividend Comrade!

Anarchist Pete

CHAPTER SEVENTEEN: KAPITAN AHAB

Rory Carlisle closed the lid of the laptop and returned it to sleep mode. So, this was it. Krendler was on board and operational. Soon 'the game' would begin. All those long years of planning and waiting; waiting for the right candidate, waiting for the right moment. And now the waiting was over. As soon as he returned to London he would send the final post to the blog...the game card itself!

It was perfect, thought Rory. In fact, it was so perfect it made him wonder whether the divine hand of Providence was pulling the strings behind the scenes. There could be no better time to attack the global capitalists than at the height of their iniquity; no better message to send to those vultures than to remind them of the fact that the exploitation of others comes at a price.

Rory walked to the window and stared out. Green tranquillity. Hillsides leading to mountainsides. Britain's own version of the Alps. Only one dark and blackening cloud in the distance threatening to spoil the idyll. Rory smiled to himself, enjoying the irony. He spun on his heel and headed straight to the mahogany drinks cabinet. It was still early in the day but he felt a celebratory Scotch was in order. The liquid practically sang as it fell from the bottle into a heavy lead crystal tumbler. Rory took a sip and felt strangely tired. The emotion of the occasion, he supposed. The fact of reaching *this* point in his plan – having an active comrade waiting for his direction; having only one more message to post before his idea became reality. It was almost overwhelming.

Rory slumped into his favourite armchair. This was it! He was about to unleash his shock trooper, his Manchurian Candidate, his Golem onto an unsuspecting society. However, no-one would ever know he was responsible for Krendler's actions. And, even if they did know, few would understand. 'This is my gift to the world,' he thought. 'Freedom from the chains and shackles of global capitalism. Yet no-one will connect the name Rory Carlisle with the actions that will lead to this freedom. I will forever remain in the shadows.' There was historical precedent, of course.

There are others whose names are unknown – ignored and unrecorded by the annals of history – who have changed the world and yet retain a total anonymity. For example, the person or persons unknown – and who will remain forever unknown – who ordered the assassinations of JFK and Martin Luther King. Of course, the names of the JFK/MLK trigger men – Oswald and Ray are universally known. But behind the trigger men – behind the mere *Patsys* –

are the people in power; the people making the policies; the people taking decisions. For every Georg Krendler – a Rory Carlisle.

And so, if you are that person or persons unknown – if you are the power-broker in the shadows ordering the changing and shaping of history itself – how much mental strength must it take to remain in total anonymity? How great must the temptation be to instead shout from the rooftops of your culpability? Rory wondered – did *he* have that same mental strength? Did he have that same character to take such a secret to the *grave*?

He drained his drink. By a circuitous route his thoughts had brought him round to his own mortality – as they so often did of late. This – BANKER BINGO – would be his legacy; his mark on society. He had no wife, no children. He had painted no works of art. He had written no novels. BANKER BINGO was his testimony; his gift to future generations; his *bequest*.

Who would truly understand such a motivation as his? Krendler? Perhaps. Yet, for all their similarities, Krendler's vision was narrow whereas Rory's was grand. Krendler merely believed in an ideology – whereas Rory *defined* an ideology. Jardine? No. Jardine might know more than anyone else on the planet (other than his employer) about BANKER BINGO – but he had no *understanding*. Jardine had no love of the cause. Jardine's only loyalty was to Jardine. His silence and his complicity was bought and coerced – and it would also be his downfall, if necessary.

Love, Gudrun Ensslin

Jardine was not a political animal. He was merely a craven serf – a lackey to whoever held the reins of power; a forelock-tugging civil servant *non pareil*. No, there would be no understanding of Rory's actions or motivations; no appreciation of the genius of Rory's plan.

Even if people everywhere *knew* – even if he *could* tell the world that BANKER BINGO and its revenge on global capitalism for its rampant greed and wilful destruction was his idea – almost no-one would *understand*. These days, it seemed, all people cared for – or understood – was the pursuit of profit and the accumulation of wealth.

Rory owned unimaginable riches, people would say – *why* then would he throw it all away on an insane political crusade to slay the capitalist dragon? Surely he was only slaying *himself*? Surely he was misguidedly attempting to resurrect a discredited and rejected political world view that belonged squarely in the past – alongside the ghosts of Stalin, Mao and Ceausescu?

How could an über-capitalist be a supporter of a radical left wing cause? They would not be able to compute the connection! They would not be able to get their minds around the concept! How – they would ask – could Rory Carlisle promote a cause that opposed everything he had taken his entire lifetime to *become*? To them, it would not make any sense.

And yet that lack of understanding was the very reason *why* Rory's BANKER BINGO project was

Love, Gudrun Ensslin

in fact so very necessary. *That* was the reason why
Rory *must* post the game card on the website and set
Krendler free. It was precisely *because* people in the
21st century had *forgotten* the evils of capitalism and
had been so *anaesthetised* by consumerism and so
subjugated by the post-Cold War status of capitalism as
a quasi-religion that they had forgotten there were *still*
alternatives to this destructive system that told Rory he
must continue with this project. It was precisely
because there were now children in schools who did
not know the word 'Communism' existed – let alone its
definition – that he must continue. It was precisely
because no-one *would* understand that he must
continue and bring BANKER BINGO into being.

Back in the day, however, it would have been a
different story. Back in the second half of the 20th
century – back in Georg Krendler's youth when
Gudrun, Andreas and Ulrike took up arms and fought
to make a difference – people surely would have
understood. Back then people would not simply have
stood idly by while the financier class feathered their
nests and widened the gap between rich and poor at the
direct expense of the masses. The irony, of course, was
there was now even *more* justification for a Baader
Meinhof Gang than there was back then. And yet –
where were the freedom fighters of today; those brave
few who would stand up for the poor and the oppressed
of our era? Clearly, it had fallen to Rory to create
them!

Had it really taken just two generations to

blind the populace to iniquity – to pacify the masses through the 'bread and circuses' distraction of 'celebrity' and the cynical fiscal control of enslaving people through debt? Was Rory really the only one who could see what was happening?

Ironically, perhaps it *was* precisely his wealth and his privilege that allowed him the luxury of the detachment one needed to truly see and observe. Freed of the need to chase every penny to pay every creditor just to meet the rising cost of living, Rory had the opportunity to see things as they really were; the chance to peep behind the curtain of Oz. And he was disgusted. How could he stand idly by and watch while the world was raped and exploited for the profit of the few? How could he join in with the greed-fuelled revelries of the ultra-rich and then look at himself in the mirror when all of the wealth they attained was built directly on the backs of the exploited masses?

No, there was no more need for self-justification or explanation. This was his *destiny*. And it was Krendler's destiny too. Life is a process of becoming. No man can avoid his destiny. In just a few days it would be time to upload the final Anarchist Pete blog post. It would be time to pass the baton and let Krendler off the leash; it would be time to change the world.

Love, Gudrun Ensslin

CHAPTER EIGHTEEN: GEFREITER SCHWEIK

Even if I had wanted to, I couldn't stop myself becoming radicalised once more. I could not delude myself any longer. I couldn't just stand by and see what I had seen – the way the world has become since The Wall fell – and continue to bury my head in the sand. I could not betray the memory of Gudrun, Andreas, Ulrike, Holger, Astrid, Julius and the others for the rest of my life. I could no longer deny what I was – either to myself or to the world at large. I could no longer tolerate what I was becoming. It was time instead for me to remember what I used to be; what I used to believe. It was time for me to turn the clock back. It was time once again for revolution.

The posts on that website by 'Anarchist Pete' – whoever he (or she?) might be – spoke to me directly; affected me in ways I thought I had either buried or forgotten. Sometimes it was really as if Gudrun was contacting me from beyond the grave. It was like the time I heard her speaking to me – in my head – at the Frankfurt Christmas Market all those years ago. It sounds insane, I know – but the passion, the phrasing, was often so much like her. Sometimes it was as if she were still with me. And Gudrun is someone I have never forgotten. How can I continue to ignore her pleas? How can I continue to neglect to honour *her* memory?

Yet should I really throw away the life I have built for myself since moving to England? The cottage, the teaching, the peace and tranquillity. Should I really renounce my renouncement of praxis? And what about another memory I have to honour? That of Inge? How can I pick up a gun and kill with the memory of Inge to consider? The decision has not been easy.

For a time I attempted to ignore the website. When the letter arrived with the code and the URL I thought it was one of my students playing a practical joke. I wondered which one would have that sense of humour – and that deep, hidden knowledge of my comrades and my past. Who amongst those naïve, privileged girls who visit me to study the German language had the hidden disposition of Ingrid and Irene, sitting 'innocently' in the hallway of the *Dahlem Institut*, guns at the ready?

But no – this was something other than my students. 'My students' – how Julius would laugh at the irony of me teaching; of *me* having students. Julius? I wondered if Julius had sent me the letter. It would have been typical of the way Julius operated to send me a covert message, to communicate through a fake persona. But Julius would be too old for this game now – if he were still alive. I was probably too old for this game now!

Love, Gudrun Ensslin

For a time I ignored the letter. But I did not throw it away. It lay in a drawer in my bedroom – silently calling to me; announcing its presence every time my memory took me back to '68, every time the further excesses of the capitalists were announced on the news. Economic downturn. National debt. Credit crunch. A widening gap between rich and poor. I logged onto the website – and from that point onwards I didn't stop. Once I was hooked, I was hooked! The Anarchist Pete posts made complete sense of what was happening all around me. It was like our old communiqués. It could only be a Comrade who was responsible! It was the present viewed through the prism of the past – and the past still made perfect sense.

I now had a decision to make. Gudrun or Inge? It was the hardest decision of my life – for it directly affected my life; its future and its destiny. Have I chosen wisely? Time will tell. Time reveals its own legacy. What will be my legacy? After six decades on this planet, *where* is my legacy? After all, I no longer had a wife and I had no children either. I had painted no works of art. I had written no novels. BANKER BINGO would therefore be my testimony; my gift to future generations; my *bequest*. My *Praxis*. I had spent too long in the world of thoughts and ideas – from my time as a Philosophy student to my time as a teacher of German. Now it was time for *action*. As Gudrun said: "Those who don't defend themselves die."

My mind is made up. I have chosen Gudrun. In

Love, Gudrun Ensslin

so many ways, I have *always* chosen Gudrun. This is my destiny. Life is a process of becoming. No man can avoid his destiny. All I need now is a gun – and then BANKER BINGO can begin. It is time to download the game card. It is time once again for revolution. It is time to change the world!

Love, Gudrun Ensslin

CHAPTER NINETEEN: DIE WAHL LIEGT BEI DIR

BANKER BINGO ENCRYPTED WEBSITE POST

Here is your **BANKER BINGO** game card of merciless, profiteering financiers and assorted capitalist swine. Eliminate **ONE TARGET PER MONTH** to build a better society! Those who profit from misery and iniquity – those who repossess homes sold on unaffordable loans, those who predicate medical help purely on cost and an opportunity to profit, those who gamble on the price of food the starving cannot afford, those who make money from misery, exploitation, suffering and death – all must receive their dividend!

A Hedge Fund Manager	An Investment Bank CEO	A Money Broker
A Building Society CEO	A Debt Collector	A Government Tax Official
A Derivatives Trader	A City 'regulator'	A Bond Dealer

CHAPTER TWENTY: DIE MASSNAHME

One of the very few benefits of the capitalist system is that it didn't take me very long – or cost me all that much – to acquire the gun. It was a Chinese-made sniper's rifle – modelled on a Russian patent from the Second World War. It had apparently been standard issue to several forces in the Eastern Bloc. Who knows, perhaps it had even once been handled by a border guard in the *DDR*. It came with a very accurate telescopic sight and several boxes of ammunition. It was simple – but effective.

I thought of the last time I'd held a gun. It was the handgun given to me by Anton. An obscenity; and an obscenity I had buried; covered with the earth – the same earth that grew the plants I tended; the same earth to which we will all return once the sound and fury of our all-too-brief lives is over. The memory gave me pause. Did I really want to do *this*? Did I really want to become like him? Did I really want to pull the trigger on another human being? No matter how much I despised the target…did I want *this* act on my conscience? How would I feel if my conscience ever awoke?

Love, Gudrun Ensslin

And yet my target was well chosen. I certainly wasn't about to kill Mother Theresa! My target had caused misery; my target brought grief and misfortune to others; my target had to pay the price. I had the opportunity to execute justice. Could it really be an accident – mere happenstance – that I found myself here…with *him* in my gun sights?

Would I really spurn the opportunity I had been given? After all, I had the gun, I had the game card, I had the passionate belief that things were so very wrong with this world and that I could change them. All I really needed was the *willpower*. I needed to execute my will in order to execute justice. I needed to get a grip! I needed to remember the one person who acted without hesitation, without question, without demur. I needed to seek my strength in *Gudrun*.

I was here…on the balcony…and he was *there*…in the crosshairs! The moment was indeed *momentary*! This was no time for questions, delays or doubt! It was true I had used my initiative and deviated from the targets that Anarchist Pete suggested. It was true I instead picked my own target! "Your problem is you think too much, Georg," Gudrun said to me. "And if you think too much, you do not act. You should trust your subconscious mind to rule your conscious mind. You should trust your *instinct* for justice – and then you will *know* how to act. You will *know* what has to be done." True – but by now – by this stage in my life I *knew* who to target…and Anarchist Pete's evil bankers could wait in line; their time would surely come. And my choice? An arch-capitalist, an uber-capitalist; an architect of the internet. I had seen the damage the internet could do. I lived through the technological change that no other generation would see. I lived before the internet even existed...and I lived now...in a world dominated by the internet and IT. It was a technology that was never going away; that would be used to enslave – to monitor, to classify, to document, to oppress. And more than this, it was the primary medium used to spread the message of hatred and division among all peoples. No, the Anarchist Pete game card was wrong. The real target all along should have been a high profile arch-capitalist master of the internet! And now I had one...caught directly in my sights!

Love, Gudrun Ensslin

CHAPTER TWENTY ONE: LIEBESTOD

BANKER BINGO ENCRYPTED WEBSITE POST

THIS WEBSITE HAS BEEN HACKED IN THE *TRUE* CAUSE OF PEACE, LOVE AND UNDERSTANDING BETWEEN *ALL* PEOPLES.

PLEASE READ AND CONSIDER THE FOLLOWING MESSAGES CAREFULLY:

Make hatred history!
Drop your hatred – not bombs!
Kill hatred – not people!
Hate hatred – not people!
Don't tolerate intolerance!

THOU SHALT NOT KILL – neither shalt thou HATE. . .for hatred leads only to MURDER!

The desire to kill someone – however justified you believe your cause – is NOT something you should keep in your heart. You must struggle to RESIST

such thoughts with ALL your being.

MAY PEACE BE UPON YOU!

PEACE-LOVING PAUL

Sacrilege! Perfidy! Outrage! Rory Carlisle could not believe it! Months, years, *decades* of planning the 'project' and now, just as it came to fruition – so soon after Krendler had been found, and downloaded the game card and decided to play – some sanctimonious lickspittle, some pansy little God-botherer, some naïve little *shit* had hacked into Rory's website and destroyed *everything* there! And what had this reprehensible usurper put in the place of Anarchist Pete's eloquent social critiques? His own trite Fortune Cookie sloganeering about "peace, love" and all things hippy. Pathetic homilies from a pathetic mind! Obtuse! Simplistic! Fatuous! 'Peace-loving Paul' – what a *bastard*! What a pity he wasn't Number One on Krendler's list!

How could this happen? How could this be? Rory had some of the finest encryption available – secure servers in remote locations backed by even more secure servers in even more remote locations ready to take over the very moment something went wrong. *Jardine*? Could *he* be behind this sabotage? Somehow, Rory decided, this was all Jardine's fault. He would summon that queer freak back to Canary

Love, Gudrun Ensslin

Wharf from Scotland immediately – he had some explaining to do! But first, Rory felt he simply had to get out of the building – get some fresh air, clear his head. He didn't want to drive, didn't want to call his bodyguards for an escort – just get himself outside and into the fresh air where he could breathe more easily! He would walk quietly around the Old Millwall Dock until his headache cleared, until he felt calm enough to know what he should do next.

He stalked into the service elevator and tried to compose himself by looking in the mirror and telling himself to gather his thoughts. Fuming, he pushed the wrong button and travelled all the way down to the basement. Cursing, Rory ran up the back stairs to the ground floor – ignoring the startled janitor who blurted a garbled "Good morning, Mr. Carlisle." He stormed past the reception desk, burst through the revolving doors and practically jogged out into the street.

*   *   *

I lay quietly prone on the balcony opposite my target's office block. Now I had the target clearly in my rifle sights; his slender form captured neatly and symmetrically by the crosshairs. It had taken me weeks to reach this stage of the operation – weeks of planning, surveillance, tracking and patience. Once the target was selected, I decided to rent a flat overlooking the office block he visited so frequently. This operation was costing me the bulk of the remainder of the savings from my father's business – but now that I had the target squarely in my sights, it was money well spent.

I made a cosy and perfectly disguised sniper's nest for myself on the balcony of the rented flat – carefully building a hideaway among the assorted pot plants, creepers and other foliage that left me totally invisible to onlookers from all directions. Only the merest hint of the tip of the gun barrel protruded through the glossy black railings. And there I waited – day after day, hour after hour – with only toilet breaks and cups of coffee to sustain me; tiny windows of opportunity for my target to appear.

Many times I viewed him in my gun sights. Already I could have pulled the trigger several times over. But, on those few all-too-brief occasions, he was always moving too fast; flanked and shepherded by bodyguards, members of the public wandering lemming-like across my field of vision. And I wanted a clear and undisturbed shot – a golden opportunity rather than a half-chance; an extended and uninterrupted moment so that I could be absolutely sure.

And so, there I lay, prone and silent amidst my cocoon of foliage, awaiting that one perfect moment. I had, in fact, enjoyed the wait. My patience felt infinite and I now felt I belonged on that balcony and had taken root every bit as much as my plants. My hideaway was my domain – my own small corner of Planet Earth; a small green oasis – a defiant island of

Love, Gudrun Ensslin

Nature amidst the impersonal glass, steel and concrete of London's soulless, corporate Canary Wharf district. Camped out thus, in the epicentre of the enemy's heartland, I felt as though I could remain forever hidden – awaiting that one opportunity I craved; and now, *finally*, that perfect opportunity arrived. Rory Carlisle had just stepped – all alone and unobstructed – straight into my gun sights!

*   *   *

"Where was Krendler?" Rory wondered. "Where was he right now – at this very minute?"

He had surely downloaded the game card and chosen to 'play' by now. That 'Peace-Loving Pansy' couldn't have managed to stop that happening. There wasn't time. So, where *was* Krendler now? And, more to the point, where was the first public slaying that should be hitting the headlines right about now? Where was that all-important publicity-generating high profile victim who would promote 'The Cause'? Where was the first random death that would have the overpaid capitalist oppressors quaking in their *Gucci* loafers? Rory had a communiqué he needed to release to the media. He wanted to give his instructions: "Take practical steps to reduce the widening gap between rich and poor…or one banker dies every month!"

Had Krendler lost his nerve, wimped out? Could Rory trust no-one, rely on absolutely no-one to do his bidding? It was bad enough that some pathetic

Love, Gudrun Ensslin

little pacifist fruit fly destroyed Rory's website...but had Rory's own puppet now voluntarily cut his own strings too? That really would be adding insult to injury! Rory stood rooted to the spot on the dockside pavement and pondered his options. Where to go? What to do? Which way to turn – to the left or to the right?

*   *   *

I knew I would only get one shot – and here was my opportunity; it was now or never. I thought long and hard about the target and decided, quite quickly, that I would not be able to follow the game card I downloaded. In this day and age of CCTV, DNA profiling and private security, there was no way I was going to achieve a 'Full House'.

Indeed, I would be lucky to even get two of the targets before being apprehended. Besides, I didn't necessarily agree with all of those selected. The rationale was certainly sound enough – destroy the architects-in-chief of our corrupt society and the whole rotten edifice will crumble – but, in my view, most of Anarchist Pete's targets were merely *symptomatic* of the iniquity in modern society rather than the root cause.

I preferred to go for the jugular – especially, as I concluded, I would only get one chance to make one spectacular kill. Hence, it had to be meaningful – both personally and in a wider context. I wanted to go for

272

Love, Gudrun Ensslin

the throat – plunge my lance directly into the belly of the Beast rather than simply cut off one of its many heads that, like the Hydra, it could simply re-grow.

No, I would not be manipulated or dictated to! I would choose my own target and it would be *appropriate*. I would hit the capitalists where it hurt most – by taking out one of their own number...a world famous leading plutocrat; a typical money-grabbing profiteer hoarding up his assets while the rest of the country starved; some soulless egomaniac engaged in a vain struggle to accumulate more than the egomaniac next door; some greedy bastard locked in a bizarre 'let's see who can piss highest up the wall' contest with other greedy bastards measured solely in terms of personal wealth; some scumbag salting away all of their ill-gotten *gelt* in a Swiss Bank vault where it does no-one any good whatsoever. It was time for me to become Robin Hood's avenging bastard son! But *who* would I choose? With so much choice – with so very many worthy candidates – who, for me, would be 'the one'?

It was the internet that provided the answer. Eventually I decided I wanted to target someone closely involved with the *internet*; someone who profited directly from the internet itself; a high profile businessman with his fingers deeply entrenched in the virtual slime of the cyberspace pie; someone whom the people of Britain – and beyond – would immediately associate with the internet...and these days that meant only one person: that odious capitalist pig Rory

273

Love, Gudrun Ensslin

Carlisle. There were other options, of course, but Carlisle with his ISP, online car business and smug self-loving smile was the *perfect* candidate.

The internet is a barometer of the human psyche and it's rotten to the core. Every filthy perversion, every slanderous lie, every hate-filled incitement to kill can be found there at the mere touch of a button. It's a sewer and a cesspool – a repository for every evil human imagining, desire or deed…and yet certain people in our society choose to *profit* from it! After all, if it were not for the internet I would not be acting like this; I would not have been tempted to revisit my past, to resurrect my old passions. The irony was not lost on me! If it were not for the internet I would not be about to betray the memory of Ingeborg Barz – and yet people like Carlisle *profit* from this sick creation! To people like him, it's just more money in the bank. And that is why I know I am *right* to have chosen Rory Carlisle for my first and only BANKER BINGO target.

And now I have him! I have my finger curled gently around the trigger – all it will now take is a steady squeeze and I will send a red hot piece of high velocity lead crashing through his fragile cranium. I have him – and yet still I hesitate. *Still* I ask myself if I really want to go through with this. It is as if an angel is sitting on my shoulder telling me that even now – at this late, late eleventh hour it is still not *too* late. I could still pack up my things and just go home – back to my quiet, unassuming life in rural Kent with no

Love, Gudrun Ensslin

harm done and no-one any the wiser. I don't *have* to *kill*. It is *still* within my power to walk away. It is still within my power to find *another* way – a *healthier* way – to change the world for the better. I am looking through the gun sight once more and this time I can see the face of Ingeborg Barz staring back at me – wide-eyed and innocent, pleading with me not to shoot.

And I ask myself: what madness, what devilry, has brought me through six whole decades of existence to this particular balcony at this particular time with a rifle in my hand and a man's life in the balance? How has it happened – and what right do I now have to play God like this...to be Judge, jury and executioner...to be he who casts the first stone? Is it really nothing other than the vanity and rage of an old fool? Have I become so bitter by my personal misfortunes, jealousies and hatred that, rather than rise above it, I am now seeking revenge on an imperfect world for an imperfect life? Am I just lashing out blindly and wildly – a victim of my uncontrolled spite – with Rory Carlisle cast as the sacrificial lamb for my grievance-fuelled bloodlust? Maybe. Perhaps. But just now – with the man himself frozen in my gun sights – these questions seem utterly irrelevant as I recognise that the time for action is upon me – and all I can think about now is pulling the trigger...and to Hell with the consequences. Quick now, before he moves away, while I can still be sure of a clear shot...

And yet *still* I hesitate! For, if I have learned anything at all in my rapidly advancing years it is that

Love, Gudrun Ensslin

every human life is a personal journey – incorporating individual, subjective choices for which nobody else can ever be held to account. And, if I have learned anything at all in my time in Baader Meinhof – and most especially from the tragic death of Ingeborg Barz – it is the certain knowledge that every human life is a sacred thing. And so, with the arch-capitalist swine Rory Carlisle still here in my gun sights I know I am facing a distinct choice that is mine – and mine alone. And the question, with my finger wrapped tightly around the trigger, is this: will I choose Death...or will I choose Life?

Love, Gudrun Ensslin

LOVE, GUDRUN ENSSLIN: BAADER MEINHOF TIMELINE (1967 – 1972):

September 1967:

Gudrun Ensslin meets Andreas Baader at a party and leaves her husband and son to become his lover

2nd April 1968:

Gudrun and Andreas firebomb two Frankfurt department stores with two associates

31st October 1968:

Gudrun and Andreas are sentenced to three years in prison

13th June 1969:

Released on parole, Gudrun and Andreas hang out in Frankfurt – raising funds and planning 'actions'

November 1969:

Love, Gudrun Ensslin

Gudrun and Andreas go on the run – electing not to
return to prison and instead resurfacing in Paris

February 1970:

The lovers return to West Germany and accept
temporary lodging in the Berlin apartment of
prominent left-wing journalist, Ulrike Meinhof.
They lodge with Ulrike for two weeks.

March 1970:

Molotov cocktails are thrown through the windows
of the Länder administrative offices in Berlin in the
first official 'action'. Andreas is subsequently
recaptured and sent to Tegel prison to complete his
sentence for the original Frankfurt department
store firebombing.

14th May 1970:

Andreas is sprung from the Dahlem Institut by
Gudrun, Ulrike and others in a daring raid. The
RAF (Rote Armee Fraktion – Red Army Faction) is
officially formed. Journalist/sympathiser Ulrike
Meinhof joins the Gang and is officially on the run.

Love, Gudrun Ensslin

Ulrike's film, *Bambule*, is banned from release.

2ⁿᵈ June 1970:

The first RAF communiqué is released.

8ᵗʰ – 22ⁿᵈ June 1970:

The RAF travels to Jordan to train with the PLO; 'training' includes a practical course in robbing banks.

9ᵗʰ August 1970:

The RAF resurfaces in Berlin – actively recruiting new members and planning bank raids to raise much-needed funds.

29ᵗʰ September 1970:

Four simultaneous bank raids are undertaken by the RAF in Berlin.

November 1970:

The Munsterlager military arsenal is raided for weaponry. Guns are also purchased from Al Fatah contacts.

15th January 1971:

The RAF raids two banks in Kassel.

15th July 1971:

RAF member Petra Schelm is killed by police in Hamburg.

25th September 1971:

Two policemen are shot and wounded by RAF members Holger Meins and Margrit Schiller as they approach the Gang members' car on the autobahn.

22nd October 1971:

A policeman is killed in a shootout with the RAF in Hamburg.

Love, Gudrun Ensslin

22ⁿᵈ December 1971:

A policeman is shot dead during an RAF bank raid in Kaiserslautern. Ingeborg Barz is allegedly one of the bank robbers.

21ˢᵗ February 1972:

Eight RAF members wearing carnival masks raid the Ludwigshafen Mortgage & Exchange Bank. One of the raiders – Ingeborg Barz – subsequently phones home and tells her mother she wishes to leave the Baader Meinhof Gang. She is never seen alive again. (In July 1973 Ingeborg's decomposed body is found at the side of an autobahn on the outskirts of Munich).

2ⁿᵈ March 1972:

RAF member Tommy Weisbecker is shot dead by police in Augsberg.

11ᵗʰ May 1972:

The RAF explodes three pipe bombs at the HQ of the US 5ᵗʰ Army Corps in the IG Farben building in

Frankfurt. 13 GI's and a Lieutenant Colonel are killed.

12th May 1972:

Two RAF bombs explode in the police HQ in Augsberg; five police officers are injured. A larger RAF bomb detonates in the car park of the BKA office in Munich; 60 cars are destroyed.

15th May 1972:

An RAF car bomb cripples the wife of intended target Judge Buddenburg in Karlsruhe.

19th May 1972:

Two RAF bombs explode (a further three fail to detonate) at the Axel Springer building in Hamburg; 17 clerical staff are injured.

24th May 1972:

Two RAF car bombs detonate within 15 seconds of each other at the US Army's European HQ in Heidelberg; a Captain and two Sergeants are killed and five GI's are wounded.

1ˢᵗ June 1972:

Andreas Baader is arrested live on German television during an early morning siege at a suburban garage in Frankfurt.

7ᵗʰ June 1972:

Gudrun Ensslin is arrested in a clothing boutique in Hamburg whilst attempting to buy a new disguise.

15ᵗʰ June 1972:

Ulrike Meinhof is arrested after a 'schili' sympathiser informs the authorities of her whereabouts. (The informant later attempted to use his reward money to pay for Ulrike's legal defence).

Love, Gudrun Ensslin

LOVE, GUDRUN ENSSLIN: GLOSSARY OF TERMS

Baader Meinhof Gang:

The name given to the Red Army Faction (see Glossary entry below) by the news media in Germany. Baader Meinhof operatives themselves never used this term – calling themselves the RAF instead. Right wingers and opponents of Baader Meinhof called them the Baader Meinhof Gang ('bunde') whereas left wingers, sympathisers and supporters called them the Baader Meinhof Group ('gruppe'). Whichever epithet you routinely applied was therefore indicative of your political allegiance.

Bambule:

A term of German prison dialect referring to a form of largely non-violent prison protest, typically the repeated banging of objects against the metal bars of a cell. The term is derived from the African dance *Bamboule* or *Bamboula*. *Bambule* is also the title of a 1970 TV movie about a group of borstal girls in West Berlin written by Ulrike Meinhof and banned after Meinhof joined the Red Army Faction/Baader Meinhof Gang. The film was not officially screened until 1994.

285

Love, Gudrun Ensslin

BKA (Bundeskriminalamt):
Federal Criminal Investigation Office. The West German equivalent of the FBI. At the time of Baader Meinhof the BKA was a fairly small agency coordinating the police forces of the various German states (*Länder*) in their crime-fighting efforts across the equivalent of county boundaries. The need to track and capture Baader Meinhof operatives caused the BKA to be greatly expanded in terms of manpower, budget and remit.

ersatz:
Fake, imitation; a substitute or replacement of (usually) inferior quality

Kommune I:
A 1960s commune in West Berlin based on the concepts of free-living and free-loving. Kommune I wrote pamphlets advocating social change and opposing capitalism. Its members engaged in low-level anti-capitalist action – for example, throwing custard-filled balloons at demonstrations.

konkret:
A left-wing student magazine founded by Ulrike Meinhof's husband, Klaus Rainer Röhl and bankrolled in its early years by East German Communist funds.

Love, Gudrun Ensslin

konkret (which deliberately avoided using capitalisation in its title as an act of defiance) was edited by Ulrike Meinhof after her marriage to Röhl and prior to her formally joining Baader Meinhof following her role in springing Baader from the Dahlem Institut. *konkret* was then edited by Stefan Aust – later editor of *Der Spiegel* and author of *Der Baader Meinhof Komplex* (both book and movie).

Krav Maga:
Israeli system of self-defence incorporating boxing, ju-jitsu, judo and other martial arts techniques. As used by the IDF, Mossad, Shin-Bet, FBI, NYPD SWAT teams and UN Special Forces.

Polizei:
Police. Divided into areas of specialisation – including the **Kripo** (*Kriminal Polizei*); criminal police and **Popo** (*Politische Polizei*); political police.

Praxis:
Putting political theory into action – within a specifically Marxist context. 'Political theory' discussed the best way to bring about The Revolution whilst 'praxis' constituted the direct action necessary to achieve revolution.

Love, Gudrun Ensslin

Red Army Faction:
Red Army Faction was the name the Baader Meinhof
Gang gave to themselves ('Baader Meinhof' itself
being a construct of the news media – and entirely
missing the point that Gudrun Ensslin was perhaps the
most significant player of all in the *RAF*). The name
Red Army Faction (*'Rote Armee Fraktion'*) served
many purposes: firstly, it allied the group with the
Soviet Red Army (and thereby with Maoist
Communism – the political ideology that really
motivated Baader Meinhof); secondly, it implied that
the organisation was larger than it actually was; thirdly,
its acronym, RAF, recalled the British *Royal Air Force*
that had bombed Germany during WW2. The logo of
the Red Army faction is a Heckler & Koch machine
pistol superimposed on a red Communist star.

Schili:
A term used to describe affluent middle-class
supporters of the radical left. The *schili* were also
known as the *"schickeria"* or the *"Raspberry Reich"*.
Schili was a largely dismissive term derived from
'schick' ('chic') and *'linke'* ('left') – largely akin to the
English phrase "trendy lefties". The *schili* were useful
to Baader Meinhof for the provision of funds and safe
houses – although they were rarely, if ever, directly
involved in violent action.

Love, Gudrun Ensslin

Stammheim:
A prison in Frankfurt. Stammheim was the prison in which Baader, Ensslin and Meinhof were incarcerated following their capture in 1972. A purpose-built courtroom within Stammheim hosted the trial of Baader Meinhof's first generation. Following *Todesnacht* ('Death Night') in 1977 when Baader, Ensslin and Raspe died, 'Stammheim' became a by-word for the abuse of power by the Federal German government.

Tegel:
A prison in Berlin – the largest in Germany.

Todesnacht:
'Death Night' took place on 18th October 1977 and is shrouded in controversy to this day. The authorities contend that on this night Baader, Ensslin and Raspe committed joint suicide in disappointment at the failure of the Mogadishu-based hijacking of a *Lufthansa* jet during which one of the hijackers' demands was the release of the Baader Meinhof prisoners. Left wingers resolutely believe the Baader Meinhof prisoners were murdered by the State in order to prevent any further hijacking demands. The 'facts' behind the 'suicides' remain a matter of debate.

Love, Gudrun Ensslin

zeitgeist:
"Spirit of the times". The term derives from 'zeit' ('time') and geist ('spirit', 'ghost'). It denotes something that both typifies and symbolises the era in which it was produced.

LOVE, GUDRUN ENSSLIN: TRANSLATION OF CHAPTER TITLES

Der Spiegel

The Mirror. *Der Spiegel* is also the name of Germany's foremost current affairs magazine – until recently edited by Stefan Aust.

Pig ist Pig!

A pig is a pig! An anti-police/anti-establishment slogan written on walls and in radical left-wing publications in West Germany during the 1960s.

Ich bin Pete

I am Pete. A pun – alluding to President Kennedy's infamous "Ich bin ein Berliner" proclamation.

Das Konzept Stadtguerilla

The Concept Of The Urban Guerilla. The title of an official Red Army Faction publication espousing RAF political theory.

Heimat

Homeland. Also the title of a TV series created by

German left-wing film maker Rainer Werner Fassbinder.

Wie Alles Anfing
How It All Began. Also the title of the autobiography of Michael 'Bommi' Baumann, leader of the anarchist paramilitary group, Movement 2 June (*Bewegung 2 Juni*) – comprised of members of Kommune I and contemporaneous to Baader Meinhof.

Praxis
Putting Marxist political theory into direct action in order to spark revolution.

Lebensweisheit
Practical wisdom; wisdom gained by experience. Literally: life-wisdom.

Kontakt
Contact.

Bambule
Non-violent resistance. (Prison slang)

Love, Gudrun Ensslin

Jugend ohne Gott
Youth without God. Godless youth. Also the title of a
1938 anti-Nazi novel by Ödön von Horváth.

Es Beginnt
It Begins.

Der Teufelswerk
The Devil's Work.

Es ist so Schön…Soldat zu sein
It's So Beautiful…To Be A Soldier. A slogan from a
WW2 *Wehrmacht* (German Army) recruiting poster.

Alles ist in Ordnung
Everything's as it should be. A phrase often attributed
to cartoon Nazis in UK comic books and movies of the
1970s.

Wahrheit
Truth.

Kapitan Ahab
Captain Ahab. A pun on the fact that Gudrun Ensslin

Love, Gudrun Ensslin

(while in captivity in Stammheim) used characters from the novel Moby Dick to denote Baader Meinhof operatives in coded messages. This chapter concerns Rory Carlisle and so is titled 'Captain Ahab'.

Gefreiter Schweik
Private Schweik. The German title for 'The Good Soldier Svejk' – the 1923 satirical anti-war novel by Czech writer Jaroslav Hasek that poked grim fun at the pomposity and absurdities of the Austro-Hungarian Empire's army during WW1 – an army into which 140,000 Czechs were conscripted without fully understanding what they were fighting for. This chapter title continues the punning aspect of the previous chapter and is called 'Schweik' as it concerns Georg Krendler.

Die Wahl Liegt Bei Dir
The Choice Is Yours.

Die Massnahme.
The Measures Taken. Also the title of a play by Bertold Brecht, written in 1930s Weimar Germany in the hope of educating the workers against the Nazis. Brecht also worked on several projects focusing on the Schweik character.

Love, Gudrun Ensslin

Liebestod

'Love Death' – perhaps better appreciated in English when written as 'Death-Love'. The title of the final climactic aria in Wagner's opera, *Tristan und Isolde*. In literary criticism, *liebestod* signifies the theme of the 'eroticism' of death – both in terms of the notion of a climax being a 'miniature death' and in terms of symbolising the power of love over death to ultimately defeat death (…love being the *only* way to attain this eternal victory).

Love, Gudrun Ensslin

Love, Gudrun Ensslin

AUTHOR'S NOTE:

Writers are most often afraid of two things – not being published and being misunderstood once they are published! There is little a writer can do to influence the former (which is the domain of the literary agent) but an Author's Note can sometimes help avert the latter scenario. My decision to write this explanatory note at the end of LOVE, GUDRUN ENSSLIN has been prompted by both the contentious subject matter within the novel and the fact that many people today remain affected by the real events of 1968-1972 that are fictionalised in my book.

As much as writers dislike explaining their work, many readers find such explanations patronising and needlessly didactic. Indeed, one of the pleasures of a novel (which is a work of art and thus open to uninhibited scrutiny) is the myriad of unique interpretations individual readers will inevitably bring to a text. In fact, astute readers can often identify themes, metaphors and sub-texts of which the author was blissfully unaware at the time of creation. When it happens, this can be a valuable and enlightening occurrence. However, this can equally be offset by occasions on which the reader misunderstands or misrepresents the work and/or its author. Thus the Author's Note exists – for the writer to set the record straight regarding his or her intentions and to lay bare

Love, Gudrun Ensslin

his or her conceptual thinking. I am now about to begin that process – so, any readers who object to an Author's Note should stop reading now. For those who remain, I shall begin.

The genesis of LOVE, GUDRUN ENSSLIN is this: having completed my debut novel RUDE BOY – a very different animal to LOVE, GUDRUN ENSSLIN in that RUDE BOY is a 'rites of passage' tale updating 'Catcher In The Rye' for a new generation – I began thinking about my next novel. It occurred to me it was impossible to switch on the television or radio (or log onto a news website) without being confronted by the twin phenomena of celebrity and terrorism – the unfortunate dual motif of our era. Thus, I determined to fuse these two aspects of modern life into a single cohesive narrative and thereby arrive at a definitive *zeitgeist* 'novel of our times'.

In preparation for writing the book you now hold, I spent four years researching the Baader Meinhof Gang – and in this endeavour I am indebted to (and must certainly acknowledge) two valuable sources of information: the non-fiction writing of Stefan Aust (the world's foremost Baader Meinhof historian) and the comprehensive website of Baader Meinhof archivist Richard Huffman (www.baader-meinhof.com). Only after this essential groundwork had been completed did I begin writing the narrative. Having completed my research, I began working on the narrative in 2005. The original title was CELEBRITY DEATH BINGO – and it was in this early guise that the manuscript was requested and read by Stefan Aust, prior to the release of his *Der Baader Meinhof Komplex* movie. However, by late 2008, I realised the entire work needed a significant redraft – and I promptly changed the title to LOVE, GUDRUN ENSSLIN. The new title emphasised the fact that the shadow of Gudrun Ensslin manifests itself throughout the entire work. Furthermore, the dual impact of the simultaneously literal and ironic interpretations of the new title were especially pleasing. Most significantly, the current title ensures the reader's focus centres on the fact that, whilst the novel indeed has two protagonists, the book essentially remains Georg Krendler's story over and above that of Rory Carlisle.

The decision to utilise the Baader Meinhof Gang and their terrorist reign in West Germany (1968-1972) as a backdrop to the events in the novel seemed to me to be particularly apposite. Not only do the politics motivating the group still carry resonance in today's global capitalist post-Cold War era (where profit and celebrity often appear to be the only things Western society values) but the Gang represents the first flowering (in Europe at least) of a ruthless militaristic approach to propagating one's political ideology through small, highly organised terrorist 'cells' – an ethos that has a direct legacy in the suicide bombers of recent times.

Love, Gudrun Ensslin

In many ways, Andreas Baader and Gudrun Ensslin – the lead figures within the Baader Meinhof Gang – were the world's first 'celebrity terrorists'; admired by West Germany's student youth as much for their 'Bonnie and Clyde' media persona as for their radical left-wing politics. In addition to being revolutionary comrades, the charismatic Baader and highly arresting Ensslin were lovers – fuelling a further Romanticism surrounding the group that served only to enhance their appeal among the rebellious '68 generation.

The Baader Meinhof Gang began on a small scale – Ensslin and Baader (along with two comrades) fire-bombing two Frankfurt department stores and (later) hurling Molotov cocktails through the windows of local government administrative offices. Following a period of expansion, recruitment and reorganisation, the Gang (now known to themselves as the Red Army Faction) travelled to Jordan to train with the PLO (during which time their 'training' included a practical course in 'how to rob banks'). On their return to West Germany, the Gang was a very different animal – it now constituted a fully-fledged terror group prepared to wage war on the imperialist/capitalist/fascist State enemy in its own back yard. There followed a succession of bank heists, raids on military weapons stores and a series of shoot-outs with police in which people from both sides were killed. The violence culminated in an orgy of killing and destruction during the month of May 1972. Between 11th-24th May 1972,

Love, Gudrun Ensslin

the Baader Meinhof Gang/Red Army Faction set off no
fewer than ten bombs (a further three failing to
detonate) at prominent locations throughout West
Germany – leaving 17 US military personnel dead, a
further five wounded, five West German policemen
injured and 17 clerical workers injured. After such an
intensive period of mayhem and destruction, the State
authorities quickly rounded up Baader Meinhof's key
players (Andreas Baader, Gudrun Ensslin and Ulrike
Meinhof) the following month. Andreas Baader's
arrest – at a protracted early morning siege at a
suburban garage in Frankfurt – was screened live on
West German television. As Baader emerged from the
wrecked building on a stretcher, his 'shades' still
jauntily in place and his spirit as defiantly nonchalant
as ever, the notion of the 'celebrity terrorist' was
forever entrenched in the media psyche.

One element of the novel that I fear may be
misunderstood (in any version) is its central message.
Whilst this is indeed a novel that has been written out
of a sense of anger and dismay at the financier class
(and global bankers in particular) it is not a hate tract
that endorses or encourages the terrorist response of
shooting people and/or bombing buildings. Rather,
LOVE, GUDRUN ENSSLIN is a book written in the
hope of emphasising our common humanity – and in
recognition of the fact that it is most often when our
common humanity is negated or denied that conflict,
hatred and exploitation sadly arise. If anything, this

Love, Gudrun Ensslin

novel encourages a greater understanding among all peoples – and aims to promote the notion that a readiness to set aside our perceived financial, ideological or political differences is the only realistic hope of a fairer society and further progress towards the attainment of true civilisation.

Love, Gudrun Ensslin

There is another matter I feel I must address in these Author's Notes – my use of the real-life unsolved murder of Ingeborg Barz within this work of overt fiction. I am painfully aware of the fact I did not seek permission of the Barz family to trespass on their grief in this manner and that it may come as a shock to them to discover their relative unexpectedly portrayed here. However, I would like to make this public assurance that I mean no disrespect to the Barz family – and I proudly dedicate this novel to the memory of Ingeborg and others (on both sides of the ideological divide) who lost their lives during the turmoil of 1968-1972. When I assiduously researched Baader Meinhof for the background to my novel, it was the death of Ingeborg Barz that spoke to me most forcefully as the central motif for the story of the Baader Meinhof Gang in its first generation. It was immediately clear to me that I should make the death of Ingeborg the fulcrum of the novel and an eloquent testimony to the enduring dangers of ideology-led violence. I sincerely hope my intentions will be understood.

Love, Gudrun Ensslin

A few further elements require brief clarification. LOVE, GUDRUN ENSSLIN is a novel of ideas – a psychological thriller – rather than a work aiming at absolute fidelity with reality (and, in particular, modern technological processes). Indeed, some suspension of disbelief will be required from the reader to get the most out of the narrative – in the same way as a visit to the theatre requires the self-same suspension of disbelief to fully enter the dramatic world of a stage play. I readily admit I am no expert in the intricacies of website encryption – and no doubt it will be easy for some techno-geek to spot a 'glaring continuity error' in the measures taken by Rory Carlisle to ensure the BANKER BINGO section of the URBANE GORILLA blog remains inaccessible and undetected. However, this would be to miss the metaphorical point that is being made: the reinforcing of the fact that the internet is now almost certainly the world's primary means of inciting hatred and dissent and in recognition of the fact that 'blogging' is now often a metaphor for a multitude of sins.

It is also worth mentioning that my use of the car industry as a thematic backdrop to the book is quite deliberate. There can be few other industries that so readily typify the ideological divide between Communism and capitalism. Under Communism the car was seen solely as a functional utility – simply a means of transportation – rather than as symbolic and indicative of the wealth and social status of the driver.

Love, Gudrun Ensslin

However, under Communism car production stagnated and entered a technological time-warp – insufficient quantities of vehicles were available to meet demand and the machinery that produced them was often outdated and decommissioned equipment that was, ironically, provided by the West. There was simply neither the motivation nor the resources under Soviet Communism to drive forward the levels of innovation within the car industry as existed in the West (with its large-scale manufacturing and widespread consumer choice). On the other hand, whilst the car industry undoubtedly flourished under capitalism – with flagship vehicles, imaginative prototypes and exotic supercars pushing forward the boundaries of technological innovation – the fact remained that only the very wealthy could afford the very best. Once again, the nature of the capitalist beast meant the majority of citizens were left pressing their noses against the windows of the showrooms only to be taunted by luxury they could never hope to afford.

Love, Gudrun Ensslin

Having now completed my apologies, explanations and dedications, I should like to close with some statements of personal gratitude. Firstly, I would like to thank Leah Redhouse for her ceaseless encouragement and tireless proof-reading of my several drafts of manuscript. I would also like to thank my dear friend, Poppet, for her immaculate cover design that, with its Warhol inspired overtones, perfectly defines the concept of a 'celebrity terrorist'. Poppet is also a very talented writer – and I would urge you to discover her work on the following websites: [www.authorpoppet.wordpress.com] and [www.poppetsplanet.weebly.com] Thanks also to Hector for continuing inspiration.

I do hope you have enjoyed reading LOVE, GUDRUN ENSSLIN and that it has proved thought-provoking and entertaining in equal measure. If you would like to discover more about me and my writing, please visit both my blog [www.simoncorbin.wordpress.com] and my website for my first novel, RUDE BOY: [www.rudeboybook.com].

Simon Corbin
August 2010

Love, Gudrun Ensslin

CPSIA information can be obtained at www.ICGtesting.com
Printed in the USA
240579LV00001B/12/P

9 781907 756672